DROWNING INSTINCT

ilsa j. bick

carolrhoda LAB

MINNEAPOLIS

Carolrhoda Lab™
An imprint of Carolrhoda Books
A division of Lerner Publishing Group, Inc.
241 First Avenue North
Minneapolis, MN 55401 U.S.A.

Website address: www.lernerbooks.com

Cover photographs: © Joseph Hancock/Photolibrary/Getty Images (girl); © iStockphoto.com/letty17 (ice texture).

Main body text set in Janson Text LT Std 10/14.
Typeface provided by Linotype AG.

Library of Congress Cataloging-in-Publication Data

Bick, Ilsa J.
      Drowning instinct / by Ilsa J. Bick.
          p.   cm.
      Summary: An emotionally damaged sixteen-year-old girl begins a
    relationship with a deeply troubled older man.
       ISBN: 978–0–7613–7752–8 (trade hard cover : alk. paper)
       [1. Emotional problems—Fiction. 2. Family problems—Fiction.
    3. Teacher-student relationships—Fiction.] I. Title.
    PZ7.B47234Ds 2012
    [Fic]—dc23   2011021239

Manufactured in the United States of America
2 – BP – 12/31/12

For AK: yes, you.

Some say the world will end in fire,
Some say in ice.
From what I've tasted of desire
I hold with those who favor fire.
But if it had to perish twice,
I think I know enough of hate
To say that for destruction ice
Is also great
And would suffice.

—Robert Frost

"**Look**," says the detective. He stares down at the girl huddled on the gurney. Despite a half dozen blankets, the poor kid is still shaking as badly as when they pulled her from the water an hour ago. Another ten, fifteen minutes in that lake, Bob Pendleton thinks, and she might not have made it either. "Just tell the truth. The truth can't hurt."

She says nothing. Christmas Muzak dribbles from an overhead speaker which, considering they're in an ER, he finds obscene in the most irrational way. His wife keeps telling him he's too sensitive to be a cop. "Jenna?"

Silence. Her eyes stare at something he can't see, but he was there when the rescue divers came up. So he imagines she's looking at something pretty terrible, a real nightmare. Her face is so white that her lips, ripe and dusky blue, look like dead worms, and her hair drags in limp, gray ropes. Still, Pendleton can see that she's very pretty and, considering what she's been through over the years and *now*, damned gutsy. She's got the

1

kind of ethereal, unselfconscious beauty some young girls possess that breaks your heart. Or theirs.

"Jenna." He covers one of her hands with his own. Her skin is cold and pale as glass. At his touch, a tremor ripples through her face. Her gaze wanders and he ducks down, so he can grab her eyes with his. "Honey?"

"Am I . . . Am I under . . . under arrest?" These are the first words she's spoken since he took her from the divers and insisted on carrying her, half-frozen and shuddering, to the ambulance. Her voice is halting and strange. "Am I . . . g-g-going to j-j-jail?"

"No, no." He gives her hand a gentle squeeze. "Of course not. You didn't do anything wrong. It was an accident."

"Which part?" she says.

Pendleton frowns. "I don't understand."

"Which part is accidental?" Her eyes, a stunning, brilliant sea-green, shimmer, and a tear dribbles down one cheek. "Before or after?"

"Before or after what?" he asks, but she only shakes her head. "Look, Jenna, I have to know what happened." He pauses. "Don't you understand? You're the *victim* here."

She says nothing.

"Look, here's what we'll do." Pendleton fishes a tiny digital recorder from his pocket. The recorder is no larger than a pack of gum. He shows her the buttons and the display and what the different numbers mean—numbers for folders, letters for files: "Like chapters in a book. I hear you like books."

"And movies," she whispers. "I . . . I like movies."

"Okay, so scenes instead of chapters. Same idea. You talk into that, much as you want. The nurses said you'll be here a while, so I'll check back in a couple hours, how's that?"

She studies the recorder and then nods. "Okay."

"Good girl." Patting her hand, Pendleton turns to go then pauses at the door. Beyond this room and in the larger trauma bay, there is chaos and urgency and motion: doctors in green scrubs, the reek of antiseptic scrub and dying flesh and cooling blood, the chatter of metal against metal, the bleep of monitors and an inarticulate babble of people talking over one another. He hears a high mosquito whine and the doctor's crisp bark: "*Clear!*"

And then, there is . . . nothing.

And more . . . nothing.

When he looks at her again, he can tell that she hears the silence, too. He says, "There's no one left to tell this but you. So I need the story, Jenna. I need the truth."

The grief in her green eyes slips then hardens and, for an instant, Pendleton sees the woman she has become and has no right being, not at sixteen. A hot needle of shame pricks his chest, as if he's barged into her bedroom without knocking, and he almost looks away.

"Right," she says. "Like the two are the same thing."

1: a

So. Okay . . . this is . . .

Okay. I . . . this is kind of creepy, Detective Pendleton. I'm sorry. *Bob*. You said I should call you Bob, like we're old friends or something. I guess that considering the *first* time we met was after the fire and then again just yesterday when you came to the hospital to see my mom . . . well, that might be true. That we're friends, I mean. Only, you know, that first time? When I was eight? I was unconscious and on a ventilator and had already died twice. So I really don't think meeting that way counts.

Anyway . . .

b

You want me to tell the truth.

The truth is . . . I am so cold. I should be dead. Maybe I am. That would be okay.

C

You know what I was just thinking, Bob? *Tell* is such an interesting word. There are so many meanings. There's telling, like spinning a tale, making up stories. I'm good at that.

Of course, in *that* kind of telling, there is another *tell*, as in telling the difference between night and day, girl and boy, fact and dream. If you ask me, this is related to a gambler's *tell*. You know, how something a player does or says tells the other players that he's bluffing? David Mamet did this *great* movie, *House of Games*, all about that. Yeah, I know Mamet. Don't be so surprised. When you spend four months on a psych ward and then the rest of the year at home in exile, you watch a lot of movies.

Anyway, you know what I liked best about that film? The bad girl; the shrink who shoots her lover, that con man who sets her up. Because, in the end, she gets away with it *and* forgives herself.

Wish I could do that.

d

So, Bob, I can tell. I can tell plenty. But the truth? I don't know what that is. I thought I knew until this afternoon, but now. . . . Even if I tell my version of the truth, then what? I'll go back to being the old me? Well, what kind of future is that?

Because let me tell you about the old me, Bob, the beta-version of Jenna Lord. Here's how Beta-Jenna thinks: *They let me go, and I'll cut. Walk out of this room and into the waiting arms of Psycho-Dad—and I'll cut. Together, we'll visit my crispy critter of a mother, who's a drunk and wants only the best for me—and I'll cut.*

I'll cut.

I'll cut.

Yeah. Going back to being Beta-Jenna makes the truth just *so* attractive.

e

The truth.

Well, the year I was fifteen completely sucked. Considering I've died twice, that's really saying something. I was a month shy of sweet sixteen when I started my sophomore year at Turing, this science-techie school just outside Milwaukee for brainiacs, which I'm supposed to be. Skipped a grade, tested out of classes, yada, yada. It goes without saying that I'm a straight-A-plus student, a quiet kid, sort of a loser, and the kind of girl no one would ever suspect.

Or notice.

Okay, other stuff, other stuff . . .

Well, my cell phone is pink. I'm a very careful driver. I've never kissed a boy, which feels . . . wrong. Because I am sweet sixteen, the age when a girl is supposed to find her prince and settle down.

I used to pretend I was Ariel. I had the doll and a blue gown for dress-up, like in the movie. I was wearing the dress the night we first met, Bob, although you probably don't remember that because by then, I'd died a couple of times; the dress was only so much ash; and there was kind of a lot going on.

I don't remember much about the fire, the one that swallowed Grandpa's house eight years ago. I do recall cowering behind the boiler and listening to Grandpa crashing around the kitchen. Then, there was the angry sputter of an argument and, later, the thud as Grandpa MacAllister passed out, a lit cigarette still pinched between his fingers and two more smoldering on the sill over the kitchen sink. That's where they said the fire started, you remember, Bob? How those lacy curtains, soaked in vodka because Grandpa knocked over the bottle when he blacked out, must've caught with a *whump*?

The next is a jumble: the churn of black smoke; the spiking scream of the alarm; the hiss and crackle of orange flames. But I do remember the fear icing my whole body, freezing me in place.

And then I remember Matt, my older brother, frantically shouting my name. His voice was a lifeline, a hook that set in my heart, and I grabbed on tight, swarming up the cellar stairs in a swirl of pale blue petticoat as Matt forced the door. But the fire was greedy. Its orange fingers snagged my dress which died in a sizzling shriek.

And then *I* was screaming because the fire was eating my back and Matt was dodging flames, running with me in his arms, but the front door was still so far away and then . . .

f

I heard my mother, screeching, wild, fighting with the EMTs: *Don't you dare . . .*

g

When they shocked me to life, I blazed back into this huge supernova. Fire hot enough to fry skin and melt fat ignites pain, too: constant and agonizing and so bad you can't die fast enough. I wanted to scream at the doctors to stop, *stop*, but I was mute. The fire had scorched my lungs and boiled my voice. A tube snaked down my throat, pushing in and then sucking out the air from my lungs. So, there was no way to tell anyone what I wanted. Wouldn't have done any good anyway because no one will let a kid die. They think they're doing you this big favor keeping you going because you've got your whole life ahead.

Well, news flash, Bob: Not. Necessarily.

Because you think there's only one kind of pain? That pain is pain is pain?

Uh, that would be *no*.

There's blood-pain. There's knife-pain. There's bang-your-funny-bone-pain.

And then there is the pain of fire, molten and alive: the swirl of flames streaming over rotten wood and naked flesh. That pain moves when you move; it mutters between every breath; it spikes your ears; it rips. You think pain can't be any more horrible than that.

Until you discover that the well is bottomless. There's always more. A different kind of pain, maybe, but more and much, much worse.

But that would be getting ahead of myself.

h

Pain's not all I remember, of course. There were bright lights. The beep of monitors. Needles and tubes. Lots of faces . . . God, now that I think of it, they brought me to this same ER. Maybe these are the same doctors, but I don't know because I faded in and out. I do recall that everyone, *every face*, was grim, like they'd read this story before and knew the end wasn't pretty.

Later, the doctors said how lucky I was that my mom and Matt had decided to pick me up from Grandpa's early. Lucky to be alive. Lucky, lucky, lucky.

Yeah, that's me, Bob. I'm just so, *so* lucky.

i

I'm beating around the bush. I know I am. I don't want to tell this story, Bob, and you know why? Because this is a fairy tale with teeth and claws, and here's what completely sucks: you're going to want black and white, Bob, right and wrong. I'm not sure I can give that to you. That's the problem with the truth. Sometimes the truth is ambiguous, or a really bad cliché.

But *this* is the truth, Bob: I'm a liar.

I am lucky, a liar, a good girl, a princess, a thief—and a killer.

And my reality—my story—begins with Mr. Anderson.

2: a

Of course, the library doors were locked.

Score another point for Psycho-Dad, who got impatient when I reminded him to double-check and make sure the school librarian would be there to let me in. "Stop worrying about it," he'd said the night before. "I talked to the school last week. They said there was no problem."

Well, wrong-o there, Dad.

b

Turing High was one of those Psycho-Dad command decisions, same as us moving to a new McMansion ninety miles north of Milwaukee after my stint on the psych ward. Or was that my breakdown? No, no, it was my "little episode," Psycho-Dad-speak for my stay in the place where the nuts feed the squirrels. My father always called it a *"little episode,"* as if my life was a sitcom and we could simply channel-surf right on past.

We were in Rebecca's office when he first floated the idea in March, and although I hadn't known it then, I'd only see my therapist twice more: another linchpin in Psycho-Dad's clean-slate campaign.

"Turing makes sense," he'd said. "Jenna's a bright, sensitive girl. She's just had a . . . little episode, that's all. When she was on the, ah . . ."

"Ward?" I prompted. I was sprawled in my usual spot, a plump, brown leather armchair. "Unit?"

Dad's lips set in this line above his chin, a fissure in granite. I never talked to my father like that at home, not unless I wanted Psycho-Dad to pay a visit. Of course, the go-to for *that* is he's a shock trauma plastic surgeon and and screws his nurse and has temper tantrums because he's just under so much stress. Not that we talk about the blow-outs or the affairs. All that's no one's business. It's a family matter. You know what I'm talking about, Bob.

But Rebecca's office was my turf. Dad had to behave himself. Doctors are very sensitive about their reputations in front of other doctors, even if the other doc is a shrink and the lowest form of life because all docs know that the med students who become psychiatrists were always pretty squirrely to begin with, the ones who went all girly around blood and guts. Rebecca *being* a girl . . . well, that was proof.

"Yes," he said. "Your teacher *there* said you were light-years ahead of the other kids."

This was true, though that wasn't saying much. In the four months I'd been an inpatient, there were only two kids who stayed long enough to need more than their regular homework delivered. One was eleven and manic half the time—when he wasn't in the quiet room, threatening to blow up the joint, that is. The other girl was seventeen, had gotten pregnant, and then started throwing up to stay thin. The baby finally starved, and she miscarried. Only she couldn't—wouldn't—stop puking. I think there was only one week where she wasn't walking around with a feeding tube taped to her nose, and a psych tech within arm's reach.

"I've had a long talk with the principal and guidance counselor at Turing," Dad was saying. "They've assured me that they are accustomed to dealing with kids who've had . . . problems."

"You *told* them about me?" I shot a glance at Rebecca, who was scowling. "Did you know about this?"

"Not exactly," Rebecca said. "Dr. Lord, don't you—"

"I didn't think it was necessary to involve Becky in the preliminary stages." Dad never called Rebecca *Dr. Savage* and even Rebecca didn't call herself *Becky*. "This isn't Becky's decision to make anyway."

"But you didn't ask me," I said, stupidly believing that maybe, oh, all those hours of family therapy had made a dent. "We didn't discuss it."

Mom, the apologist, jumped in. "Your father didn't mean any harm."

"Why can't I just go on being homeschooled?"

"That's a nonstarter," said Dad.

"Why?"

"Because. Emily has her hands full with the bookstore. I've got surgeries scheduled every day, and that's not counting emergency reconstructions. I'm at the hospital six, sometimes seven, days a week. Neither your mother nor I have the time to babysit you."

That drew a little blood, as Dad had intended. I looked away, chewing on my lower lip, willing the tears not to fall. I turned to Rebecca. "Please. Say something."

Rebecca sighed. "Unfortunately, your parents have a point, Jenna. You *do* need to be around kids your own age, and preferably ones without serious problems. You won't get that if you hide in your house. Being alone is when you've run into problems."

"Yeah, but I was in *school* when it hap—" I let that die. I couldn't argue. Even though I hadn't cut for over six weeks—a new record for me back then—the urge was there, all the time. It was like what that bulimic girl from the ward said: *If I go an hour and don't think about throwing up, I worry there's something wrong. Puking's the new normal.*

Slicing and dicing myself would land me back in the hospital, though, and I knew it. All the doors in the new McMansion had locks, but I wasn't allowed to use them. Sometimes after I showered, my mom would barge in as I was toweling off with her patented: "Oh! I didn't know anyone was in here." Uh-huh. I saw how her eyes flicked fast, up and down, searching for new cuts, fresh scabs. I knew she checked the trash for bloodied tissues or used Band-Aids. Heaven forbid they ever looked behind the false panel beneath my vanity and found my nail scissors. I hadn't used them since I'd been home, but they were . . . insurance.

I thought of something else. "Wait a minute," I said to Rebecca. "Don't you need my permission before you release records or something?"

Rebecca shook her head. "Not technically. You're only fifteen."

"I'll be sixteen in September."

"It doesn't matter. Until you're eighteen, your parents have full say over release of your records. Legally, I can't stop them."

Dad snapped his fingers to get our attention. "Let's stay on track, shall we? The point is, Jenna, you are perfectly capable of being around kids your own age, and Turing's an excellent private science and tech school."

"Who said I'm going into science?" I demanded, although that was probably the stupidest thing I could've said. The best Christmas gift I'd ever gotten was this Edu Junior Scientist Kit Matt bought with his own money when I was five. Mom had a fit when I filled the basement with orange smoke. "Doesn't *my* opinion count?"

"She has a point," Rebecca said. About time, too. "I'll be honest, Dr. Lord. I was under the impression we were *discussing* Turing. I had no idea Jenna's records had been released, much less that she'd been accepted. I haven't even gotten a request for a summary letter from Turing's guidance counselor."

"Wait." Mom looked at Dad. "They don't have a letter from Rebecca?"

"No," Dad said, and then he sighed as if he was just so *sick* of having to get us all up to speed. He spoke slowly and distinctly, like we were morons. "It's bad enough that Jenna's wasted *months* of her life, recovering from her . . ." He waved a hand to swat my past away. "I see no reason why we should burden her further by prejudicing them with Becky's observations. Jenna's out of the hospital. She's on no medications. She's at home, not in a straitjacket. She comes here, what, twice a month? Becky, no disrespect, but there are one hundred and sixty-eight hours in a week, out of which my daughter spends,

14

exactly, one hour with you. No, less than that: fifty minutes. Your involvement is minimal. I doubt you have much of an impact at this point."

"I see." Rebecca's tone dripped acid. "So what, exactly, is your point, Dr. Lord?"

"My *point* is that we are grateful to you. We acknowledge the help you've given Jenna. But her future will not depend upon the fifty minutes she spends here, nor an assessment based on limited exposure."

"In other words," I said to Rebecca, "you're fired."

Psycho-Dad blustered a little bit, said things like *outgrown* and *hatched* and *time to spread her wings*, like I was some kind of baby bird Rebecca just wouldn't let out of the nest, she was so protective. But it all boiled down to this: Dad decided I needed a fresh start. Turing was in, and little Becky was out. My opinion didn't count. God hath spoken.

Something that happens a lot when your dad's last name is Lord.

C

That summer, I stayed put in my parents' new McMansion, which never felt like home. While I was an inpatient, Dad had gotten rid of all my old furniture. I now had a four-poster with a frilly canopy that I completely hated, which was kind of ironic considering how hard I'd begged when I was younger because all princesses had canopy beds.

I weeded the garden, mowed the grass, clipped around the trees, painted the picnic table that no one sat on. Given my mom owned a bookstore, there was always plenty to read, so I devoured at least three books a week. When I wasn't reading or doing chores, I single-handedly kept Netflix in business.

And I e-mailed Matt, although I didn't tell anyone. I'd never even mentioned it to Rebecca, who would've freaked. All our e-mails were on a separate e-mail account that I set up on this ghost server run out of Israel, if you can believe it. I know it sounds like overkill, Bob, but I had to be über-careful. My parents hated that Matt enlisted. I think what really ate at Psycho-Dad was that once Matt was eighteen, he was free and our father couldn't do a damn thing about that.

And what Matt wanted was to run; to get the hell out. It didn't work out the way he planned—or, maybe, you know . . . it did. Once he was in Iraq and gone, my parents wouldn't talk about it, or him. So, if they found out we were keeping in touch, my mom would've had a nervous breakdown. Dad's head would explode. Really, I didn't need the headaches.

I didn't blame Matt for running. Before my life came crashing down around my ears, I was on the cross-country team. That summer before Turing, I thought about starting up again, doing some serious training. Except I never did—not then, anyway—because I think I knew, somehow, that I could run and run and run away into forever and still never get anywhere.

The truth is, Bob, that no matter how far or fast you go, the past always follows: an inky, faceless thing tacked to your shoes that only the harshest light can kill, and then just for those few moments when there is nothing but the strongest fire from the brightest sun, breaking over your shoulders, burning that shadow—and your past—to ash.

So now, at quarter past six in the morning, I stood in the semi-dark of a strange high school, staring at locked doors and wondering what to do. Mom was long gone, her taillights flashing as she took the circular drive and headed back down the access road which bled into the highway and east toward her mother's—my grandmother's—old bookstore. Mom wouldn't be back for another twelve hours when we would wash, rinse, repeat every single school day for some unspecified time in my bright, sunny future. That is, until she—or more likely, Dad—decided I was normal enough to get my license. Given everything that had happened, I thought that would be a long time coming.

Where was everyone? My watch said I still had almost ninety minutes before that first bell. The office staff probably wouldn't show for at least a half hour. I could sit tight except my backpack weighed a ton and I had a cup of sickly sweet cappuccino I didn't want, but Mom had insisted on buying—like coffee was some kind of rite of passage, a ticket into my new life. Maybe I could put away some of my notebooks at least? I remembered from orientation that my locker was upstairs and to the left. The stairs I needed were all the way down this next hall, I thought, past the cafeteria and—

"Hey!"

I whirled, a scream-bubble at the back of my throat. The guy was squat and burly, with a bottle-brush mustache and a grimy red rag threaded through an empty belt loop.

"I . . . uh . . ." I swallowed my heart back into my chest. "I came early . . . I have . . . I have permission . . . uh . . ."

"Doors don't officially open for almost another hour."

"They were open. My dad was supposed to arrange it. Me waiting in the library, I mean, so I thought I could come in." This was crazy. Did this creepy guy want me to go back outside and wait on the curb while he locked the front doors?

"Librarian isn't here." His eyes kept drifting from my face to my chest.

Maybe he was a little slow. "I know."

"Didn't anyone tell me."

"I'm sorry. The doors were open."

"You said that," he said, speaking to my breasts. "That's not supposed to happen either."

"Well, there are two cars in the lot."

"The pickup's mine."

Which left a Prius with an empty bike rack on its roof. "So maybe one of the teachers came in early and left the door open?"

"Maybe." His face folded in a scowl. "You got ID?"

All I had was my learner's permit, which I fumbled from my wallet. He stepped close, squinting at the picture, his eyes clicking from it to me and back again. He stank of cigarettes and sweat and ammonia. Finally he said, "Okay. Library's down the end of the hall."

"I know. It's locked." When he opened his mouth again, I said, "Yes, the librarian doesn't come in for another hour, I know. Do you have the key?" He nodded. "Can you unlock the door?"

He shook his head. "The librarian has to be there."

"Well, can I go to my locker, please? Maybe by the time I put my stuff away, the librarian will be in." I could tell he didn't like the idea, but I was already moving away, heading for the stairs, not waiting for permission.

He let me get maybe ten feet then called, "Hey!"

Now what? I looked back. "Yes?"

He held up that damn coffee, the one I'd set down when I tried the library doors. "This yours?"

₿

By the time I made it to the second floor, my stomach was churning. Great. I couldn't even handle a perv janitor. No way I was going back downstairs, not while that guy was around. Maybe hide in the bathroom? Bathrooms were safe, even in the dark. Especially in the dark. Lock myself in a stall, plug into my iPod, tune out, and let the blackness fold around like a blanket.

The upstairs hall was quiet. Lockers lined white cinder-block walls, which were broken at intervals by closed classroom doors.

All except one, on the right. A spray of fluorescent light splashed onto the floor, and there was music, something lush and bittersweet.

Well, okay, so a teacher was getting a jump on the first day of classes, so what? I was going to my locker, no big deal. I'd just slide by, pray my locker door didn't make a racket, then dump my stuff and duck into the bathroom at the other end of the hall.

I moved fast, on the balls of my feet, quiet as a mouse. The music was everywhere. It billowed. Walking into the swell of violins was like passing into a fine mist, and I couldn't help it. I slowed, just a little, tossing a quick glance to the right—

And stopped dead.

Because Oh. My. God.

3: a

It was your standard chemistry classroom: desks and chairs in the center ringed by lab benches and high stools, with a demonstration bench up front. Chrome spigots, sinks. Nothing special.

Nothing, that is, but him.

His back was to me. He stood at the far side of a lab table, staring out a bank of windows overlooking the woods to the northeast. The sky was a clear, crisp cerulean blue. The rays of the rising sun bathed his shoulders and back, which were flawless and very muscular, a rich, warm gold.

Because he was naked.

b

I had turned to stone. I just . . . Bob, I just couldn't move. You have no idea, or maybe you do. Like when you first saw the girl who would be your wife. . . . Maybe it wasn't a thunderbolt moment for you, but even my parents, as messed up as they are, remember the instant they first laid eyes on each other. So I remember every second of that first time.

He was . . .

He was *beautiful*, like something out of a dream. When he shrugged into a pale blue button-down, sunlight rippled over valleys made of muscle and that smooth, smooth skin. His hair, dark and curly, fired with red and blond highlights. His movements were fluid and graceful and utterly unselfconscious because he thought he was alone. He was a demigod, and I was, well . . . *awed*. Like someone this perfect just couldn't *be*.

I know that sounds hokey to you, Bob. But that's how I felt. That's the truth and that very first moment of sun and light and beauty is one I will never, ever forget.

C

Maybe I made a sound. Or he knew he was being watched. Either way, he sensed something because he began to turn and move away from the windows. That's when I saw he wasn't naked but wearing khaki slacks cinched around a trim waist. His mouth unhinged in surprise. "Wha—?"

"Sorry!" And then I was bolting, a freaked-out little bunny scuttling down the hall. Bathroom, bathroom, where was the bathroom . . . there! I darted for the door at a dead run, thinking: *If I can just get away. . . .*

Of course, it was locked. I hit pretty hard, too. The impact balled in my shoulder then shivered down my right arm. I staggered back and then the lid of that stupid coffee cup popped like a cork from a bottle of Champagne. A gush of tepid cappuccino sheeted over the door and sloshed over my skirt and bare legs. Sticky liquid crawled down my calves and leaked into my shoes. *Oh no no no . . .*

"Whoa, whoa, hey." He was in the hall now. "It's okay, it's okay; relax, I'm not going to hurt you; it's *okay.*"

I burst into tears.

4: a

His name was Mr. Anderson, and he taught chemistry, which I had eighth period. Back in his classroom, he handed over a wad of paper towels and pointed me to a back room: "There's a sink. Plenty of soap. Take your time."

The back room was a kind of office with a couple computers, a coffeepot, a fume hood, and a short hall leading to more doors and a storage room lined with shelves of chemicals. Music swelled from a Bose stereo squatting on a windowsill.

The putty-colored stain on the khaki skirt I'd laid out so carefully the night before was dark and precisely centered over my crotch. A fist-sized splash of coffee splotched my shirt. Even after everything dried, I would look—and smell—as if I'd taken a bath in a coffeepot. Great. At least my canvas slides were dark blue.

There was a cake of Dove at the sink. I washed off my arms and splashed water on my face then inspected myself in a small mirror hanging on the wall. My eyes were raw and red as if someone had thrown a fistful of sand, but otherwise I didn't look too bad. Only now what? God, I was so embarrassed. Maybe I could just hide out here until the bell rang and—

"You okay back there?" Mr. Anderson called from the classroom. "Need anything else?"

How about a new life? "No. I mean, I'm fine, thanks. Be right out."

Come on. Forking a handful of hair from my forehead, I hefted my backpack onto a shoulder and blew out, the way I used to right before a big race. *He's only a teacher; he's not going to bite. Just apologize and go.*

Mr. Anderson was back at his windows, in a wedge of bright sun, sipping coffee from a black *X-Files* mug. When he heard me, he looked over and smiled. "Better?"

I nodded, tongue-tied, all the words I'd thought about saying jamming up behind my teeth. Mr. Anderson's face was lean but square with high cheekbones, just the suggestion of a cleft in his chin and a broad forehead framed by thick, dark curls. His eyes were a startling, bright, silver-blue, like ancient ice, and his skin was bronzed from time in the sun. "Th-thanks," I finally managed. "I'm . . . I'm sorry I made such a mess."

"Don't worry about it. You were just lucky that coffee wasn't hot. While you were cleaning up, I did the hall. One less thing for Harley to complain about." He raised his mug. "Need a cup?"

"No," and then thought that sounded rude, so I added: "I don't really like coffee. It was my mother's idea."

"Smart woman. Coffee is the elixir of life." He hesitated. "Look, uh, about earlier . . . what I was doing . . ."

"It's okay," I said, quickly. "Honest."

He put a hand up. "Let me apologize, okay? All I wanted to say was I'm sorry I scared you. You kind of caught me out. I wasn't expecting anyone around this early, *obviously*." The way he rolled his eyes made me giggle and he grinned. His teeth were square and very white. He had a nice smile. "That's better. I'm training for an Iron Man. Summer's no problem but once school starts up, I have to squeeze in time when I can. You a runner?"

"I used to run cross-country," I said and then wondered why I was telling him anything. Well, he *had* been nice. He could've kicked me right back downstairs.

"For real? What's your time for a 5K?" I told him, and he made impressed sounds. "Not bad. You done any middle distance? Eight or fifteen hundred?"

"No. I haven't run in a while, actually. I mean, I haven't been training. Anyway, I just liked to run. I like . . . speed." That wasn't quite what I meant to say, but *to fly* sounded, well, weird and I was supposed to be acting normally.

"I like the power," he said. "You know, when everything's working the way it should and nothing hurts? You slip into that zone where you're skimming the ground, almost like you're running alongside the earth instead of on it."

"Slipstream," I said. It just came out.

He nodded, his eyes serious. He wouldn't be the kind to laugh even if he thought I was an idiot, I knew that. "That's right. Only real runners get that." He paused. "So . . . you interested in training again? I'm the track and cross-country coach and, well, I could always use another pair of legs, especially varsity girls."

Then he ran a hand through his hair and let out a little laugh. "Sorry. School hasn't even started and you're new and already I'm trying to sell you on a sport. You'd probably like to settle in before getting yourself weighed down with a million obligations. Come on, I'll walk you downstairs to the library just in case Harley's still lurking."

He waited as I checked my left palm where I'd penned my locker combination that morning. Unfortunately, between the coffee and washing up, the writing was faded and blurred, and I messed up the combination twice. Mr. Anderson waited a beat then said, "You have to twirl it twice clockwise to reset the mechanism and . . . Here, let me." He reached past. "What's the combination?"

I told him. This close, he smelled of sunlight, pine needles, and Dove soap. He spun the knob right, then left, then once around clockwise, and then stopped on the last number before giving the handle a yank. The locker clanked open.

"Thanks." After I'd stowed my stuff, we walked back down the hall, past his classroom. That lush music was still playing, and I said, "That's really nice. I've heard it before—in a movie." I thought a second. "*Blume in Love*, that last scene where they're in St. Mark's square."

"Yeah?" Cocking his head, he closed his eyes, listened a moment, said, "You know, now that you mention it . . . that's right. But George Segal?" He gave me a curious look. "He's not even *my* generation. How do you know the movie?"

If there's one thing you have plenty of time for on a psych ward, it's watching DVDs. But I couldn't say that, so I just shrugged. "I like movies. So, what's the music?"

"It's from an opera, *Tristan and Isolde*. Wagner was kind of a Nazi, but I love his music. Like the helicopter scene in *Apocalypse Now*? That's Wagner, too."

"Really?"

"Mmm-hmmm. 'Ride of the Valkyries.' Robert Duvall is . . ." And Mr. Anderson kept that up all the way down the stairs, this steady patter about opera and films with classical music scores. *2001* even *I* knew, but *Alien*?

Harley was nowhere to be seen. As we neared the library, Mr. Anderson said, "So where do you live that you have to come in so early?"

"Lakeside."

His eyebrows lifted. "Yeah? We're practically neighbors. I live maybe twenty miles west, a little past Plymouth in the Kettle Moraine. Why are you going to school here?" He listened as I gave him the SparkNotes version of my rehearsed speech: *We live up north, only my mom's bookstore is down here and Turing is such a great school, so blah, blah, blah.*

"Which bookstore?" he asked.

"MacAllister's."

"Really? Cool. My wife's a big reader."

"Oh." That he had a wife was like a pinprick. I felt myself deflate, which was completely stupid. Of course, he was married; he was *gorgeous*. Was he wearing a ring? No, I didn't think so, but no way in hell I was going to look, not then. Not *ever*. Jesus, how many different ways can you spell *loser*? "What does she like to read?"

"Romance, mainly, and literary fiction. She likes someone local . . . uhm . . . Simmons, I think."

"Meryl? She's a really good friend of ours. My mom's known her since they were kids. Mom usually has a big writers' party the last weekend in September and Meryl comes down from her farm up north to, you know, sign books and stuff."

"Seriously? My wife will be impressed."

"Maybe I can get her an autographed book. Or Mom can invite you to the party." I was babbling. What did I care if his wife had a signed copy of Meryl's latest? As we got to the library doors—open, mercifully, and the lights were on—I finished, lamely, "For the reading, I mean."

"Sure, that would be nice," he said, but his eyes were already dropping to his watch and I could tell his mind was leapfrogging ahead to the rest of his day. "Well, you'll be okay now. See you eighth period, Ms. Lord."

The librarian was half asleep and sucking from a gallon coffee mug. She just gave me a vague wave and grunted that I could sit anywhere I liked. I prowled until I spotted a solitary desk snugged beneath a window at the end of a stack. I knew as soon as I saw it that this was the perfect spot: books to my right and a window on the world to my left.

Only much later did I realize that the view faced northeast, same as Mr. Anderson's windows. We might even be looking at the same thing at precisely the same moment, although I had a feeling that whatever he saw would be different. After all, I was on the ground level and he was directly above, with a clearer, sharper, brighter view.

And that . . . well, I don't know, Bob. But when I realized that?

It just seemed like this really good omen.

5: a

The first bell rang, but Ms. Sherman didn't flinch. Her fingers toyed with her letter opener: long and pointed with a blocky handle fashioned out of green stone. "Of course, all our students are exceptional. It's not that I want to give you the wrong idea, that you're somehow all alone, dear," she said. Dropping the opener, she twined her fingers together. For a second, I worried she was going to start praying. "But it's not uncommon for very bright students to be more . . . *sensitive* or socially awkward. I just don't want you to feel as if no one understands."

"Okay," I said, "thanks." Not five minutes after I settled down in the library, Ms. Sherman had ambushed me for a little face time to see how I was getting on. Considering school hadn't started yet, she probably wanted to reassure herself that the crazy new girl wasn't going to go postal her first day. I was only glad she hadn't seen me almost break my arm running away from Mr. Anderson.

Ms. Sherman and I had met during orientation two weeks earlier. She was like all guidance counselors: earnest and eager to convince me that it was safe to open up about all my troubles, what we said was confidential, blah, blah, blah. Her eyes were moist and dark brown, like a cocker spaniel's.

"There are other students here who are under a psychiatrist's care or been in a hospital or institution," she said, clearly deciding to abandon the nuanced approach. "So there's no need for you to feel alone. How often are you seeing your therapist?"

Shit. If I said twice a week, that sounded like I was barely holding it together. Every week was only a little better. Of course, since I wasn't seeing *anyone* . . . "Every month," I lied. "I used to go more often, but . . ." I let that dangle.

"Curious." She thumbed open a manila folder, flipped through papers, ran the manicured ice pick of a fingernail down one page. "Your parents neglected to give us your therapist's name and number."

"Why do you need it?"

"Just in case."

"In case what?"

She paused, studying me with her big wet eyes. A thought-bubble ballooned over her head: *Oh hell, I hope she's taken her medication this morning; is she on meds; where* is *that panic button?* "In case you run into difficulties," she finally said, only gently, like she'd just walked into a sickroom with a terminal patient. "We like to know who to call."

Ghostbusters? God, Bob, I *swear* that was on the tip of my tongue. The moment was so *perfect.* But, no, she might not have a sense of humor and then I'd only sound weirder than I already was. "Wouldn't you just call my parents?"

"Jenna." Her lips compressed. She was all through being sweet and understanding. "Is there a reason we shouldn't know who you're seeing?"

"Because it's private? It's none of your business?"

"Really, Jenna, there's no need for hostility. We only want—" She broke off as her phone buzzed. She picked it up, said hello, listened for a few seconds, then said, "I'll be right there." Hanging up, she scraped back her chair. "Look, I don't want to be blunt or cruel about this, dear, but we simply don't want to risk a repeat of your, ah . . . difficulties."

"I thought you said you guys were used to kids with problems."

Her face set. "Wait here." She left, pulling her door shut with a sharp, incisive snick.

I waited. A skinny rectangle of reinforced glass—the kind with chicken wire—was set in the office door. From my chair, I could see into the hall for only a few feet in either direction. I heard muffled voices, the buzz of a phone. A woman walked by, her arms full of papers. She flicked a bland look through the caged window the way you might eye a drab zoo animal of no particular interest and kept going. There was a clock above the door that ticked off the seconds in loud, percussive pistol shots.

I stared at Ms. Sherman's letter opener. The blade was brassy and pointed and looked pretty sharp. My fingers moved in a spastic little twitch, like the legs of a hermit crab. I fired a glance back at the door. No one in the window.

The letter opener was much heavier than I expected. I balanced the tip on the pad of my left index finger and pressed, grinned as the skin dimpled. You could put your eye out with that thing.

For the first time in months, the scars on my stomach squirmed. The skin grafts between my shoulder blades bunched. My ears roared and I had to close my eyes. I wondered how hard I would have to push to draw blood. Not hard, I decided.

A few seconds, that's all I'd need.

Then I heard the second bell and thought, *Screw it.* My morning had been pretty crummy so far, but doing *that*, no matter how much I wanted to, would be admitting I was a complete head case. Besides, another half minute or so and then I'd be late for my very first class on my very first day and there was just no way.

So I didn't wait for Ms. Sherman. And I put her stupid letter opener back before I slid out the door.

6: a

The halls were too bright and jammed with other kids all chattering and laughing. Until that moment, I hadn't been around that many kids for almost a year, and I just stood there, in shock, a rock in a fast-flowing river that parted and eddied and swirled on. Snatches of conversation spun past like leaves swept along a swift current:

". . . his mom went ballist . . ."

"He said what?"

"No way, I told him, I'm not that kind . . ."

". . . and then Dad saw the car and he *totally* flipped out. . . ."

"Oh, here comes Robbie, I don't . . ."

"My mom was *so* pissed. . . ."

"He said what?"

I spawned upstream and made it to trig before the late bell. The teacher wore smudgy Lennon specs that made him as bug-eyed as that fish-headed commander in the first *Star Wars* movie. (Come on, Bob, you know: the one where the Muppet-alien shouts, "*It's a trap!*") Fish Eyes squinted through smears and studied the attendance card Ms. Sherman had insisted on, probably because she wanted to, well, *alert* everyone about just who the crazy new kid was. Then Fish Eyes aimed a stubby finger to an open seat in the middle of the class: "We sit in alphabetical order."

Great. You know that very last scene in *The Birds*, Bob, the one where Rod Taylor and the old lady who played his mom are trying to get Tippi Hedren into the car, only they have to run this gauntlet of seagulls and crows that might just peck their eyes out? Well, this was like that. I swear, it felt like a gazillion eyes drilled my back, all these other kids watching and waiting for me to trip or burp or fart, or maybe all three. I made it to my desk without any drama and that seemed to be the general cue for everyone to go back to gossiping, which was fine by me.

Then, maybe ten seconds after I slid into my seat, I felt a tap on my right shoulder. I couldn't help it; I flashed to Harley and that dumb coffee cup: *This yours?* I turned.

"David Melman." He had dark eyes and a mop of muddy brown hair. When he smiled, a dimple showed at the left corner of his mouth. He stuck out a hand. "Welcome to Turing."

"Jenna Lord. Uhm, pleased to meet you." His skin was soft, but his grip was very firm. The handshake was weirdly comfortable and formal all at the same time.

"Everyone will tell you that I'm just being nice because I'm running for student council," David said. "They're partly right."

"About the student council part, or the being nice part?"

"Oh, I'm running. Looks good on the résumé. If you haven't gotten that speech from your advisor yet, you will. Do you know who that is?"

"I'm too busy trying to find my way around."

The tardy bell rang. David dropped his voice to a whisper, "Well, if you need any help or don't understand something, just ask, okay?"

"Sure." I gave my perkiest *you bet* grin and faced forward. But, to tell you the truth, Bob, I was a little pissed off, too. Like, did I *look* as if I needed the help?

This is just like the ward. I inched a little lower in my seat. *Don't shout, don't make a fuss, smile at the doctor and we'll all be just fine.*

The first day of all classes is virtually the same, regardless of the school. Trig was no different. Fish Eyes finished calling attendance and then got a couple students to hand out textbooks. We spent the next twenty minutes going through the books, looking for stray marks, and noting where other students had scribbled in answers. Then, in the fifteen minutes that were left, Fish Eyes snorted and snuffled his way through the first chapter, all of it review, and assigned homework—"Even problems, one through sixty"—with maybe thirty seconds to spare before the bell shrilled.

Thank you, GAWD. I gathered up my books as everyone else started jabbering like caged parakeets. All the noise was the perfect cover, though. I figured to just slip in behind those three girls and glide on out—

David slid in at my elbow. "What do you have next?"

"Ah." I had to think about it a sec. "Honors English."

"Oh, you'll like Dewerman." He grinned. "He's really—"

"Ms. Lord," Fish Eyes called just as we got to the door. "A moment, please."

I braked so quickly that David nearly tripped over my feet. "Sorry," I said.

"It's okay," he said. "You want me to wait?"

"Ah . . ." Everyone else was spilling around us, some tossing curious glances and others smirking: *Yeah, sucks to be you.* To be honest, David was getting on my nerves. I wasn't a lost puppy, for God's sake, just the crazy new kid.

"No, I'm good, thanks," I said. David opened his mouth to say something else, but I was already doing a quick about-face.

"David, if you'll close the door on your way out?" Fish Eyes called.

"Sure," David said. "See you, Jenna."

"Yeah," I said but didn't look around. I heard the door snick shut. The room was dead quiet except for the shush of my slides over linoleum as I walked back to Fish Eyes's desk.

"Yes, sir?" I wasn't sure if I ought to say *sir,* but I blanked on the guy's name and *Fish Eyes* would probably be a mistake. "Is there a problem? Did I do something wrong?"

"Wrong? Oh, no, no." Fish Eyes tugged off his glasses and dragged a cloth from his front pocket. Without his specs, his eyes dwindled to lead pellets. "I just wanted to let you know how delighted we all are that you're here, Jenna. . . . May I call you Jenna? Good. . . . I've, uh, had the opportunity to look at your record—your placement exams and those you took while you were homeschooled—and they are impressive, most impressive. Particularly." He *hawed* on one lens and rubbed with the cloth. "Particularly given your, ah, peculiar circumstances."

37

I said nothing. I could feel the heat rising up my neck and splashing over my face. My God, was it going to be like this with every teacher? No, wait, that wasn't fair. Mr. Anderson hadn't treated me like a freak. Yet. Maybe he just hadn't placed the name with the diagnosis.

"We, uh, know that you've had quite the, ah, *struggle*," Fish Eyes said. "A very bad, very tough time of it. I want you to know how sorry I am about—"

"Thanks." In five seconds, my twitching skin would rip itself from my bones and go screaming down the hall. All I wanted was to run run run and find someplace to cut in peace. "I should go," I said, flashing a bright, chipper little grin. "Wouldn't want to be late my first day." Which was true enough.

"No, of course not." Fish Eyes slipped on his glasses. "I just want you to know that if you, ah, need anything, any *special* help, just want to *talk* maybe . . ."

"Thanks," I said, edging away, grinning my frozen little rictus of a grin. "Thanks a lot."

I didn't exactly run, not like I had from Mr. Anderson. Oh, I wanted to, but my eyes stung and I would probably have bashed into a wall. And, anyway, running was just too pathetic. But I was still moving pretty fast and so, of course, as I burst through the door and into the general swirl, I didn't look where I was going.

Bam!

I plowed right into David Melman so hard that even *he* staggered. My notebooks, bright M&M colors, fluttered like broken-winged kites. My trig textbook promptly got turned into a hacky sack by assorted legs and feet before some kid scooped it up on the fly and backhanded it to David.

"Whoa, you okay? Here, let me." David stooped just as I bent to pick up my notebooks and we banged heads. My vision sheeted white. This time, both our trig books went to ground. "Jeez." David put a hand to his forehead. "Are you all right?"

"I'm fine," I said for what must be the millionth time that day. How many hours had I been at this already? I could feel a knot beginning right above my left eyebrow. Great. Now I'd look like a rhino. "Are you okay?"

"Yeah." David started piling notebooks into my arms. "I just hung around in case you needed, you know, help getting to your next class."

"No, I'm good," I said, as the second bell rang. "But I've got to go. See you, okay?"

"Wait." David grabbed my elbow. "You won't get there in time if you go that way. Come on, we'll take a shortcut through the cafeteria."

This time, I didn't argue. We pretty much jogged down the stairs and into the lunchroom, which already had a sprinkling of kids in small knots, drinking coffee and munching doughnuts. Someone shouted at David, but he waved them off and then we were blasting out of the lunchroom and into a side corridor.

"Okay," David said. He was panting a little, and his dark hair was mussed. "You go all the way down the hall, last door on your left. I have to go upstairs now, but I'll be back in time to take you to your third period class. And we've got the same lunch. Sit with me and I'll introduce you around."

"I don't need an escort," I said as he started for a narrow stairwell.

"Yes, you do," he said over his shoulder. "You just don't know it yet."

7: a

Honors English, second period: I blew through the door after the tardy bell. Of course, the only seats left were in front. I scuttled into one closest to the wall. Everyone ignored me, which was fine. The teacher, Dewerman, was nowhere in sight. Most everyone was chatting with someone else except for one girl two rows back who didn't look away. She was pretty in a sporty kind of way, with a long blonde ponytail, good skin, and preppy clothes, the kind of girl who might be either a cheerleader or captain of the soccer team. When my eyes skipped over her, she turned to whisper something to another girl, who shot a glance, made a face, giggled, and whispered something back.

I looked away. A survival tactic I learned on the psych ward was how to quickly size up potential enemies or garden-variety badasses. Ponytail did *not* like me, that was clear. *Fine. You don't bother me, I won't bother you.* But I wondered what I'd done to tick her off. Unless she disliked new kids on general principle.

My gaze skimmed the walls. Dewerman liked posters, the ones with celebs urging you to read, and art reproductions: Van Gogh, Rembrandt, Picasso. Behind his desk and snugged along the wall to my left were three bookcases crammed with hardcovers and paperbacks, arranged alphabetically. My eyes ran over the spines—and then the title of a very familiar book hooked my gaze like the business end of a steel barb.

Oh shit. My stomach bottomed out. My eyes cut away, but the title was burned onto my retinas the way the sun scorched if you looked too long. *Relax; he doesn't know; no one here does; just let it slide. . . .*

"Welcome back, boys and girls!" Dewerman barreled in, an enormous mug clutched in one paw. My God, Bob, every single adult in this place was this major addict. Dewerman was this bearded 1960s throwback: a Teletubby in tie-dye, suspenders, and thinning hair scraped back into a stringy gray rat. "All right, let's roll."

He did the attendance drill. Ponytail was Danielle Connolly, which fit. I gave my prepared *Hi-I'm-Jenna* spiel and was about to sit back down when Dewerman shot me a curious look. "Your mother owns a bookstore? Is it MacAllister's?"

"Uh." *Why* had I mentioned the store to begin with? I knew he had the book. It was like I was daring him to put two and two together. I could've lied. Maybe I should've. But, instead, I said, "Yeah."

"Well, I'll be damned." Dewerman bustled over to the bookshelf, fingered out the paperback I'd recognized and held

41

it up. It was one of the reissues because *THE COMPLETE UN-EXPURGATED EDITION OF THE SHATTERING NOVEL* screamed from the cover.

Because, of course, Dewerman was a fanboy.

b

A little sidebar, Bob, because you don't look like the bookish type. That's not a slam, it's just . . . well, it's probably a fact. If I were directing the movie of your life, I figure you must've been a star athlete in high school, probably football. Ten to one, you were angling for a scholarship, only you messed up your knees or back, and that's why you became a cop. Only I bet you got bored or sick of standing by while EMTs scraped people you knew—friends, old drinking buddies, maybe a girlfriend— off the pavement. Maybe you cut one too many people out of crushed cars. You had to think that, hell, making detective's got to be better. Break-ins, assaults, drug deals, but not a lot of bodies. You had to think that there just aren't many homicides this far north. Maybe one or two a year, tops.

Of course, at the time, you hadn't met me.

Anyway . . . my grandmother was Stephanie A. MacAllister. To everyone else, my mom's mom was this brilliant writer who started sleeping around when she was ten. Honestly, Bob, if you believed her, Grandma MacAllister had sex with just about everything but a gerbil and then wrote about it. Give her enough time, she might have figured out the gerbil, too.

Of course, the book—*Memoirs of a Very Good Girl*—was banned and burned and trashed, so just about everyone read and talked about it. My mom always says there is no such thing as bad publicity. By the time she was thirty-five, Grandma MacAllister had made a fortune, started a pretty famous artists' colony, opened up her bookstore, discovered new talent, promoted reading, blah, blah, blah. She never wrote another book. I never asked why because I hadn't been born when she hanged herself from a sturdy wooden closet dowel in a swank New York hotel the night she won some award for lifetime achievement.

She left the store to Mom, which pissed off Grandpa—he of the drunken, chain-smoking, torch-the-house rampage. Mom used to be a poet and did pretty well. Although after Matt was gone, she bought up all the copies of her one collection she could find and burned them in this giant bonfire in the old, pre-McMansion backyard.

After Grandma died, Mom poured everything into the bookstore. That hummed along fairly smoothly until 2003, which is when Matt left. Since then, sales have crashed, publishing has cratered, and Mom and the store . . . well, it's like handing a bucket to a bulimic, Bob. No matter how much you vomit, the bucket's never quite full enough.

C

As Dewerman rambled on, my back began to burn, and I felt the wings of my skin grafts, the ones between my shoulder blades, straining to tug free. My throat tried to close against the memory of thick, acrid smoke. Until that instant, I had been the new kid, a nobody, just another transfer. Only my teachers knew anything about my *little episode*, but no one had made the connection to my gerbil-screwing, sex-crazed grandmother. Now everyone would look her up, if only to suck up to Dewerman. Would there be anything about our family? Me?

"...comparison analysis." Dewerman's voice leaked through. "Suicide is a highly individual choice. The psycho-analysts would tell you there's an intimate connection between creativity and madness."

Danielle raised her hand. "Doesn't suicide run in families?"

Dewerman opened his mouth, but I beat him to it. "Well," I said, trying to sound all jokey, thinking—stupidly—I could salvage something by being so very über-cool, "*I'm* still alive."

"Well," said Danielle, "so far."

8: a

I motored out of English fast enough to blur. If David was there, I didn't see him. I don't know what freaked me out more: Dewerman's gushing, people finding out about my crazy grandma, or Danielle's razor-sharp eyes.

I clicked to crisis mode, my go-to where the world smears and I slide into a parallel reality, like when I'm running. Rebecca called it *depersonalization*, but that's bullshit, Bob. I never float along and watch *myself*. I watch you guys. Think Ariel in a fishbowl. The world becomes water and I bob along in my glass bubble, right alongside. You see me, I see you, but we inhabit different bodies of water. You can't touch me, and I can't touch you and that's just fine.

I floated like that through honors-level world studies and on to fourth period gym where I made like Clark Kent's girlie clone, changing in a bathroom stall instead of a phone booth. No one cared. The teacher spent half the period talking about safety and the other half making us shoot hoops. No stress, no fuss.

So, by lunch, I was starting to relax.

Big mistake.

b

I don't know what I was thinking. Once the fire happened—and especially once Matt was gone—I learned to hate the cafeteria, that momentary pause when a thousand eyes scanned and then dismissed me, the whispers trailing like bad odors as I made my way to a solitary corner. But this was a new school, right? My get-normal campaign? Things had to get better. Besides, David said he'd save a seat.

Right away, I spotted Mr. Anderson standing just inside the door. Okay, good omen. He was talking to another student, but as I scooted by, he nodded and said, "Ms. Lord." I kept on another four steps, heard my name and, yes, there was David standing at a far table, waving both arms. I started that way—

And then spotted Danielle on his right.

Okay, this was bad. Even across the lunchroom, I read her expression: *Stay away or I'll scrape your tonsils out with a fork.*

Yeah, see, this was just more trouble I didn't need. So, without breaking stride, I did this abrupt midcourse correction, a complete one-eighty—which was my second big mistake.

Someone yelped, "Hey!"

A split second later, I collided with a taco salad, salsa, French fries, and a large Coke. The guy carrying the tray cursed. Sticky brown fluid sloshed across my chest. Ice chattered to the floor like dice. A squishy gob of sour cream and black beans glued itself to my left thigh.

And there was Absolute. Complete. Total. Silence.

I could hear Coke raining onto the floor. No one was moving except Mr. Anderson, who was already starting over. Everyone else gawked at the freak, the alien who'd just beamed down. David stood, a look of shock leaking across his face. Danielle smirked.

"Whoa," said the kid whose lunch I was wearing. "Are you okay?"

Mr. Anderson was ten feet away. "Ms. Lord . . ."

"I'm okay." My voice was strangled, gargly, strange, and then I was moving fast, scuttling out of the cafeteria and down the hall, banging into the bathroom. Empty. No one at the sinks. I gulped air like a hooked salmon dying of slow suffocation. The remnants of the kid's taco salad had oozed down my thigh and fallen off somewhere along the way. I looked around for paper towels and found nothing but a bank of blow-dryers. Great. A very progressive, environmentally minded school. I dove into the first stall and slammed the door. Hunkering on the toilet, I hugged my knees. Stupid, stupid, *stupid*.

A few minutes later, the bathroom door opened again. A swell of hall chatter ballooned in. Peeking, I saw four feet as the girls crossed to the sinks. I heard the unzipping of purses, rummaging sounds.

"Oh my God," one girl said. "I almost died, it was so funny. Did you see her *face*?"

"She's in my English class," said the other, and I recognized Danielle's voice. "Her grandmother was some kind of crazy famous writer. Dewerman almost had an orgasm."

"I saw David with her."

"So?" Smacking noises as Danielle inspected her lipstick. "He was just being nice. That boy and his strays . . . The more broken they are, the better he likes them, just like Anderson."

"Mr. Anderson's nice." The click of a compact. "I thought you liked him. You said he was cool."

A pause. "He is. You know, he talks to everybody, and he writes these killer recommendations. I just wish he'd decide already if I can take over David's TA slot once the fencing season gets started. God, I hope that girl's got Schroeder for chemistry. Otherwise . . ." They went on like that for a while, eventually moving on to other losers. Then they left.

I stayed in my stall. Not in school a full day and I'd already made the gossip rounds of the mascara-and-lipstick crowd. At least, I now knew why Danielle hated me. She didn't have to worry. From that moment on, David Melman wouldn't get a drop of encouragement.

I peeled off my soggy shirt to inspect the damage. My skin was alien and yellow under the bathroom fluorescents, the lumpy scars pale as tapeworms, the donor sites on my thighs only the faintest of rectangles.

My body was a memory quilt, a patchwork of scars and moods and deeds best left to fester in the dark. *Here*, Matt ran with me from the house as my back boiled. *There* is where Mom smothered me with her coat. And that pucker on my belly there is where Grandpa MacAllister, still alive after the fire and senile, tried pinching my ass so I twisted a staple out of an informational pamphlet on Alzheimer's and jabbed until the blood bubbled.

(Mom, screaming: *Don't you dare save . . .*)

I wanted so badly to cut, I could taste it. But the thought that someone like Danielle would tip the balance made me mad. No way would I give that bitch the satisfaction.

C

I crept out about thirty seconds after the second bell. The river of kids had dwindled to a trickle. Mr. Anderson was leaning against the wall at the foot of the stairs but pushed off when he saw me coming. Too late, nowhere to run. The day wasn't even done, and I felt as if I'd spent my whole life running into things and away from him.

"Here." He dealt me a late pass. "You might need this. You okay?"

No. But I gave an all-purpose shrug, hoping he'd read it as *yes* and let me slink away.

"It'll get better. Just give it time."

"I should get to class." Then I remembered: "Actually, the library. I've got study hall."

"Then walk with me for a second."

I remembered what Danielle had said about Mr. Anderson liking the broken ones. Well, if that was true, what was *her* problem? Whatever. "I'm okay."

"All right," he said, easily. "No pressure."

All of a sudden, I felt bad. He was just being nice. "I'm sorry."

"What for? You have nothing to apologize about, Ms. Lord. You're allowed your feelings." He hesitated then said, "Look, I run or bike every other morning. You get here so early, if you ever want to come along, you're welcome to. Runs are always nicer when you've got a partner. And no pressure to join the team, I promise."

"Thanks." I knew I wouldn't take him up on his offer, but the fact that he *had* bothered made me feel better. "I'll think about it."

"Liar," but he smiled as he said it. "Well, the offer always stands. Come on, we'll go to my room. It's my planning period, and I've got a blow-dryer you can use for that shirt. Back room will give you plenty of privacy."

"What about study hall? Shouldn't I go to the library?"

"What for, Ms. Lord?" Mr. Anderson said. "You're with me."

9: a

And the rest of that day...

Oh, who cares? You know, Bob, school is school, one of those life experiences we kids all have to get through in order to become you. Then we wonder what all the fuss was about, especially while we're cleaning up your little messes: toxic waste, war, bank bailouts. Honestly, if we ran up debt the way you guys do? You'd ground us, take away our cells, and make us clean toilets with a toothbrush until we'd paid back every penny.

Anyway, things haven't changed that much from when you went, I bet. The only people who love school are either the über-popular kids with about a bazillion Facebook friends and no credit limit, or the truly geeky. Or the sports people, I guess. The rest of us fly below the radar, or try to, anyway.

So here's the only other important thing. Well, two things, actually. Okay, three.

b

One:

In chemistry, Mr. Anderson did not make me stand up and give my spiel. Oh, he took attendance. When he got to my name, though, he never looked up, didn't pause, just kept right on rolling so my name was lost in the general blur. Maybe he figured I'd had enough. Pretty much everyone knew my story by then, anyway. So I would've been one of the anonymous masses except . . .

c

Two:

Danielle threw a whisper to a classmate right after he called my name. Nothing audible, but when they both snickered, Mr. Anderson paused, drilled Danielle with a look and asked if she had anything she'd like to share.

Danielle looked stunned, like she couldn't believe he'd call her out like that. "*Excuse* me?"

"I said, would you like to share, or take your conversation into the hall?" Folding his arms, Mr. Anderson leaned back against the board. "We'll be happy to wait until you're done."

The class was deathly quiet. Everyone was looking at Danielle, even me. Well, I couldn't help it; I'd chosen the very last row. So I saw the color ooze up her neck.

"No," said Danielle, finally. Her voice was very small. "I'm sorry. It won't happen again."

"Excellent," said Mr. Anderson. "Now, where was I? Ah, here we go . . . Jim Morris?"

ₐ

And three:

Mr. Anderson lectured for about thirty minutes on safety, the curriculum, blah, blah, blah. But then he did an experiment.

"Let's look at what happens to liquid hexane in air and on glass," he said, after turning off the lights. We were goggled up and clustered around his demo bench. He squirted a few drops onto a huge glass spatter plate as big as an elephant's contact lens. Next he held a flint over the plate and scraped out a shower of sparks.

The hexane caught with a faint *bah*. The flame burned slowly, but it was also clean and very bright, almost white. Everyone oooohed and from where I stood, Bob, the way he palmed the glass? Mr. Anderson had scooped up a handful of flame with his bare hands.

"Now, watch what happens when the hexane's in a plastic bottle. You might want to stand back a little for this one." He coated the inside of the bottle then carefully slid a long rod into the mouth and set off a spark.

BUMPH! The hexane erupted in a bright, violent fountain of flame that spewed from the bottle like a blowtorch. Everyone gasped; a couple people clapped. Someone said, *"Whoa."*

"Yeah, very *whoa*. So here's what you've got to remember, people. The conditions under which an experiment is performed are key. Change a single parameter and you might alter the outcome. On the watch glass, the vapors dissipated. It's still hexane and it's no less volatile, but you get a nice, controlled burn. Yet ignite that same hexane in an environment from which the vapors can't escape, and now you'll get an explosion, no less beautiful," Mr. Anderson said, "but deadly."

10: a

The thing about starting school a week before Labor Day is you go to school for four days and then you have a long weekend. There's no time to get into any kind of groove, and the next week's going to be short, too. So you're all, I don't know . . . discombobulated. At least I was. If I were normal and had, oh, a social life, I'd be as thrilled as every other girl not to be in school that next Monday. Instead, I got dragged along on our monthly guilt-pilgrimage to see my grandpa.

Well, it's not like I was ever like any other girl anyway.

b

"Stephie, honey." Even before the fire, Grandpa MacAllister—husband of my nutty, sex-crazed grandmother—was a gargoyle, with his beaky nose and bright, button-black eyes. The whole left side of his face was drippy now, like molten candle wax, because of a stroke he'd had in the ICU. The good news was, most of the time, he didn't know who I was. He'd mistake me for Grandma Stephie or Aunt Betsy, my mom's sister who'd wisely moved to England and never came home, or someone named Helen, a woman no one knew. (Given the leer on Grandpa's face I was happy not knowing.) That Grandpa sometimes thought I was his wife—Mom's mom—drove Mom up a tree. "Stephie, you bring me a carton of those Camels I asked for?"

"Dad," my mom said wearily. She looked up from the windowsill where she was perched with her Crackberry and studying the store's spreadsheets. I don't know why she bothered to call what she did "visiting." "Mom's dead. That's Jenna . . . your granddaughter?"

"Don't you tell me what's what, Betsy." Grandpa's lips puckered to a wet, fleshy, liverish rosebud. A permanent trail of drool slicked the left corner of his mouth down to his jaw. "You think I don't know my own wife?"

"It's like I keep telling you," my father said. He was standing on the threshold of Grandpa's room, either because the air was better there or he could bolt that much faster. "They've got to up his meds."

My mom ignored him. "I'm Emily, Dad. Betsy's in Greenwich. Mom's dead, remember? She hanged herself in the hotel?"

"Don't I know it." Grandpa's face darkened and his gnarled fingers tugged at a fleshy wattle under his chin. Grandpa was Wisconsin-farmer stock. Of all the various . . . ah . . . *life-forms* she screwed, Grandma never wrote about her husband. Maybe when Grandma was young and famous and they were still rich (before Grandpa drank or gambled the rest away), he'd cleaned up pretty good. When they met, she was twenty-five, but he was over forty, widowed once and already boozy. So maybe he left her alone, never screwed her much, loved his vodka better. . . . I don't know. If he couldn't get it up, Grandma might've been relieved.

Anyway. Since the stroke, a lot of Grandpa's meanness poked through, like the skin of the mask he wore was sloughing off, leaving just the snake.

He said, "Left me her goddamned mess to clean up like she always did. I'll bet those maids couldn't get the stink of her shit out of the carpet for weeks."

"I'm telling you." My father rocked back and forth on his heels. "Meds."

Mom glared. "Would you shut up? You wouldn't be like this if it was your father."

"My father would never be like him."

Grandpa squinted at me. "What's wrong with those two, Stephie?"

"I don't know, Max," I said.

"Jenna, I wish you wouldn't do that," Mom said.

"Oh, what's the harm?" Dad said. "You think he's going to remember this in five minutes?"

"It's not respectful," Mom said.

"Like your father's ever been respectful."

"It's okay," I said. "Whatever makes him happy." That was a lie. I didn't care about making Grandpa happy. I hoped he never recognized the real me ever again.

"See? I know my own wife." Grandpa reached to pinch my ass.

Mom stiffened. "Don't touch her, Dad."

"It's okay," I said, pulling back before his fingers got a good hold. His touch made me wish I could peel my skin like a glove. Luckily, he couldn't get at me because the staff had strapped him to the wheelchair. To Grandpa: "I'm sorry I didn't bring you any cigarettes. I forgot."

"Figures." Grandpa turned sullen. "Stupid bitch."

"*Jennaaaa*," said Mom. "Don't get him excited."

"Don't blame her." Dad jingled change. "She can't make him any more confused than he already is."

"Shut up, you cocksuckers," Grandpa said. "She's my wife, not yours."

The doctors had explained that Grandpa's stroke was *disinhibiting*, which was a fancy medical term for Grandpa now said what he wanted whenever he wanted. Come to think of it, that wasn't much of a change.

"I told you about listening to those doctors." Grandpa waggled the stub of an index finger in my face. He'd been such a bad smoker, there were nicotine stains all the way to his knuckles. "Bad enough I got to sit here all day long. I can't have myself a good smoke?"

"It's not allowed, Max," I said. "I know it's hard. I'm sorry."

"Jesus," said my mother.

"Sorry." Grandpa made a sound that started out disgusted and came out a phlegmy, gargly hawk. He spat into his claw-hand, only half landed on his chin and dribbled onto his neck. He smeared the rest of his chest-snot on the twig of a thigh. "You always were one sorry bi—"

"*Dad*," my mother said.

"What?" said Grandpa, but you could tell Mom had broken his concentration because Grandpa's gaze went muzzy. "All right," he said, mildly, "all right." His claws rasped over stubble on his cheek and then his eyes traveled over my face and he blinked once, twice, like a sleepy lizard. "I'm just talking to

Betsy, we're just having a nice . . ." He fumbled for the words. "Father-daughter talk."

"Here we go," said Dad.

Mom: "Dad, that's not Betsy either."

Grandpa, to me: "So, girl, where's that husband of yours?"

Me: "Oh, you know, back at the house, mowing the lawn."

Mom: "Jenna, that's not funny."

Grandpa: "He finally doing some work? About time. I told you not to marry him. Anyone with half a brain could tell he didn't have his heart in it when it came to women."

Me: "I know, but what I can say? I was in love."

Mom: "*Jenna—*"

Dad: "I think it's pretty funny."

Mom: "He's not *your* father."

Dad: "Thank God for that."

Grandpa: "I am not deaf, Stewart, thank you very much."

Dad: "Glad to hear it, Max, but my name's Elliot. Max, what year is it?"

Mom: "Elliot."

Grandpa: "What's that got to do with anything?"

Dad: "What day?"

Mom: "*Elliot.*"

Dad: "What? I'm just orienting him. Who's the president, Max?"

Grandpa: "Nixon. Hah! Thought you'd trip me up."

Dad: "You're sharp as a tack, Max."

Grandpa: "Damn right. And, Stewart, don't think for one second I don't know you voted for that damn Kennedy."

Mom: "Oh, for—"

Dad (thought-bubble): *Told you.*

Grandpa: "Smooth-talking, skirt-chasing son of a bitch. Screw anything with a ho—"

Mom (stabbing her Crackberry): "Yeah, we've definitely got to be going."

Come to think of it, Bob, maybe Grandpa and Grandma deserved each other.

C

While Mom went to complain to the nurses, I tried to air-kiss Grandpa good-bye. Only when I got close, Grandpa's eyes sharpened and I knew he was seeing *me*-me.

"Jenna, such a sweet thing, you're my little sweetheart." His breath reeked of ancient tobacco, that morning's scrambled eggs, and chest rot. "You come back and visit your old grandpa anytime."

"Yeah," I said, stepping back fast as he made another grab but came up short. "Sure."

And then we were out of there, Dad peeling off to go break it up between Mom and the nurses while I ducked into the bathroom. The toilets smelled of baby powder and old farts. All the seats were higher off the ground and handicap-equipped. I huddled on a seat and clasped my arms around my stomach. If I'd been at a computer, I'd have e-mailed Matt, which sometimes helped, but that wasn't an option. My belly was twitching and my skin grafts burned as raw and fiery as they had when they were new. (Memo to Bob: What they don't tell you is that not only do the grafted sites *kill*, but the donor sites hurt as much as second-degree burns, and for just about as long. I was on fire, in one way or another, for a good year and a half.)

The metal prong of my watchband was nowhere near sharp enough, but I had to, I *had* to. That patch of unblemished skin on the left, below my navel, that would be good. *Yeah, yeah, come on, come on.* I really worked at it, coring and digging and twisting, the skin trying to jump out of the way. Cold sweat pearled my upper lip, and a bead crawled down the back of my neck to trickle between my skin grafts. *He touched me he saw me he touched me.*

(Mom, howling: *No, don't you do it. . . .*)

Finally, a red bead oozed and ballooned, and I sighed with relief as my blood bubbled and drew out the poison that was Grandpa.

There was this other cutter back on the ward. She etched words and letters. But I didn't.

Honestly, Bob: how do you carve a scream?

11: a

My parents started in as soon as we pulled out of the lot.

Mom: "Well, that wasn't so bad, was it?"

She said this every time. Dad always stared straight ahead and let the silence spin out.

Mom (an edge creeping into her voice, daring someone to disagree): "I thought he looked much better this time around."

Dad: "He was thinner and more confused, Emily. His tremor is worse and he's clearly not oriented. You should make him a DNR."

Mom: "That's not what he wants."

Dad: <mumble>

Mom: "I didn't catch that."

Dad: <silence>

Mom: "Excuse me?"

Dad: "I said you'd be doing all of us a favor if you'd change his status to a DNR. That last stroke would've killed him but, no, you had to pull out all the stops. Emily, you keep doing this guilt thing. Let him go."

Mom: "I won't be a party to murdering my own father."

Dad (grunting a laugh): "That's rich."

Mom: "What did you say? What the *hell* did you just say?"

Me: "Guys, don't fight. Please."

Mom: "He needs better care."

Dad: "You need to let him go."

"Don't tell me what to do with my—"

"We can't afford—"

"I promised—"

"I wouldn't be surprised if he put the noose around your mother's neck—"

"How *dare* you—"

"Oh, look who's talking. First him, and then your daughter, and now you and that damned bookstore sucking us—"

"I'm working as hard as you are—"

"You know where the mental illness in this family comes from? Not from *my* side, my father's—"

"Don't you bring up—"

". . . still got it together—"

". . . my *mother*! Don't you give me that crap! Jenna's problems are *not*—!"

Like that. On and on. They hurled daggers, and the air split and tore and howled.

Me, I screwed in my buds and turned up Nine Inch Nails until my ears bled.

b

Home.

My parents stomped into the kitchen to continue their "discussion." I bolted upstairs to my room, put on Hurt, pulled up my ghost account and reread Matt's e-mail for that day.

To: Jenna Lord
From: Lord, Matthew SSG
Subject: re: The Home Front

Jenna, you should never feel bad about telling me what's going on. For the longest time, I would think about you every day, all alone with them and probably going crazy. Remember when I left for basic, and only you and Mom came to see me off?

Yes, I remembered. I clutched a miniature American flag and Mom sobbed. I didn't want Matt to worry about me but, inside, my guts shriveled. Matt was my protector. Now there was no one between me and our father, me and our parents, me and the flames.

In the beginning, I kept thinking about that day, focusing on what I'd left behind, looking over my shoulder at you guys, you know? But go outside the wire for the first time, and you're in the present, real fast. If you're not, you're toast. All you can afford to see is now. So you worry about that boot lying in the middle of the street, the way the shopkeeper slid back into his shop and, it's quiet, it's too damn quiet, where are all the kids? It's when everyone disappears that you know something bad's going to happen.

So I pretend. Or maybe it's lying, I don't know. But to get through the day, you have to decide that there is no past, no family to come back to. You tell yourself that you're already dead and buried. . . .

"That is not *true!*" Mom's voice was shrill, loud enough to shatter crystal. "You *know* I'm working as hard as I—"

Dad: <something hard and mean I couldn't decipher>

Mom: ". . . *excuse* . . . for trying . . . always shooting me down!"

Dad (louder, meaner): "Don't push . . ."

Mom: ". . . who . . . screwing *this* week!"

Dad (really loud now): ". . . drinking . . . won't be *goaded* . . . "

Mom: ". . . don't have the *guts* to—"

There was a sudden, massive BOOM that made the panes of my windows chatter and Mom scream.

Shit. My heart scrabbled up the back of my throat. I bolted out of my room then skidded to a stop on the landing, not sure what was best. You have to understand, Bob. It's one thing to run to an accident that's already happened to see if you can help. It's another to jump in the car right before it wraps itself around that tree. "Mom? Dad?"

Silence.

"Dad?" I slid onto the first step and then the second, the third. My scars writhed; the grafts between my shoulders clenched as if trying to hold me back. "Mom?"

More nothing, which didn't necessarily mean anything one way or the other. Maybe five seconds since the BOOM, and now I had a choice: go downstairs, or back to my room and pretend I hadn't heard a thing.

Three guesses, Bob.

C

The kitchen was . . . bad.

My mother was half-cowering, her hands stalled before her face. My father was puffing like a bull. Blood and drywall smeared the knuckles of his right hand. A cloud of grit hung in the air and more sanded the kitchen floor. A fist-sized crater had caved in the wall beside Mom's left ear.

Without taking his eyes off my mother, Psycho-Dad said, "Go back upstairs, Jenna."

"But, but . . . Dad," I said. "*Mom*."

"I *said*, go upstairs." Dad's blood dripped in big, ruby teardrops onto the cream tile. "What part of that did you *not* understand?"

I didn't budge, although the patchwork of new and old flesh on my belly and back tugged and fisted. I thought, fleetingly, of calling 9-1-1—but to tell them what, exactly? My psychotic father killed the kitchen wall? "Mom, do you want me to . . . I mean, should I st—?"

"No. Go on, Jenna." Her voice was flat, eerie, almost dead. "I'll be fine. Be a good girl and go to your room."

If I went—if I did what they said—this was more pretend, like the ward and school, too. Pretend you haven't heard this, Jenna. Go listen to your music, Jenna. Tell yourself a nice story, Jenna, and everything will be just fine.

Tell yourself you're dead, the way Matt does, so the past can't hurt you.

Well, Bob, I wish I could say I dialed 9-1-1. I wish I could say that I stood as a human shield and told my father that if he needed to hit anyone, he could start with me. Matt might have done that. He certainly tried to protect me, even if that hadn't always worked out.

I wish there was some other story I could tell you, Bob.

But you wanted the truth, remember?

So, here it is: I was a very good girl and did as I was told.

12: a

Five minutes after I heard the garage door chug up and then down, there came the dull thud of cupboards and then the bony clatter of ice against glass. I knew what was going on. Any second now, Mom would drag out the Stoli hidden behind the jumbo-sized box of Cascade and pound back the first slug of her evening. It was always like this when she and Dad fought, and since they fought at least twice every weekend, my mom went through a lot of Stoli.

A few moments later, the television began to mutter. Food Network, probably. When Mom got started with the Stoli, she confused watching other people make food with actual cooking.

I crept downstairs an hour later. Mom was passed out on the couch, a washcloth over her eyes. Paula Deen was spazzing about peach cobbler. I covered Mom with an old comforter she'd crocheted when she was pregnant with me.

Ever study someone who's sleeping, Bob? I mean, *really* looked at them? Maybe your wife? In movies and books, lovers do that all the time. There was this one television show from way back—science fiction, Bob, so my guess is you being so black and white, it never crossed your radar—where this alien race has this ritual. Each partner spends the whole night awake while the other sleeps because that's when everything artificial falls away. What you see then is what's behind the mask: their true face.

Which begs the question, Bob: when you stared down at me after the fire, what did you see?

Who?

b

And speaking of masks, let me tell you a secret, Bobby-o.

When I was little, I played dress-up. Not just Ariel. I used to sneak into my mother's closet and slip into silken dresses that smelled like spicy roses and wobble in high heels.

When I was little, I sat at my mother's vanity, an antique with five mirrors, so there were many me's, each in her own world. Each me brushed her hair with our mother's heavy silver brush. We drew in lips and eyes and colored our cheeks with our mother's makeup. Each me was different from the other and yet the same, like the angles of a triangle or the facets of a diamond.

When I was little, our family gathered for pictures. We smiled. We touched each other. None of that was a lie yet.

There's this great Coppola film, Bob, *The Conversation*, where the real story lies in nuance: how who you are and what you're prepared to hear influences your perception of what's actually said. There's this one scene where this woman stares down at this drunk and then says something about how this poor guy was once someone's baby. Once up a time, someone loved him; he was cherished, but now he was just a used-up lush.

That's us, Bob. I look at those pictures and remember I was my parents' baby girl. Matt wasn't gone yet, and we were a family.

What I remember of them, Bob, is love.

Asleep, my mom's mask was gone, and there was the ghost of a pretty girl who'd been brave enough to read her poetry to a young and handsome Harvard surgery resident while they picnicked on a beach by the clear blue sea.

And I remember, Bob, how when I was little?

My mother was a queen and I wanted to be just like her.

Only here I was, almost all grown up and still just me, with a mom who got shit-faced six nights out of seven and a psychotic asshole of a dad. Matt was the only pure one left, and he was gone.

C

After I tucked my mom in, I made myself a PB&J with the dullest butter knife I could find and ate over the sink. Then I loaded my dirty plate and Mom's empty vodka glass into the dishwasher. If I had any guts, I'd have pitched the Stoli, but we both know better, Bob.

Instead, I slotted the bottle into its hiding place. I turned off Paula, and then I went to bed.

13: a

Almost a month later, I watched from my hiding place in the library as Danielle and the other girls on the cross-country team did speed drills. Danielle led, her blonde ponytail streaming like a mane, but that wasn't saying much. She might be fast but only because the other girls ran on their knuckles. Danielle's form was crap: a human pogo stick with way too much up and down instead of glide and push, glide and *push* and *stretch*. If you're a runner, Bob, you'll know what I mean. All her energy was going into lift, not speed. Mr. Anderson stood with a stopwatch in one hand, and when Danielle passed, he said something, which seemed to piss her off because she peeled out of formation, hands on hips, and scowled as she scuffed grass.

I glanced at my watch. Her time for the two hundred was in the toilet, five seconds slower than just the week before. I looked up again in time to see Mr. Anderson blow his whistle and then motion for the other girls to finish up and gather round. Danielle was doing her Drama Queen sulk on the bleachers. Maybe she'd gotten into Mr. Anderson's face one too many times and he'd made her sit out the rest of practice. About time. I'd watch her cop an attitude—in class, on the track—and marveled that he kept her on. The guy had the patience of a saint.

Either that or he liked the abuse.

b

School had settled down. My classes were easy; my favorite was chemistry (big surprise); I got along with . . . okay, okay, I avoided most people.

Except Danielle.

I wasn't sure it was all about David. David was Mr. Anderson's TA, and so I couldn't help but see him every day. We said hello, and he tried talking me into being on the homecoming decorating committee so I could meet other people. I begged off with the excuse that I lived so far away, blah, blah, blah. Eventually, he stopped trying but was still friendly enough and that was fine.

Still, Danielle never wasted an opportunity to make some kind of snarky remark. When Dewerman got it into his head that we would do this extra project all about creativity and suicide, that was, of course, all *my* fault. We were supposed to pick a name from a list of famous writers who'd killed themselves and then figure out if there was something in what they'd written that explained why suicide was an option for them. Thank God, Grandma wasn't on the list. Not even Dewerman was that clueless.

"Be creative, people," Dewerman said. "I want you to decide for yourselves whether what you're reading is great literature or simply called great because the author checked out. Examine the web of connections that make up a person's life and then follow the strands, see if they really are connected."

Confusion. One guy raised his hand. "Uhm . . . but what's the assignment?"

"Socrates said the unexamined life is not worth living. Is the only reason we read these books because a critic tells us to?"

"No," said some wit, "because it's assigned."

Danielle, scowling at me but talking to Dewerman: "So, I'm confused. Does this mean you want us to write a paper or maybe a poem or something in that writer's style, or paint a picture or what?"

"Yes," said Dewerman, which set off another gust of laughter and only made Danielle shoot more death rays my way.

To date, I hadn't chosen anyone from Dewerman's dwindling list. I don't know what I was waiting for. Inspiration, maybe. Or maybe I figured my person would be the writer no one else wanted, which would be fine.

C

I know you'll find this hard to believe, Bob, but despite how nice he was, I avoided Mr. Anderson, too. Maybe my lizard brain— the part that tells you when to run and when to blend into the scenery—was sending up flares or something. Or I was keeping my head down, I don't know. I just wanted to get through the day with a minimum of drama.

But avoidance isn't the same as being oblivious. I wasn't. I . . . I watched him. From my spot behind glass in the library, mostly, or if the librarian wasn't there when I arrived in the morning, I waited outside, on the curb, out of sight. That way, I could watch as Mr. Anderson came in from his morning run (Mondays, Wednesdays, and Fridays) or bike ride (Tuesdays and Thursdays). The woods were west of campus, so when Mr. Anderson burst from the woods, the rising sun caught and held and turned him golden, like a Roman god. I liked watching him move, the glide of his body parting the air, the cords of his muscles as they worked. You could see how strong he was. He might have suspected I was there, but he never let on and didn't look my way. When I walked to my locker every morning, there was always music swelling from his classroom—jazz, classical, opera, some oldies—and I could smell him, fresh from his shower: wet and dark green and mysterious as the woods.

Yet, in class, he treated me like everyone else, so much so that our very first hour together on that first day took on the quality of a story I'd told myself. Not a lie, but not exactly real either.

I also wasn't the only one to notice him. One day when he announced that he'd be looking for a new TA, a girl beside me muttered she'd be happy to *assist* Mr. Anderson any way he wanted. Which made all the girls snicker, even Danielle. Not me, though.

I made it to lunch maybe twice a week, whenever I could screw up the courage to wolf down a sandwich at a corner table where no one else sat. David threw the occasional meaningful look, usually when Danielle was busy gabbing with one of her minions, but my gaze always skipped away. Mr. Anderson would glance my way, maybe nod or smile but never approached in front of the other kids. I like to think he was sensitive enough to know how that would make me look more pathetic than I already felt. Since he had cafeteria duty three times a week, he knew I skipped lunch more times than not. Considering I had gym the period before, my go-to excuse—showering, changing back into school clothes—was legit. For the rest of the lunch period, I also got to know the graffiti in just about every stall in every bathroom.

Maybe two weeks after school started, though, I had a close call. The first bell had already rung, and I was stepping out of the bathroom, figuring to scoot to the library for study hall, when I looked up and saw Ms. Sherman standing there, her arms folded over her chest. She aimed a forefinger. "You were supposed to stop by my office last week. We had an appointment right after lunch, if you remember. I know you got the slip. Why have you been avoiding me, Jenna?"

"Uh . . ." Had I gotten a slip? I couldn't remember. "I'm . . ."

"Ms. Lord?" Both Ms. Sherman and I turned as Mr. Anderson came up. "Ms. Lord, what are you doing? We need to get started. . . . Oh, hey, Rosalie. I'm sorry, did you need Ms. Lord? Can it wait?"

"Well." Ms. Sherman looked as surprised as I felt. "I was just checking in. She missed an appointment." To me: "So you've been helping Mr. Anderson during your study halls?"

"Uh," I said. "Some?" Had I made that sound like a question?

"She's been great," Mr. Anderson said. "I keep asking her to be my TA, but she's playing hard-to-get." He lifted his eyebrows as he looked at me. "So? Today?"

"Oh." I tried again. "Sure."

"Well then, I won't keep you, Jenna," said Ms. Sherman. "It sounds like you're adjusting and things are going fine."

"Yeah," I said, finally. I know: very articulate. "Things are great."

"Excellent. Don't look back," Mr. Anderson said as we took the stairs. The tardy bell rang and the halls emptied except for one or two stragglers. When we got to his room, he said, "Well, here's where I get off. You're welcome to work here during your study hall, you know that. Or—" His lips twitched into a grin. "Eat the sandwich you haven't gotten out of your locker yet."

I didn't know if I should thank him. "Why did you do that?"

He shrugged. "You looked like you could use the rescue. She was hassling you. People like The Tank make me tired. She means well, but I can't think of anything worse than being constantly reminded of things you'd rather forget. What exactly does she think you're going to say, anyway?"

All the things I wouldn't mind telling you. That's what I thought, Bob. Of course, I kept quiet. We said good-bye and went our separate ways. I don't remember if I ate my sandwich that day.

That seemed to . . . start something, though. Some nights, he dropped by the library on the way to his car—to see how I was getting on, he said. He would talk about the cross-country team, which was not doing well, but he didn't pressure me to join. Other days, he didn't come in but looked toward my window on his way through the lot and raised a hand. The windows were polarized, so I don't know if he saw me wave back. But he knew where I was, Bob, he knew.

d

Then, ten days before Mom's book party, on a Tuesday:

6:45 P.M., and still no Mom. It would be dark in another ten minutes. The library would close in fifteen. Through the library windows, lights glowed on a soccer game on the lower field. The football team was scrimmaging on the upper field. Beyond was a dense thatch of blackness where the woods began.

When the library closed, I didn't know what I should do. I didn't have a cell yet. I couldn't go anywhere. Even if I could, I was afraid Mom would come, not find me, and then get pissed. She was really stressed out about the store and the book party. Times were tough at the store, and she'd let two employees go, leaving just her and Evan, the store manager, to do everything. The last thing she needed was for me to go MIA. So, better for me to wait on the curb when the librarian shooed me out. If I got too spooked, I could always move under the lights in the breezeway.

One of the dubious perks of coming early and having to stay late all the time was I got my homework done, and I could use the library computer to write to Matt, which was safer than home because I wasn't allowed to lock my bedroom door either. (Honestly, Bob, it's amazing how much an open-door policy is just like living in a jail. There are so many things you just don't—can't—do.) Now, I found the sentence where Matt asked how things were going and started my reply again.

What's going on with me, the boy asks. Hah. After everything you've been through? You are so brave. My life is nowhere near as exciting. School is, you know, school :<P. But it beats the hospital. My favorite class is chemistry. I've got this awesome teacher. . . .

"Hey."

I was so startled I actually jumped. The librarian always retreated to her office so she could count down the seconds until I would stop being this major inconvenience and just leave already. No one else used the library this late. I'd been so absorbed, I hadn't heard anyone come in. I craned my head around.

"Oh," I said. "Hi."

"Hi." David's dark hair was damp, and pearls of sweat stood on his upper lip. He smelled of locker room soap and leather. A backpack hung from his right shoulder and a gym bag large enough for a cello dangled from his left. "Want some company?"

"Uh," I said. "What are you doing here?" Brilliant: like the guy had no right to be in the school library.

"Fencing practice." He hunched his left shoulder with its huge bag. "I saw you from the hall. Actually, I see you here every afternoon, but you're usually gone by now."

He'd seen me every day? The idea that anyone who wasn't a teacher or guidance counselor would even think to look— or care—was a little jarring. "Yeah, I . . . I have to wait for my mom. She's late."

"That sucks. Have you called her?"

"I don't have a phone."

"No way. No *cell*?"

"Well, I . . . I just never needed one. I mean—" I tried to be all jokey about it. "Who's going to call me?"

"If you don't have a phone, how will you ever know?" His eyebrows pulled down in a frown. "Seriously, you should have one for emergencies at least." He made a move for a front pocket of his jeans. "You want to use mine?"

"No, thanks. My mom probably got delayed at the store, that's all."

"Okay." David studied me a moment. "How come you don't have a car?"

How long you got? "I might get one." I didn't have a license either, but he hadn't asked about that. "Maybe this summer."

"Well, that sucks," he repeated. "Waiting around must be a drag."

"I don't mind too much." Then, all bright and chirpy: "I get all my homework done." God, that sounded pathetic.

"I'd hate having to depend on my folks all the time. It would drive me nuts."

Been there, done that. I didn't know what else I could say, though, so I kept quiet. Why was he even talking to me? Student council elections had come and gone. (Yes, Bob, he won.)

After another moment's silence, David thumbed off his gym bag, which settled with a dull metallic clatter to the floor. "So," he said, dropping into a chair alongside mine, "what are you working on?"

"Oh." I made a move to minimize the screen, but he was crowding in at my right elbow, his eyes skimming the words. This close, I could see the fine film of sweat along his temples, too. He smelled . . . really nice. "It's, uh, a letter. To my brother."

"Yeah? Where is he?"

"Away," I said, and then I did close out of the account. "It's private."

"Oh, okay. Sure," he said, and easily enough that I didn't think he'd seen the word *hospital.* Or maybe he was just nice enough not to let on. No, on second thought, the word passed him by. David was a decent guy and didn't seem to be that good a liar. Believe me, Bob, it takes one to know one.

More. Awkward. Silence. I glanced at the librarian, who was studying us through her office window. God knows what she thought was going to happen. She caught my eye then did the whole checking-her-watch routine. Like I always had guys drop in at the last second just to piss her off.

I turned back to David. "So how was practice?"

"Not so great." Wrinkling his nose, David tipped his chair back and then gave this long and very languid stretch so his shirt rode up and I could see bare skin. "My focus is crap. I'm making a lot of dumb mistakes."

"Oh?" His stomach was staring me in the face, so I couldn't help but look. David was a couple cans shy of a six-pack, but his belly was still muscular and trim—and crisscrossed with bruises. Some were fresh, angry, purple wheals; others, a mottled yellow-green, were healing. He looked as if he'd been whipped. "What happened?"

"Hunh?" Startled, he followed my gaze and then rolled up the edge of his shirt and studied his skin as if seeing it for the first time. "Oh. Those are saber cuts. You get used to it."

"But don't they hurt?"

"Oh yeah, but saber's not like foil or épée. You can score with the whole blade, not just the tip, and everything from the waist up is target area. So it's really fast, and there's a lot of cut and slash." He gave a lopsided grin. "It's why I like it, I guess. But this year the coach thinks I'm more interested in just beating the hell out of people."

"How come?" My eyes zeroed in on the tail of very pink scar tissue, as thick as my little finger, snaking down along his left side, just below his ribs. Take it from a pro, Bob: that slice had been deep and bad.

"Pissed off, I guess." His laugh was humorless, more like a bark. "You know . . . just stuff."

Just *stuff*. Well, that was an invitation for a follow-up if ever there was one. Because the truth, Bob, is that I'd kind of forgotten how to talk to normal people. You know: the give and take, the little lies you let stand, the black holes you avoid because all friends know what shouldn't be said? The sucky thing about a psych ward is that you have to watch what you say. Therapists love hidden meanings, especially when their patients morph into these mini-me's. It's like the more people who agree with you, the truer whatever you think becomes. Complete psychopaths really get into it because they're total suck-ups, the best liars around, and when the therapist's watching, they'll hammer until you either get angry or break down and agree that, yes, yes, what you said isn't what you meant. Silence is not an option, either. Silence is *resistance* and, as we all know, resistance is futile.

David wanted to talk. That was clear. Why else would he bother with someone like me? So the normal response would be: *like what kind of stuff?*

Instead, I pointed. "What's that from?"

An arrow of surprise shot across his face. "Where? Oh." He pulled up his shirt even further, and now I could see how the cut had unzipped his skin all the way to his armpit. "It's from last year. The other guy's blade broke in the middle of a bout and got in under my jacket. It happens way more than you think."

"Really? Why?"

"Because a saber blade is really whippy and light, so you can go fast. Blades break all the time. The doctors said I was lucky this one went up instead of in, though. There was blood everywhere. Totally freaked out the coaches and the ref. Me, too."

"Wow," I said, and then my hand was floating into the space between us before I could call it back. Or, maybe, I really didn't want to, Bob. I don't know. But it was like watching myself in a dream, the way my fingers homed in.

His skin jumped at the contact. No way to hide that flinch. I heard the tiniest suck of air as he pulled in a gasp, but he didn't say anything. Didn't tell me to stop. Looking back on it, Bob, I don't think he wanted me to. Or maybe he was just too stunned.

The scar was very smooth. Warm. The feel changed, too, as my hand followed the trail of tissue over the hard shelves of his ribs. David still didn't move or speak; I think he was as astonished—as hypnotized—as I. The scar finally petered off over his left pec. His heart was knocking so hard I felt the flutter against my fingertips.

My head went a little airy. I could see the sudden throb of his pulse in his neck. His lips parted, and something spirited over his face, very fast. He blinked and said, roughly, "It doesn't hurt anymore."

That broke the spell. "Oh," I said, and exhaled a shaky little laugh. I took my hand back. "Sorry."

"That's okay," he said, tugging his shirt back down around his waist. Scarlet dashed over his cheeks. "I . . . uh . . . I still carry that broken saber around. Want to see it?"

"Sure," I said, but he was already turning away and reaching down to unzip the large blue gym bag. I heard that metallic chatter again as he rummaged. I spotted at least five different swords. "How come you have so many?"

"Because some weapons are for bouts and others for practice," he said and then tugged out the broken saber. "Here."

The bell guard was broad and bright silver and curved, like you see in a movie, but the blade itself was a little disappointing: just under a foot long and dull gray. No real heft, either, or weight. Maybe he read my disappointment because he said, "It's really light, but the tip, where it's broken? Here." He proffered the ruined weapon. "You don't want to be on the business end of *that*."

He was right. The saber's jagged metal was very sharp. I thought about how easy it would be to draw blood. Mind you, I wasn't tempted. Just . . . interested. Handing it back was easier than I thought it would be. "Why do you keep it?"

He hunched a shoulder. "I don't know." He turned the broken weapon over in his hands. "I think, maybe . . . to remind myself, you know, I could've died. Guys do, every once in a while."

"So why keep fencing?"

"Because the danger's half the fun." His eyes flicked up from the broken blade to touch on mine. "You could come watch practice sometime, if you want. Maybe you'd like it enough to want to try it out yourself."

I thought of Mr. Anderson then, how he'd pressed about the cross-country team. "You recruiting me?" God, had that come out sounding like a line? Had I meant it that way? Was I flirting? Maybe.

"Well." That scarlet splash on his cheeks deepened. "You'll never know if you're any good unless you try. It might be fun. Do you do sports?"

"I used to run." I paused. "Cross-country. Like Danielle."

"Oh." He gave me a careful look. "So how come you're not on the team?"

Oh, because your girlfriend might cleat me just for the hell of it? That was part of it, Bob, really. But there was also something about showing myself in front of Mr. Anderson that . . . that made my throat kind of fluttery. If you know what I mean. It wasn't about my scars or grafts; my tank and shorts gave just enough cover. So he'd never see *them*.

But I thought that I might want him to watch *me*; to stand there, stopwatch in hand, and be completely focused on *only* me. Which was completely weird, considering how much I avoided him.

"Just not into it this year," I said.

"Oh," David said again. There was a moment's silence which he filled by glancing at his watch. "Look, uh, the library's going to close. You want to get a coffee or something? We could call your mom. I could take you to her store, if you want."

It was so unexpected—so nice—I almost glanced over my shoulder to make sure there wasn't some other person standing there. I wanted to say *yes*, but then I remembered Danielle's face from that first day and what she'd said: *The more broken they are . . .*

And that made me wonder, again, just why the hell David was bothering. Hadn't he just said he was having a crappy year fencing? That he was mad? *Stuff* going on, was how he'd put it, and *stuff* had to equal Danielle. So this wasn't, like, a date or anything. Even someone like David must need someone to talk to. So, maybe we could be friends. That wasn't a bad thing.

But something evil clicked in my brain then, all the little gears meshing and mashing and grinding out hidden agendas. Blame the psych ward for this one, Bob, and all those times therapists tell you that what you say is not what you mean.

"That's really nice of you," I said, "but I should probably stay put. My mom might be on her way now, and if I'm not around, she'll freak out." This all had the benefit of being true. If David had stopped right there, things would've been fine.

But he didn't. "You shouldn't be alone," David pressed. "You want me to wait with you?"

Yes. No. Why don't you do the thinking for both of us? But I wasn't Ilsa Lund; he was way better-looking than Humphrey Bogart; and this wasn't *Casablanca*: it was Wisconsin. "That's okay."

He was quiet a second. "Is it because of Danielle?"

Bingo. "Kind of. Did you guys, like, have a fight or something?"

"What does that matter?" A silly, half grin played over his lips, but his eyes were suddenly wary. "It's just coffee. It's not like a date or anything."

Oh yes, it was. "What if someone sees us together? Won't she be pissed off?" *Isn't that what you want?*

"Is that what you think? This is, like, getting back at her?"

"Isn't it?" I said. That just squirted out. Oh, all right, I let it happen. Whatever. I could hear Rebecca's ghost in my head, too. Every word out of her mouth was this creepy little verbal feeler, like an antenna: *I think; I sense; I wonder.* Like she didn't want to get caught committing herself one way or the other, so she would never be *really* wrong. Anything she'd said was a *guess*: an *I think*. "Because, yeah, I kind of wonder."

Of course I was right. You should've seen the look on his face: shock and surprise washing his skin purple as a beet. Even his ears pinked.

And, Bob? You have no idea how much seeing *that* hurt.

David was using me. He was being kind of a tool, you want to know the truth. This was all about hitting back at Danielle.

I was convenient; that was all. But just because I thought I was right didn't mean I wanted to be.

"I'm sorry," I said, although I was probably talking for both of us. I felt the sudden sting of tears I couldn't afford pricking the back of my eyes. "It's none of my business."

"Don't worry about it." David's face closed tight as a fist. He was such a bad liar, Bob. So, probably a good guy despite all that, you know? Hitting back at someone who's hurt you or for whom you care is human—well, unless you're a shrink, in which case you can think your way out of it. Better yet, make it all someone else's fault, preferably your parents.

"I got to get going." David abruptly shoved the broken saber into his bag and stood. "Forget I said anything, okay?"

Yeah, I wish. Five seconds later, David was out the door and heading for his car. I gathered my books and tried willing my brain to gray. The librarian rolled out of her office and started flipping lights before I even had my coat on. But there was still enough light that I could see my reflection in the window—and David.

He was in his car, behind the wheel. Just sitting there, the dome light washing the car a weak orange, and he was staring. At me.

He was too far away, so I have no idea what was *in* his eyes. There was no way to read him. But it was like each of us was on the screen of our own movie: him behind his windshield; me in my little library fishbowl.

The invitation was right there, again. David was waiting. Whether he was doing that for me or him, I don't know. Maybe he was waiting for both of us.

And the horrible thing? That moment was just like a film. If the girl would just turn around, she'd see the guy who was trying to save her life. She'd get in the damn car or not hop on that subway, and everything that was gearing up to unwind in one way would unspool another.

Sure, in some ways, my night would still have played out the way it did, but the characters would've been different. And then this emergency room, Bob, my story? Never would have happened. Maybe.

But I let the moment spin out, blow past. Evaporate.

The dome light winked out. His headlights came on. The librarian cleared her throat, and as I turned from the window, David drove away.

14: a

8:10 P.M.

David was long gone. The soccer game was over. Cars had streamed away, their lights like beads on a string. The opposing team's bus had chugged off. From my spot hugging the wall just outside the library, I'd watched the players trickle off the upper field to the locker room and then emerge again, heading for their cars, shouting insults at one another.

And. No. Mom.

She'd never been this late before. The store closed at 9 P.M. on weekdays, but since I'd started school, Mom let Evan close. So, figure she got delayed and left at 7, or even 7:30. A half hour max to get from A to B. If there'd been an accident or traffic jam, maybe longer. Maybe that's what had happened.

Or . . . could she have forgotten me? How do you forget your own kid?

There had to be a simple explanation. Things had been crazy at the store. She'd gotten wrapped up in her work and

I'd completely slipped her mind. Maybe she was on auto-pilot, already halfway home and still thinking about what had to be done before the big party. I bet any second she would remember. She was probably looking for a place to turn around.

But what if she'd gotten into an accident?

Shivering, I hugged my knees. Tomorrow would be October, and this being Wisconsin, the air was already crisp and very cool. I tried to think of what to do. Call her? Regardless of his motives, I should've taken David up on his offer. I'd been so stupid to wait here, wasting time when I could've used his cell or found a phone somewhere. Maybe the office, or something. Or maybe there were pay phones down by the field? I clambered to my feet, brushing off my hands on my jeans. I would go down there and see if maybe I couldn't find—

"Hello?" I'd been so preoccupied I hadn't heard the front doors open. To my left, Mr. Anderson stood in a spray of light beneath the breezeway. "Who's . . . My God, Ms. Lord, what are you still doing here?"

It was David-déjà vu all over again but, this time, all I felt was this sudden-surge of relief. I should've thought of Mr. Anderson, but I hadn't seen his car and figured he'd gone home sometime when I hadn't been looking. Probably when I was busy alienating David. He listened as I explained and then reached into his pocket. "Call her now," he said, offering his phone.

This time, I didn't argue. He had to show me how to use the thing; his was an iPhone and all I'd had any experience with was Mom's old Blackberry, but I was getting a little too freaked to be embarrassed now.

Mom wasn't answering her cell. I called three times and kept getting rolled to voice mail. So I tried the store next. Evan picked up. More bad news: Mom had left before closing. "She should've been there by now," Evan said. "I'll try her, too, and tell her you called, okay? Give me the number."

"Ah . . ." I looked at Mr. Anderson. "What's your phone number?"

"Here," Mr. Anderson said, and then took the phone. He rattled off the number, listened, said, "Anderson," listened some more, and then handed back the phone.

"Who is that?" Evan said. His tone was sharper now, a little suspicious. "Are you all right?"

"Of course, I'm fine. It's my chemistry teacher," I said, mortified.

"Mmm-hmm." Pause. "Do you want me to come get you, honey?"

"No, I'm fine, Evan. Really. Just . . . if you hear from Mom?"

"Will do. You call me if you can't track her down, all right? Worst-case scenario, you stay with me and Brad."

"I'll be fine," I said again. "Just, you know, call me if."

He said he would, and I thumbed off. "Sorry," I said to Mr. Anderson. "About Evan, I mean."

"It's all right. It's good that people are worried about you. Who's next?"

"My dad." But his cell was off, too, and when I called the hospital, the page operator said he'd left for the day and was off pager.

Mr. Anderson said, "Is there anyone else you can call? A relative, brother, sister?" When I shook my head, he added,

"Then maybe you should call Evan back."

"No, I'll be okay. She's just late. It's probably nothing."

"If you think I'm going to drive off and leave you here . . ." Mr. Anderson ran a hand through his hair, looked down the empty approach road, blew out. "Come on. Let's go over to your mom's store. Maybe Evan's mistaken. If she's not there, then I'll take you home, okay? You can keep trying her from the truck."

I protested, pointing out that if my mom showed and I wasn't here, she'd have a heart attack. But Mr. Anderson wasn't having any of that. "No way I'm leaving you here. We don't live that far from each other anyway. I'm sure your parents will understand. Come on."

I'll be honest. I was so freaked out he really didn't have to try all that hard. The one thing I didn't want was to stand there, by myself, in the dark. God, why hadn't I taken David up on his offer? I could've been having a cup of coffee with a nice guy who was just trying to be friendly. Okay, fine, he was having girlfriend problems, but it wasn't like Danielle was my favorite person.

I followed Mr. Anderson to a red Toyota pickup. "Prius is in the shop," he said. The truck was neat as a pin and smelled like him: clean and green. There was a shoe box of CDs he'd mixed himself and he told me to pick whatever I wanted. The mixes were all classical and jazz, so I just slid in a random CD. A snappy blast of jazzy brass, piano, and drums, which he said was Duke Ellington, filled the car. I stuck my pinkie in one ear and kept trying on Mr. Anderson's cell, but all I got was Robo-Mom who always told me to leave a message and have a nice day.

b

At the store:

"Hey, sweetheart." Evan kissed me on the cheek. He shook Mr. Anderson's hand, and I could tell from the way Evan's eyes narrowed that he was trying to decide if Mr. Anderson was okay.

"You hear from Mom?" I asked.

"No," Evan said. "She's not picking up. I don't have any idea where she could've gone, unless . . ."

"What?" I asked.

"Well, Nate Bartholomew's in town. You know, the guy who wrote *Sandlot Blues*?" He hooked a thumb at a display. On the cover, a dejected-looking pitcher, who looked suspiciously like Kevin Costner, was kicking a spray of red dirt from the mound. "Nate's in town for a few days and she said something about going out to dinner," he said, then added to Mr. Anderson, "She does that, sometimes. She and Nate have always been friendly."

Actually, no, she never did that. Mom liked books, not writers. Except for Meryl, she said all writers were prima donnas, drunks, social misfits, pompous, or depressed. Brilliant, maybe, but completely crazy. (Really, Bob, this comes under the category of it takes one to know one.) She'd rather stick pins in her eyes than voluntarily eat a meal with any author, no matter how famous.

"Do you know Mr. Bartholomew's number?" asked Mr. Anderson. When Evan shook his head, Mr. Anderson looked at me. "That's it," he said. "I'm taking you home."

I followed him out to his truck. To be honest, Bob, I was so panicked by then, I couldn't have argued even if I'd wanted to.

We left the lights first of Milwaukee and then Mequon and darkness closed like a curtain. There were fields and farms to my left, and the invisible lake unspooling on my right, and us, driving north, following the truck's headlights on a knife edge of interstate. Mr. Anderson had me pop in a mix of Cyrus Chestnut and talked about the similarities between jazz and classical. I knew he was trying to keep my mind off what might be going on with my mom, but I only listened with half an ear and grunted monosyllabic replies and after a while, he went quiet, too.

I stewed. Dad being MIA was standard. Probably screwing a nurse or something. But *Mom*. . . . Why would she make an exception for this guy, Bartholomew? Unless . . .

Oh my God. Was she *sleeping* with him? No, no, that wasn't my mom. Was it? Maybe she'd been in an accident. Should I call the police? A hospital? What if she'd just disappeared?

Or . . .

Or . . .

Oh . . . *shit*.

"What is it?" Mr. Anderson asked. "Are you all right?"

I must've gasped out loud. "Uh . . . no . . . yes . . . I'm okay." But what I thought: *Oh shit, shit; please not that, please.*

"You know," Mr. Anderson said, "if no one's at your house, I'm not really comfortable leaving you alone there."

"What?" I stomped on the hyperactive hamster that was my brain. "No, I'll be okay. I've been alone before."

"Under more controlled circumstances. This is definitely not that. If your parents aren't there, or their cells are still off, I'm staying until somebody gets there."

"*No*," then added: "I mean, I can't let you do that. I don't have anyone to call, but I'll be okay. I'll lock the door and in the morning, I'll just . . ." And then I stumbled to a halt. Just *what*?

Mr. Anderson said what I'd suddenly realized. "If no one shows up, how will you get to school?"

I didn't know. This was all suddenly too overwhelming. My eyes burned, and I bit down on my lower lip, worrying a piece of loose skin. My mouth filled with a taste of dirty pennies. God, why couldn't I be back at the hospital? Someone got in your face, you called a psych tech. Your meals came on little trays with plastic utensils. They did your laundry. Things were under control. Yeah, the ward was a little like a prison; mouth off and they locked you up or slapped you in restraints, but still.

Mr. Anderson said, "Let's just get you home and take it from there, okay?"

"I don't want to put you out." But my heart wasn't in it. I didn't want to be alone either. I wasn't sure how I would handle it if something horrible had happened. "What about Mrs. Anderson? Won't she be, I don't know, kind of mad? You not coming home? It's so late."

"No." Pause. "My wife is away."

"Oh." I didn't know what to say. Then I thought about Mr. Anderson always at school so early and there so late.

"She's visiting family. Her dad's been sick, so I'm baching it. So it's no problem."

We drove. Chestnut became Coltrane became Armstrong became Judy Garland singing "Somewhere over the Rainbow." I could tell the recording had been made when she was older. Her voice was throatier and sadder somehow, and when she tried for the high note at the end, her voice faltered. It was so, so sad.

Mr. Anderson must've been thinking the same thing because he said, "You can hear how broken she was by the end.

You know she got hepatitis in the '50s? When they told her she might always be an invalid and never sing again, you know what she said? That she was relieved."

"Why?"

"Because she was off the hook. She finally had a legitimate reason to stop performing. She could just *be*."

I knew what that was like. After Matt was gone, I'd always felt such pressure to be perfect, to make up for all the things Matt hadn't accomplished for Mom and Dad.

But I said nothing. The CD turned out to be a bunch of '50s songs, not just Garland but Sinatra and Dean Martin and Sammy Davis Jr. As Sammy was beginning the beguine, Mr. Anderson said, "You know, I've never asked. What do you do in that library every afternoon to keep busy?"

God, shades of David. "Homework, mostly. I read." I don't know why, but I added, "I write to my brother."

"Oh?" A beat passed, then two. "Where is he?"

This, I would never have told David or anyone else at Turing. "Iraq."

Another beat-pause. "Still? Even with the drawdown?"

"Yes." I swallowed. "Fallujah. Camp Baharia."

"Oh, so he's a Marine." Mr. Anderson nodded. "My brother's over there, too, only he's army. Special forces."

"Where is he stationed?"

"I have no idea, really. Somewhere in Afghanistan is all he'll say. Scares the hell out of me when I don't hear from him and then when I do, the relief just sucks everything out for a little while, like I've run fifty miles instead of twenty."

I knew how that felt. "How often do you hear from your brother?"

"Casey?" He thought about it. "Once a month? Not very often. Everything he does is classified. What about you?"

"Matt gets off an e-mail about once a week, but I write to him almost every day. It makes me feel better. Like I'm doing something. Like—"

"What?"

"Like I'm keeping him alive. Like our e-mails are—" I wanted to say *lifelines*. If I wrote to Matt, I was keeping him close. But I couldn't say any of that. I'd sound insane. I'd said too much already. So I kept quiet.

He waited. Finally, he said, "Do your parents know?"

It seemed an odd question. I shot him a glance, but Mr. Anderson's gaze was on the road. "No." I told him about how they'd been against Matt enlisting. "The last thing I want is to upset my mother more than she already is."

"I think she'd be more upset if she found out you were keeping secrets."

"She's got enough to worry about." I paused then added, "You won't . . . mention this to anyone, will you? To Ms. Sherman or anyone?"

"The Tank? No. But . . . is this something she *should* be worried about?" Before I could answer, he held up a hand. "Sorry. Not my business. I can keep a secret. But you know, Jenna . . . your brother's not the only person you can talk to."

Was that the first time he'd used my *name*-name? "I don't know anyone else."

"Well, you know me." He paused. "And you could make more of an effort to get involved in school."

Now he was sounding like an adult. "How? I don't have a car. I don't even have a cell."

"Don't you have a license?"

"My parents haven't . . . My mom hasn't had time to take me to the DMV."

"What about your father?"

"He's . . ." My brain went into prerecorded robot-mode. "He's really busy. He works all the time. He's under a lot of stress."

"Everyone has things to do. He should make the time."

Maybe in Mr. Anderson's perfect world, there were parents who were more interested in their kids than their own problems, but I had to live in mine. "I'm okay. It doesn't matter," I said. "It's not like I can exactly run out and do stuff with anyone, anyway."

"Do you want to?" When I didn't answer, he said, "That's what I thought."

Honestly, Bob, what could I say?

C

The good news: as we pulled into the McMansion's driveway, I could tell from all those yellow rectangles that just about every single light downstairs was on.

Then, the bad news: the garage door was down, so I had no way of knowing just who was home. I couldn't slide out of having Mr. Anderson come inside either. He just wouldn't budge and I was too worked up to argue.

I didn't hear the television from the front foyer, but that didn't necessarily mean anything. "Mom?" Pause. "Dad?"

No answer. I moved deeper into the house, Mr. Anderson following close behind. Every step felt like a march to a scaffold. The light was so bright and blazing it hurt my eyes.

Please. I turned down the short hall for the kitchen. *Make me be wrong, please, please. . . .*

No such luck.

15: a

Her head was down on the table: face turned away, cheek cradled on her arms. By her right elbow, a water glass, half-full of clear liquid and ice, squatted in a puddle of condensation. The cupboards beneath the sink were open. The Stoli bottle was on the counter. The kitchen smelled of fried eggs and rubbing alcohol.

I was aware of Mr. Anderson standing just behind me. He didn't say anything and I couldn't look at him. Instead, I put my hand on my drunken mother's shoulder. "Mom?" When she didn't respond, I said, more loudly, "Mom? Wake up, it's Jenna. *Mom?*"

"What?" She gasped and sat up so quickly she missed clocking my face with her head by inches. I couldn't tell if the sharp alcohol stink I smelled was from her, or the open bottle. Her eyes were puffy, but they weren't ticking from side to side—a good sign. "Jenna? What . . . ?" Her eyes widened. "Who . . . ?"

"Mitch Anderson." Mr. Anderson held out his hand. "I'm Jenna's chemistry teacher."

"Emily Lord," Mom said faintly. She made a move to take his hand then stopped, her fingers twitching a little like the legs of a dying spider. "What . . . why . . . ?"

Mr. Anderson waited a beat then slid his hand into a pocket. "When you didn't show up at school or answer your cell, I brought Jenna home."

"School?" Mom's hand flew to her mouth. Her cheek was slick with drool. "Oh my God. Oh, Jenna, honey, I'm so sorry, I was so overwhelmed. . . . I just wasn't thinking; I was on autopilot. . . . I . . ." Her gaze clicked to her drink and she swallowed. "I wasn't thinking," she said again.

"It's okay," I said for want of anything better. Her words weren't slurred. Maybe she hadn't drunk much. Maybe she'd been so tired, she'd fallen asleep right here at the kitchen table. Maybe pigs could fly.

We all stood there a second and then Mr. Anderson said, "Mrs. Lord, you look pretty beat. Have you had anything to eat? When did you get home?"

"Nine, I think. I don't remember. I went out with Nate . . . Mr. Bartholomew for a few drinks and then we . . . I came home." She ran a hand over her lips. She looked at the kitchen, maybe seeing it for the first time. "I was just going to sit and collect my thoughts. I guess I fell asleep."

And in all that time—having drinks with Nate, the ride home, walking into an empty house, pouring out her vodka—she hadn't once thought of me. "Where's Dad?" I asked.

"He left a voice mail. He's covering for Dr. Kirby and was just going into the OR."

I'd spoken to the page operator and that, I knew, was wrong. Before I could say anything, Mr. Anderson put in, "Well, that's all good then. Tell you what, Mrs. Lord, why don't you get cleaned up and we'll make tea and maybe some sandwiches? You'll feel better." He put his hand on my mother's elbow and gently got her on her feet. "Jenna, you want to help your mom? Maybe turn on the shower?"

I knew what he wanted me to do. "Sure. Thanks."

He did me the favor of not smiling. "No problem."

"I'm so sorry, honey," Mom said as we went upstairs. Her breath was sour. "I didn't mean to embarrass you. It was just . . . Things aren't getting better at the store and . . ."

"Oh, Mom. I was just scared something had happened. And you didn't answer your cell. Why? Is the battery dead?"

"Yes," Mom said, after a moment. "That must be it."

b

When I got back to the kitchen, Mr. Anderson was loading the last of the dirty dishes into the dishwasher. "Hey," he said, then tilted his head at the Stoli, now capped. "Where should I put that?"

"In the trash?" I was almost too exhausted to be embarrassed. I hugged myself and shivered. The house felt chilly, but I always got cold when I was tired. "Mr. Anderson, you should go home. I'm sorry about my mom—"

"Stop." He put a light hand on my shoulder and squeezed. "Lots of families have problems. Now . . . you like tuna fish?"

I pulled out bread and opened cans. Mr. Anderson chopped celery. Overhead, water gurgled through pipes as Mom showered. As I spooned in mayonnaise, he said, "You know, my dad was a drunk. The worst kind. He'd get nasty, then drink some more and get violent. When I was young, I called the police more than once. He only stopped because I got old enough and strong enough to beat the crap out of him."

My gaze went to the kitchen wall my father had cratered a month before. The drywall was patched and the wall repaired, but I still saw the hole every day. "I'm not that strong," I said, stirring in mayo.

"I don't know about that. You could've had a meltdown, but you didn't. You took care of your mother, and that's probably more than she's done for you, lately. Just remember, though, that no matter how bad it may seem now, you'll be gone in a couple of years. You'll go to college and . . . No, wait, try this." He shook several squirts of soy sauce into the tuna fish. "Go on, stir it in. . . . Don't give me that look. It's really good. Trust me, Jenna."

"Oh, Mr. Anderson, I . . ." My throat clogged. "I never . . . I . . ."

"Hey, Jenna, it's okay," he said. "Just because your mom has a problem doesn't mean I think you're a horrible person. I'm not thinking what a loser you are. I'm thinking that you're a brave, smart, tough girl who's doing the best she can under really crummy circumstances."

I gave a weak, watery laugh. "You don't know me."

"I know what I need to know for now," he said.

C

Mom was all apologies when she came down fifteen minutes later. Her face was scrubbed clean, and she looked better. We had jasmine tea and tuna fish sandwiches. (And, Bob, tuna really *is* better with a little soy sauce.) Mr. Anderson got Mom talking about books, which was the absolute right thing to do. She jabbered on about the store and then told Mr. Anderson about the big October party: "It's next week. You should come. Please, we'd love to have you. Bring your wife; I can introduce her to Meryl."

"Well, we'll see," Mr. Anderson said, noncommittally, and then glanced at his watch. "I really ought to be going. School night, you know."

At the door, Mom shook his hand. "Thank you so much for looking after Jenna. I don't know how to begin to repay your kindness."

Fail. Looking after me? Mom made it sound like I was about five years old. She continued, "Please do think about coming to the party."

"I will, but only if you stop apologizing," Mr. Anderson said, and he took her hand in both of his. "But if you want to do something for me, you can get Jenna a cell phone. She should have one, even if it's for nothing other than emergencies. Tonight, she was lucky I was still there. It might have been midnight before you realized you'd forgotten her, and there is no pay phone at the school."

"Oh," Mom faltered. "Yes. Well—"

"And she ought to have a license and, maybe, a car. If she drives herself, it wouldn't be so much pressure on you. Or, if that's really too much trouble, I could bring her by your store after school. It's virtually on my way anyway."

"Well," Mom said again, looking a little breathless now. "I wouldn't want to put you out."

"No trouble at all. But this isn't out of the goodness of my heart. To be honest, I have ulterior motives. I want your daughter to join the cross-country team and for that, she'll need wheels. Of course, I could take her sometimes or arrange a car pool with some of the other kids, but life's easier all the way around if she can take care of getting herself back and forth."

By the end, Mom had agreed that a cell phone was a good idea and she would take me to the DMV on Saturday. Oh, and I was going to start training with the cross-country team.

"Great," said Mr. Anderson and gave my mom's hands a final squeeze. "Oh, and Jenna, don't forget. Be in my room bright and early tomorrow morning. I need to get you up to speed if you're going to be my new TA."

"Sure," I said.

"My goodness," Mom said as she closed the front door. "He certainly is persuasive." She looked a little stunned, like she'd been blindsided and wasn't quite sure by what.

Me neither. This was so surreal. I felt a little like those times when I detached and went into slipstream, watching all the players in my life at a distance. Because had anyone asked me? Uh, that would be *no*. I stood there like an idiot as the adults talked around me, planned out my life, decided what I should have and when. Sure, I *wanted* my license and a phone, but it was so weird, the way Mr. Anderson was able to get it done. It was as if my mother was a wall and Mr. Anderson knew where she was weakest, how to get through the chinks without disturbing a single brick. No, better: he knew how to get *around* her.

It was, come to think of it, a little like a kinder, gentler Psycho-Dad making one of his command decisions: exactly the same, only without all the fuss and blood.

And the thing is, Bob, Mr. Anderson looking out for me, being there, taking *over* like that?

I liked it.

I ... *liked* it.

16: a

"Corrosives here, inorganics here. Obviously, we keep the corrosives under lock and key. Anytime you need something, you ask and I'll unlock the cabinet. . . . Jenna, you with me?"

"Mmm." I swallowed the bubble of a yawn. Although my sleep had been dreamless, it had been fast: only five hours before struggling out of bed, ripping off my old clothes, showering, dressing, and then piling into the car for the drive down. For the first time, I'd drunk half of the cappuccino Mom's barista had whipped up. It wasn't half-bad. Well, not vile.

Mom had looked rough, though not as bad as some mornings after a long evening with Rachael Ray or Bobby Flay. She hadn't said much either, not until dropping me off at school when she handed me one of Meryl's books: "For your teacher's wife. It's autographed, though not personalized. Tell him that if he and his wife show up at the party, I'll be sure they meet Meryl. See you this evening, okay? I won't be late, I promise."

Mr. Anderson had been reading the newspaper on his computer when I dragged in, and said he was running later in the day: "I slept in a little this morning myself." But that was all he'd said and when I gave him Meryl's book, he'd thanked me and gotten down to business.

My biggest job would be to catalog and organize the storeroom. Apparently, David had gotten sidetracked by setting up labs and then fencing practice and left the storeroom in kind of a shambles. We went over the bottles and boxes of chemicals arranged on open gray metal shelves. Mr. Anderson kept his already-assembled experiments in a series of plastic tubs for days if he was really rushed and hadn't time to drag equipment out of storage.

"What's that?" I'd asked, pointing to a wooden door. The door was the only one on a very short hall and to the right of a separate entrance off an emergency stairwell, marked by a dimly lit exit sign overhead.

"Ah." Mr. Anderson looked sheepish as he dug out the keys. The room was narrow and long, with two large sinks and counters on the right, a cot on the left with a bookshelf affixed to the cinder block right above and a shower stall. Two beige towels hung from a towel bar. A pair of running shoes was squared on a mat next to the cot. The room smelled of Dove and the faintest touch of musky sweat.

"My hideaway," Mr. Anderson explained. "This used to be a darkroom but then got converted to storage. When they added more classroom space, I renovated a bit. I was refurbishing a cabin I've got on my property and brought the old shower stall down one weekend. This way, I can work out and shower and no one's the wiser." He grinned as he shut the door. "Well, except you."

We spent more time going through the computer program in which I would have to record the storeroom's contents because the school had to pass OSHA inspections. Organizing and cataloging took top priority, he said. "I'd start with the inorganics to get used to the computer program. I'd help, but I've got a meeting. Budget. Blah. I have to go militate for more test tubes."

"Really?" That seemed a stupid thing to sit through a meeting for.

"No. Actually, I need burettes and graduated cylinders and, maybe, I'll harass the administration for a PCR machine.... Right, you're not interested."

I had a hand to my mouth again. "No. Really. I'm fine."

"Yeah, right. I'm falling asleep just looking at you. Help yourself to more coffee."

"I'll be okay." Then I ruined it by yawning.

"Uh-huh. You eat anything?"

"I'm fine." I actually *was* starving. At the mention of food, my traitorous stomach picked that moment to complain, loudly. We stared at each other a moment, and then laughed. That kind of broke the tension, mine mostly. I hadn't known how to behave with Mr. Anderson, but things felt . . . normal. No—better than normal. Things felt safe. Like he would be my friend and keep his promises.

"Whatever you say, kiddo. Oh, and here." He bent over his desk computer, typed in a few commands and then straightened. "Okay, you can access anything through this computer that you can through the library. In case you ever want to, you know, hang here."

I did my best eye roll. "Like I'll ever have any free time. The storeroom's a mess."

"Blame David. Listen, if you're ever on the computer and I'm not here when you're done, just log out, make sure the lights are off, and close the office door, okay? I'll get a couple spare keys made so you can always get in if I'm not around."

I spent the next forty-five minutes cataloging chemicals. The work was easy and kind of brainless. I could see why David kept putting it off and then I wondered what time he came in—if he still did. Had Mr. Anderson told him I'd be picking up the slack and then taking over? I didn't see how; Mr. Anderson had made his command-decision only, what, eight hours ago? It felt like my whole life had suddenly changed.

The radio was playing, something classical. A window next to the computer overlooked the parking lot, and as I worked, I could see cars pulling up, teachers trickling into the building. Pillars of puffy clouds towered over the gray-blue smudge of Lake Michigan on my right. It was a very nice, very pleasant view.

Sometime during all that, I poured more coffee into my Starbucks cup. The pot squatted on a gray metal filing cabinet directly across from the cataloging computer and adjacent to Mr. Anderson's desk. As I sipped, I let my eyes run over a corkboard to which he'd tacked schedules, a calendar, a couple *Get Fuzzy* comics. Then, after a second's hesitation, I slid into Mr. Anderson's black leather chair. He'd sat in it so often, it was molded to his shape. I didn't fit quite right, but it was comfortable and I decided to relax a minute. The chemicals had waited this long, and I really *was* tired. The coffee was strong, but I'd dumped in about a pound of sugar and creamer so my teeth wouldn't curl. My eyes drifted over

Mr. Anderson's desk: the computer, a small desk lamp, his *X-Files* mug, an organizer, a stack of textbooks. A John Sandford novel: *Winter Prey.*

My fingers trailed over the desk's drawers. There were four: two stacked on the left, one in the middle, and one on the right. I inched open the lower left-hand drawer: lesson plans, lab sheets, articles, and other papers. Above that were supplies, a box each of pencils and pens, rubber bands, staples, paper clips. The right held four lab books, each labeled by section and level with various labs done in a walk-through in Mr. Anderson's neat, tight handwriting.

There was one more drawer: long, centered, equipped with a lock. When I put a finger underneath and tugged, it moved. So. Not locked.

People always had one drawer where they kept the really good stuff. Stuff that was personal.

I listened for a moment but heard nothing other than the tick of the clock and a glissando run of piano. I tiptoed to the office door, scanned the empty classroom. Tiptoed back.

Mr. Anderson had been gone for almost an hour. School would start in another forty minutes. The first buses would arrive in twenty.

Just a peek.

b

Loose pens and pencils.

A roll of Life Savers (cherry).

A double-handful of loose change in a small Pyrex dish.

A small digital camera.

A hand-bound leather journal with a tie strap wrapped around a brass button shaped like a flower.

And under the journal . . .

A knife.

Don't do it! My brain really did scream that, but I was already reaching in that same, dreamy way that I'd run my fingers over David's scar. *Don't touch it; don't, don't!*

Yeah. Like I listen so well.

C

So, Bobby-o, you into knives? I'll bet some cops are. I know I am. *Duh.* Well, let me tell you about this one.

This knife was beautiful in the same way that Mr. Anderson was. That knife felt so good, so balanced. A perfect knife.

Inset in the staghorn handle was a tiny brass shield with two birds and the words, *Kissing Crane.* I slid my thumbnail into the nail nick and unfolded the blade, which locked into place with a tiny *click.* It wasn't your usual Swiss Army knife but more of a stiletto, a little like David's saber, only this was three bright inches of shining, very sharp carbon steel. . . .

"Mr. Anderson?" A boy's voice, coming from the classroom.

My heart did a quick double-thump. Oh, shit, *shit* . . .

"Mr. Anderson?" The boy's voice came again, closer now because he was walking through the classroom for the back office. "Mr. . . . Oh, hey, Jenna. Uh, what are you doing?"

"Me?" I was back at the computer, industriously typing. "Just, you know, TA stuff."

"Oh." David looked surprised. His hair was rumpled, like he'd just rolled out of bed and I thought I recognized the same shirt from the day before. "Yeah, okay, that's cool. I figured Mr. Anderson would get someone else, but I thought he was going to ask—"

"David?" Another voice that I recognized and I thought: *oh, how perfect.*

"David, is he . . ." One good look and Danielle's eyes first popped, then slitted like a cat's. Her lips peeled back from her teeth. "What are *you* doing here?" she snarled.

"Uh," I said. "Mr. Anderson asked me to be his new TA and—"

"What? No, you're not. *I* was supposed to be Mr. Anderson's assistant, not *you.*"

"Hey, take it easy." David put a hand on Danielle's arm, which she shrugged off. "There's more than enough work for two people," he said.

"Wanna bet? *She* gets here early *and* stays late and . . ."

"And what, Danielle?" Mr. Anderson was suddenly there, with a napkin-covered cafeteria plate and a smell of fried potatoes.

"What's *she* doing here?" Danielle demanded. "*David's* your TA and *I*—"

"Danielle, calm down." Mr. Anderson set the plate on his desk. "As I recall, this is my office. Don't you think you have enough going on?"

"What's that got to do with—" Her lips trembled. She looked to David who avoided her eyes, and then back at Mr. Anderson. She screwed her fists onto her hips. "I asked *first.*"

"You really want to do this now, Danielle?" Mr. Anderson asked mildly. He crossed his arms over his chest. "Jenna's here earlier and on a consistent basis and, as you pointed out, she stays later. You've got cross-country, schoolwork, band and . . . other things."

Her face changed, and that's when I really noticed, for the first time, these deeply purple smudges under her eyes, like she wasn't getting much sleep. Come to think of it, she looked as rough as David—and weren't those yesterday's jeans? "That's not fair. Don't I get a say?"

"No. This isn't a democracy, Danielle. This is my decision."

I didn't need to hear this. There was way more going on here than I knew. "I should get going." Without waiting for permission, I gathered up my things and made a beeline out of there.

Mr. Anderson caught up with me at the classroom door. The halls were filling with other kids. "She's upset," he said, and then sighed. "I wasn't thinking; I should have told her first."

I didn't think I was going to say anything, but I surprised myself. "Why didn't you pick her?"

"Honestly?" Mr. Anderson looked me in the eye. "Because she thinks that keeping herself distracted will make everything else just go away."

I didn't know what any of that meant, so I said nothing.

"Here." Mr. Anderson handed me the covered plate. "You need to eat. Don't worry about Danielle. See you after school, okay?"

"Oh, sure," I said.

◊

In the girls' bathroom, I peeked under the napkin: scrambled eggs, hash browns, a carton of orange juice.

He'd bought breakfast for me. A sweet and thoughtful gesture. Something Matt would've done.

I dumped the food in the trash.

e

After school, I went straight to the library. I kept expecting Mr. Anderson to come find me, but he didn't. Or maybe he did, but I'd made sure not to sit in my usual spot. More than likely, though, he'd gotten the message when I hadn't stayed after class. Because I couldn't see outside, I don't know if he went running or biking or coaching cross-country, or kept busy sticking Danielle together with superglue. I didn't want to know. It was none of my business. Live with a psychotic father long enough, watch enough psych techs do enough takedowns while nurses come scuttling down the halls with syringes and needles out to *here*. You get a pretty good idea of when someone's *this* close to the edge, and Danielle was right there. Her kind of trouble I just didn't need.

Mom came on time. Oh. Yay. When we left, Mr. Anderson's truck was still in the lot. I didn't look up at his windows. If my brain had been a hard drive, I would've hit <delete>, or crashed it, or whatever.

"So?" Mom chirped. "How did your teacher like the book?"

"He liked it," I lied. "He said to thank you."

"He seems like *such* a wonderful man," Mom gushed. "I envy his wife. I like the way he's taking an interest in you. You need someone like him."

"Uh-huh." I did a quick mental calculation: only seven hundred and eighty days left until graduation.

Seven hundred and eighty days of Mr. Anderson: in class, in the halls, at lunch . . .

Bursting from the woods in a blaze of early morning sun.

Lucky me.

17: a

Dad was home for once, having pawned his on-call off to Dr. Kirby, his partner. We had a civil meal and no one screamed. After dinner, Dad retreated to his study to do dictations. Mom asked me to do the dishes because she had to work, and then she sat down with a pot of jasmine tea and her spreadsheets. While I was scraping dishes, I noticed the empty Stoli bottle in the trash.

Staring at that Stoli was when I started feeling bad. What was I *doing*? Mr. Anderson really had put himself out for me. He did that for everybody, as far as I could tell. Look at the slack he cut Danielle. And how many teachers would not only drive a kid home but bring her breakfast? Convince her mom to lighten up, act more responsibly? My mom had dumped that vodka because of Mr. Anderson. She'd been on time because of Mr. Anderson, and I knew she and Dad must've talked last night because they were behaving—because of Mr. Anderson. My family was semi-normal, for that night at least, and I owed all that to Mr. Anderson, and here I'd treated him like he had the plague.

I thought about him, all alone in his house. He probably was standing over the sink, eating a yogurt or something. Or maybe not eating anything. His house would be clean and smell like lemons or, maybe, roses but there would be silence when he walked in. So he would put on music because the silence was a blanket that could suffocate a man if he didn't kick it off. What would he pick? Something soft and soothing. Not Bach. Bach was for the morning; Bach was marching orders and mathematics and setting the world just so. Not Mozart either (too happy). I couldn't think of any other composers except Wagner and Beethoven. Jazz, then, or blues. But there would be music because that was the kind of man Mr. Anderson was. If there was silence, it would be because he'd chosen that, not had it forced on him.

Then I wondered. Maybe he took care of other people because no one was taking care of him. His wife was away. He must be lonely. Maybe he gathered, well, *strays* to feel better.

After the dishes, I told Mom I was going upstairs to do some work and then get ready for bed. She kissed my cheek. Her lips were warm from the tea, and she smelled like a flower.

I knew which floorboards squeaked, and I'd read somewhere that the squeakiest place on steps or in any hallway is right in the middle because that's where everyone walks. I walked normally to my room, flipped on the light, closed the door from the outside. Then I tiptoed out, hugging the wall all the way to the spare room.

The hinges cried but so softly only I heard. Matt had never lived in this house, so there was nothing of his here at all: not his trundle bed or baseball glove or football helmet or books. Still, if Matt were to come back, somehow, this is where he would sleep. I quietly pulled the door shut, heard the slight tick of the catch, and stood a moment. I knew the layout well: bed to the left, a bureau straight on, a desk against the right wall between two windows—and a telephone.

Mr. Anderson said he lived twenty miles west and south, give or take, and I thought I remembered the town from when he'd pointed out his exit the night before. The operator found him right away—"On J?" A county road; that's the thing about Wisconsin, a bunch of roads don't have names but numbers and letters because they're all just threading through farmland. I said yes and then no, thanks, I'd dial it myself. When I did, I made sure to block caller ID, just in case . . . Well, just in case.

I listened as the numbers bleeped and blooped, and then the phone rang. Once, twice, three times . . . On the fifth ring, someone picked up. "Hello?"

A woman's voice. Or a girl? Someone young but not younger than me. Everything I'd been about to say—what *had* that been anyway?—turned to dust on my tongue.

"Hello?" She sounded tired and a little mad and about to get madder. In the space behind her pause, I heard music: disjointed notes from a piano whose melodic line I couldn't follow because then she was back, angrier now: "Hello? Is there anyone there?" Then: "Is that *you*?"

Another voice, in the background but getting closer. Male, asking who was on the phone . . . Was that Mr. Anderson?

"I don't know." Her voice was muffled, like she'd put her hand over the receiver. "I thought it . . . him . . . no ID . . ."

The other person said something else and she said: "...
know what he ... doesn't know ... here."

"Hang up." I heard that pretty distinctly. "He told us
not ..."

Click.

After a few moments, a recording snapped on and helpfully
suggested I hang up.

I did.

b

Okay.

His wife, probably.

Unless it wasn't.

Mrs. Anderson was in Minnesota, he'd said. And had that
been Mr. Anderson's voice? Well, how would I know?

Whatever.

Mr. Anderson had a life.

He sure as hell didn't need me in it.

c

That night, I read one of Matt's e-mails. He'd had a bad day.
His convoy had taken sniper fire, and he'd had to do building
sweeps, which he's said can get you killed just as fast as an
IED. He managed to take out two snipers, but the third shot
his partner and got away. The story was depressingly familiar,
one I'd read before. This time, though, I had trouble forming
a reply because I really, really wanted to talk to someone real
and not just electrons thrown halfway around the world. But

I also knew that the kind of questions I had Matt just couldn't answer.

In the end, I sent nothing back. For the first time in forever, I didn't have the energy to make up a nice story, and that made me feel worse. Just because Matt was gone didn't mean he didn't need me.

Before bed, I went into my bathroom, closed the door. I turned on the shower and, as the water heated up, peeled out of my clothes. The right front pocket of my jeans was heavy, which was weird—until I remembered why.

❑

I didn't recall slipping the knife into my pocket, but I'd found it at lunch, while I hid in a bathroom stall. I wondered if Mr. Anderson noticed the knife was gone. If he had, did he suspect me? He'd been all business during class, and then I'd gone to the library. So either he knew and didn't care, or he didn't know. Whatever. I would have to figure out a way to slip it back into his desk.

Mr. Anderson's knife—the *Kissing Crane* stiletto—was warm from my body heat. I studied the blade as the shower thrummed and steam fogged the mirror, which was a good thing. I didn't like looking at myself—you know, my face or anything—and forget the donor sites on my thighs. I never got the urge to inspect my back. (Doctors, though, they love that kind of stuff: *oh, that's scarring very well.*)

You know, Bob, there's this movie, *Secretary*, that got part of it right—for me, anyway. The girl's a cutter. The guy she falls in love with is kind of creepy-kinky, and it becomes this whole big sex thing; her suffering proves how much she loves him; blah, blah, blah . . . that kind of stuff. To the guy, her scars are part of her beauty. He bathes her, washes her hair, kisses every inch of skin, tastes every wound.

And now, here was Mr. Anderson's kissing knife. I liked the heft, the weight. How solid it was, like a promise. For a while that morning—before Danielle—I'd felt safe in Mr. Anderson's back room. Last night, he'd taken care of me.

I eyed the bathroom door.

I could. It would be so simple. A quick flick of the wrist. A little pressure. I could do it.

So I did. For the first time in months, Bob . . . I locked the door.

18: a

The knob was cool and moist with condensation. The lock engaged with a tiny *snick*.

My heart was pounding. Still clutching the knife, I drew aside the curtain and slipped under the shower. Water drummed over my face and neck, sheeted over my chest, and swam down my stomach and along my thighs. The shower was already warm, but I inched the knob over, felt the sudden surge of heat. I kept going, letting the heat build, gasping as the hot water needled my breasts. The sound—a rushing, gathering roar—was nearly identical to the bellow of that fire so long ago and yet always with me. There was heat and steam and pain raining down—and Bob?

It wasn't all . . . *bad*.

Because there was the knife. *His* knife. I pulled out the blade, felt it lock into place. This was the knife, the knife, his kissing knife. . . .

The staghorn was rough, but the stiletto was smooth, bright steel that was first cool and then began to warm. I ran the ball of my left thumb along the edge . . . *careful, be careful* . . . and felt how keen that blade was.

Careful.

Then I drew that tip, sharp as a pick, over the swell of my left breast, tracing myself . . . carefully. Slowly. Like drawing myself into being, if that makes any sense. I gasped at the feel of the knife against my tingling skin because it . . .

It was . . .

It was what I wanted. Not blood, not from the kissing knife, no shriek, not that kind of pain. I walked along that knife's edge in the heat as my blood thundered in my ears and—

"Jenna?"

I flinched.

The kissing knife slipped.

There was a sudden, bright, white lance of pain, and I stared, horrified, as a red rosette bloomed, the blood welling from where the kissing knife had nicked the skin just to the right of my heart.

"Jenna!" My mother knocked on the door. The knob rattled. "Why is this door locked?"

"I . . . Mom, I'm . . . I'm in the *shower*!" I managed through a sudden flutter of panic. Shit, shit! I forced my shaking fingers to explore the cut then breathed out a tiny sigh of relief. The slice wasn't deep, just the tiniest of nicks made by the stiletto's razor-sharp point and barely there. An accident, it had just been an accident; I'd slipped; I hadn't meant to really *hurt* . . .

"Jenna, open the door this instant!"

"No!" I watched as the water splashing over my breast pinked then paled. The bleeding was stopping already. God, that was a close call. What had I been thinking? This was *crazy*.

There was no such thing as *good* pain. Was there? No, *no!* That was a movie; the mousy little secretary got her guy, but this was real life. Besides, there *was* no guy. "I'm in the *shower*."

Mom went on about how this wasn't part of the bargain, but I kept shouting back that I was in the shower and what did she say, what, *what?* By the time she huffed off, the bleeding had stopped completely. I knew this wasn't the end of it, of course. Once I was out, Mom would march me into her bathroom for a strip inspection because the light was even better there.

But she would miss it. For one thing, I always cut my stomach, my hips. For another, the slice was so clean, so neat, the lips entirely bloodless, there was no way she'd spot it.

By the time I unlocked the door, the kissing knife was hidden, too: snugged right next to that pair of nail scissors behind my vanity.

Knowing the kissing knife was there? That I got away with it? That I could get at that knife—hold it, carry it, touch it whenever I wanted?

That I had a real piece of a memory—of Mr. Anderson caring about me, of a safe place—that wasn't *all* bad?

It was good, Bob.

It felt good.

Because it was mine, Bob. It was *mine*.

19: a

On the Wednesday before Mom's big party, Dewerman corralled me after class. "Congratulations. Since you're the only student who hasn't chosen someone for a project, it's my pleasure to name you the lucky winner of Procrastinators Anonymous. First prize is one week in New Jersey and"—he presented a note card with an elaborate flourish—"the only person no one else wanted. Be grateful. Second prize was two weeks in New Jersey."

I scanned the card. "Alexis Depardieu? Like . . . the actor?"

"No relation. *This* Depardieu was the Rachel Carson of marine mammology. She studied whales and dolphins, mainly, and wrote one book, *Ladyfish*, published posthumously the year after she died."

"Uhm . . ." As I remembered it, we'd had to choose from people who'd written novels or poetry or plays. Maybe that was why no one had chosen Depardieu. "So why is she on the list? How did she kill herself?"

Dewerman showed a thin smile. "She didn't. Her ship collided with a whaling vessel off the coast of Japan in November 2000."

"An accident?"

"That's one way of looking at it. Clearly, if she's on the list, maybe I have questions, right? So, go." He made shooing motions. "Learn. You've got all next week to work on a proposal while we're on fall break. Now, git."

I gitted. As I went out the door, I saw Mr. Anderson coming down the hall to my right, so I peeled off to the left. When I looked back, Dewerman was gesturing with his mammoth coffee mug and Mr. Anderson's hands were in his pockets. Neither man looked my way. That was fine.

b

The library didn't have Depardieu's book, so I ordered it through interlibrary loan and then did a Google search. The Wikipedia entry was pretty dry. Here's the SparkNotes version, Bobby: Alexis Depardieu was French-Canadian and an only child whose father had died when his swordfish boat went down in a gale in the North Sea. Alexis was nine when her mom remarried a well-to-do lawyer; went to boarding school when she was twelve; was premed at McGill but switched to marine bio. Cambridge for a PhD and then she moved around a lot: Quebec, New Zealand, California. Taught at Berkeley, Stanford; started publishing on dolphin behavior and communications, blah, blah, blah.

In the late 1980s, Alexis connected with another marine biologist named Stephen Wright, a professor and a member of the Sea Stewards, this radical environmental group. Alexis and Wright got arrested a bunch of times trying to free dolphins from aquariums and stuff. Got themselves fired from Berkeley and then joined up full-time with the Stewards, who were kind of Greenpeace-y, into harassing whaling ships, things like that.

Then, in 1997, off the coast of Antarctica, Stephen Wright was washed overboard as he piloted his Zodiac between a Japanese whaler and a humpback. This didn't stop Alexis for long. A year or so later, she was back with the Stewards aboard their flagship, *Mystic Dreamer*.

Then it was late 2000 and depending on whom you believe, *Mystic Dreamer* either accidentally collided with a Japanese whaling vessel or deliberately rammed it. *Mystic Dreamer* foundered. According to the survivors, Alexis ordered the crew into life rafts but stayed at the helm and radio where she continued to broadcast a Mayday. (The Japanese steamed off. I guess they figured the *Dreamer*'s crew got whatever they deserved.) The last person to see her alive was the first mate. *Mystic Dreamer* went down and then it was *au revoir*, Alexis. The rest of the crew was rescued sixteen hours later by an Australian ship responding to *Dreamer*'s Mayday. The end.

There wasn't much else, some links to follow-up articles about how pissed the Japanese got, lawsuits, and stuff like that. There were links to some essays, a couple unauthorized biographies, blah, blah, blah.

I hadn't a clue where to go with this. So I logged out and decided not to think about it.

20: a

Mom's big Oktoberfest gig was on a Saturday, and it was a good thing I had the whole next week of fall break to rest and recover. The party was my crazy Grandma Stephie's idea way back when. They started out serious, the Wisconsin equivalent of the Algonquin Round Table—only instead of famous writers and literary critics and actors meeting for lunch in some swank New York restaurant, snarking about their friends and drinking themselves into a stupor, Grandma cultivated Milwaukee beer barons, shipping magnates, and guys who owned brownstone quarries. Basically, anyone loaded enough to make the trip up to Lake Superior got a weekend of drinking, gorging, schmoozing, and general debauching with New York and Chicago writer-types. In exchange, the fat cats all coughed up a tidy sum for books at their full retail price. A pretty good deal, all the way around.

When Mom took over the store, the parties continued but scaled down and moved south: first to our old house and now to the McMansion. She invited mainly regional authors, some famous but most not. Mom supplied the books and invited a bunch of book clubs and other, mostly pretentious and preferably wealthy, people who liked (or pretended to like) and discussed (or pretended to discuss) books. But mostly they hankered for free food and free booze.

The only problem was the bookstore had been losing money on the parties for years now, mostly because people came to drink and eat and didn't cart books away in wheelbarrows the way they used to. So, like clockwork, my parents spent the morning after arguing about how much more money Mom had lost and how cost-ineffective the parties were and blah, blah, blah. Dad always threatened to pull his support until Mom groveled enough and the issue got tabled for another year.

My job was always the same: meet and greet, trudge upstairs to Mom and Dad's room with coats, trudge back, circulate between the house and the patio where Dad had the fire pit going and, in general, be charming. I had my stock answers down pat: *fine, working hard, thinking of a place out East, maybe a doctor but I don't really know yet*. Most of the guests were people I'd known for years, so I didn't mind and I really did like listening to some of the writers.

Well, most of them.

b

Nate Bartholomew was even more handsome than the picture on his dust jacket. Judging from the adoring faces of a bunch of the women—and a couple of Evan's friends—he was going to walk away with a whole new fan base. He talked about *Sandlot Blues* and the movie and how he and the stars went for a round of golf in the dead of winter.

Mom sat in the front row and beamed. Every now and again, his eyes would meet hers and I swear she blushed. When he posed for pictures, he hugged Mom a lot closer than was strictly necessary. Later, she hovered as he signed autographs, making sure he had plenty of pens and a glass of water and whatever else he needed, which was sort of standard. I mean, she did it for all the writers, only I noticed that she laughed a lot at Nate's jokes and put her hand on his shoulder.

I thought back to the night she hadn't been at her store, when she said she and Nate Bartholomew went out for "a few drinks." Now, I wondered if knocking back a couple was really *all* they'd done.

So I watched, carefully, as Bartholomew whispered something in my mom's ear and a flush crept up her neck. Her eyes sparkled.

Oh yeah.

Oh . . . *yeah.*

C

Maybe four hours in, I escaped. The guests were fed and watered and since I wasn't the main attraction, no one noticed me ease into the house. As I dragged upstairs, I was thinking how lucky I was that I'd started running again—on my own, just to blow off steam and no, Bob, I did *not* think about Mr. Anderson when I did—or else my legs would've turned to wet noodles with all that up and down and in and out.

I hadn't bothered with a light because both the downstairs and outside spots were on, filling the upstairs hall with a thin, silver glow. So it was just enough for me to notice what was wrong.

The door to Matt's room was open. Just a hair. Which was wrong because that door was always shut. Mom made sure of it.

Then, I heard something so faint it was almost no sound at all. What? I crept to Matt's door, reached for the knob, and then froze as the sound—sounds—came again.

A low, urgent murmur . . . A man's voice, I thought. Next, there came the creak of bedsprings—and then, a weepy little cry that was almost a groan.

Holy shit.

d

Okay, time out.

Bob, I may have a few problems, but I am not some sicko Peeping Tom. To tell you the truth, when I was younger, I sometimes heard Mom and Dad, which completely grossed me out. (Come on, Bob, admit it. You overheard your parents, too. Don't tell me you thought those were mice.) That had been in the days before Matt had gone and things were better: Mom not drinking herself into a stupor; Dad not screwing nurses; and me most definitely not a slice 'n dice away from a psych ward.

So I knew what people in bed sounded like. I didn't need a map. None of my business, right?

Looking back, this was another of those key moments, Bob, when my story could've taken off in a very different direction.

Because if I'd only pretended nothing was there, the fight would never have happened.

21: a

But I didn't pretend.

Instead, I inched forward and eased open the door just a hair more. Why? Mostly because the guy's tone wasn't right and now, this close, I could make out words: *Relax, baby, just relax, come on come on.* . . .

So I looked. There was just enough light for me to get the general idea. Honestly, in retrospect, better I should've stuck pins in my eyes.

They were on the bed. The guy was on top. He was the only one moving. He was still talking, but now I could hear, much more clearly, how frustrated he was: "C'mon, c'mon, let's *go*." Actually, he sounded pissed.

The woman was limp and only moaned every now and again. Not a good kind of sound, Bob, if you know what I mean. Not like she was having fun but more of a sick, hurt, what-the-hell-is-going-on moan: the kind of thing I'd heard on the ward from kids who couldn't get the voices in their head to stop torturing them. And I remember her hand, Bob, hanging like a dead flower over the edge of the bed.

I didn't know what to do. I'm sure this kind of thing—people sneaking into rooms and hooking up which, considering how upset adults get when kids my age do it, is pretty hypocritical, if you ask me—had been going on since Grandma Stephie's time. Knowing *her*, she probably took notes. Hell, these two might even be married, but I didn't think so. You had to be there, Bob, but the vibe was all wrong.

Then I heard the hitch in the man's breath as he felt my eyes. His face was a silver blur as he looked over his shoulder and sucked in a quick gasp: "What the *fu*—"

I gitted. Spinning away, I yanked the door shut and then bolted down the hall for my room. I slammed my door and didn't bother with a light but scurried for the far side of my bed where I huddled, the wooden frame biting my back. My eyes felt like someone had taken a blowtorch and melted them right down to the sockets. My windows were open and there was background chatter, voices running together like water over rocks, the pop and crackle of the fire pit, and gusts of laughter. The band was playing a jazz set and that made me think of Mr. Anderson, which I immediately wished I hadn't. *He* would have helped that woman. I was such a coward. This was like Psycho-Dad killing the kitchen wall and me turning tail like a scared little bunny rabbit. I should have done something. Screamed. Yelled. Turned on the light. Pulled the creep off. Something.

Time passed. I don't know how long. Over the thud of my heart, I heard the man's footsteps as he came into the hall and then turned into the bathroom—*my* bathroom. A light flicked on, the glow seeping through the seams along my doorjamb.

Water ran and splashed in the basin, gurgled down the drain. Then a brief, quivering silence.

And then footsteps. A dark tongue of shadow licked at the light at the base of my bedroom door.

"Jenna?" He didn't knock or try to come in. "Jenna, you in there, sweetpea?"

b

Sweetpea.

Now I knew who he was.

"Sweetpea," said Dr. Kirby—my dad's partner and a guy I'd known since I was old enough to know anyone. "Jenna, sweetpea, it'd be better for me if you didn't say anything. I know you know that, right?" When I didn't reply, he said, "I didn't force her."

Oh no, she was just dead drunk. She couldn't have consented to save her life. Dr. Kirby said something else stupid, I don't remember what, and then the shadows of his feet vanished and he went away. I waited a few more minutes just to make certain and then eased out of my room.

The woman was on her knees by Matt's bed. His room was close and stuffy, and when I bent down, she had a hand to her mouth. "I think," she gulped. "I think I'm going to be . . . I'm gonna be . . ."

We made it to the bathroom just in time. I held her hair as she hugged the toilet. The stink was like this black oily cloud, bad enough that I held my breath and concentrated on keeping what little I'd eaten where it was. When she was down to spitting, I ran cold water over a washcloth and sponged off her face and neck. The first three buttons of her blouse were gone and her stockings were ripped and there were scratches on her neck.

"I'm really drunk," she said, stating the obvious. Her words were all mushy. She struggled to focus on my face, but her eyes kept clicking from side to side like ball bearings. She sagged against the tub, her mouth slack, her breath fruity and sick.

"Did you come with someone? What's your name?" I had to ask a couple times. When she finally got the sentences out, I said, "Okay, I'm going to get your husband. Just stay here. Don't move, all right?" Like she was in any shape to go anywhere.

Her husband was a surgical nurse, she'd said. Once outside, I scanned faces and asked around until a doctor's wife pointed me in the right direction. After pulling the guy aside and explaining, I led him back to the house. Dr. Kirby tried catching my eye, but I only glanced once and then didn't look back.

Between her husband and me, we got her on her feet and downstairs. At the front door, the husband looked over his shoulder. "We had a wonderful time," he said, which was completely weird. His face was so saturated with shame, I wanted to tell him everything would be okay. But I kept quiet, watching at they staggered down the rumba line of cars snaking along the drive.

The cold air settled my stomach. There was no moon and too much light pollution from the McMansion, but I could make out some stars. I didn't want to go back inside that house. But if I didn't belong there, where could I go? I had this sudden, wild urge to steal my parents' car and go north, to Lake Superior or Canada. Of course, I didn't do any such thing.

But boy, Bob, I should've.

C

Instead, I went back to clean up the mess. Maybe halfway up the stairs, it occurred to me that I'd have to do Matt's room, too. The idea of stripping his sheets made my scars bunch. They would never be clean enough. Burning them would be better.

Right about then, I began to float. A familiar numbness dripped through my veins, and my head felt hollow as a helium balloon. Slipstream, only I wasn't running—or maybe, metaphorically speaking, I was.

Still floaty, I cleaned: Comet on the sink, Clorox toilet cleaner in the bowl, about half a can of Lysol to get rid of the stink. I splashed water into the tub even though it wasn't dirty. I scrubbed, hard, and thought about nothing at all.

So that probably explains why I never heard him.

d

One minute I was sloshing blue water down the tub drain and the next, I felt someone watching. I looked over my shoulder.

"Hi, sweetpea." Dr. Kirby was big enough that he blocked the door. "I thought, maybe, we should talk."

22: a

I said nothing. I didn't move. My skin tightened over my skull.

Dr. Kirby slid into the bathroom. "I know what it looked like, but we're all adults here, right? You're old enough to understand how things work?" He spread his hands and that's when I saw Ben Franklin's face pinched between the first two fingers of his right hand. He took another step as I stood and then he was reaching, leading with the money, ready to tuck a hundred bucks into the breast pocket of my blouse. "I know you know how to keep your mouth shut."

"I . . ." I swallowed against the lump in my throat. "I don't want your money, Dr. Kirby."

He froze, his hand hovering like a tarantula over my left breast—the one I'd nicked with the kissing knife. He was watching my eyes, maybe trying to figure out if I was going to scream, which I wasn't. He said, awkwardly, "Think of it as an early Christmas gift. What teenager doesn't need a little extra cash?"

I shook my head. "I don't need anything, Dr. Kirby. I'm fine."

"Oh, come on," and then, somehow, he was even closer, easing the money into my pocket, fingers grazing my breast, a slow stupid smile spreading over his lips. "We used to be friends, remember? I know how to be gentle," he said. His breath was rank, and then I was against the wall and he was leaning in, his hands reaching up to cup and squeeze.

"No," I said. "Don't, Dr. Kirby," I said.

But he didn't stop. First one hand and then the other and then he was pressing me against the wall, his slobbery mouth on my neck and then mashed against mine, his fat tongue worming between my clamped lips to lick my teeth. . . .

Oh God, Bob. Did I do more? Sock him in the jaw? Stomp on his instep? Kick him in the groin and then drive my knee into his chin as he doubled over in agony? Bite off his tongue? Did I even scream?

No. I didn't. I could lie and say I did. No one but me and Dr. Kirby would ever know. But that's not what happened. I don't know if you'll get it, Bob, but think of that cold slap of shock the first time a parent spanks you or gets dead drunk or stammers an explanation to a cop about why he ran a red light—and you'll understand. Those are betrayals, moments when that thin membrane separating your life as a child from the real world tears just a little bit more. The first couple of times, you put a Band-Aid over the rip and the tear knits together. Sometimes there's a scar, but maybe not, and you go on. You try to pretend that the worst betrayals—when you discover your parents don't love each other, say—have healed. But, eventually, the cuts are too deep and the membrane shreds and that curtain can never be drawn again. Maybe that's when you grow up.

This was Dr. Kirby, my godfather. Our *friend*.

So I didn't fight. I *did* say no and I began to cry. All that should've been enough—hell, the thing should never have *begun*—but it wasn't. Dr. Kirby fumbled at my blouse, jammed his knee between my legs and levered them apart. A button from my blouse popped then another and another, and I pushed at his shoulders and said *no Dr. Kirby no no no—*

"*Hey!*"

Dr. Kirby started.

Eyes streaming, I looked past his shoulder—and then I simply wanted to die.

Because—of course—it was Mr. Anderson.

23: a

Dr. Kirby jumped back as if my skin was acid. "Oh, hey," he said.

"What's going on here?" Mr. Anderson's eyes flicked from Dr. Kirby to me and then dropped to the floor and my buttons scattered there like tiny white Tiddlywinks. His face changed, shifting from shock to comprehension to black fury.

Dr. Kirby saw it, too. "I was just leaving," he said, bullying his way out the door and practically lunging for the stairs. "Jenna, tell your parents good-bye, all right?"

"Hey," said Mr. Anderson as Dr. Kirby clattered down to the foyer. Mr. Anderson started for the stairs. "*Hey*!"

I found my voice. "Mr. Anderson, I—"

"Stay here, Jenna, just stay here!" And then he was banging down the stairs after Dr. Kirby.

I took off after them both. By the time I hit the foyer, Mr. Anderson was already out the front door. I heard shouts. The cook came scurrying out of the kitchen in a flutter of white apron. "What—?" she began.

"Get my parents! Get *help*!" Then I was out the door, too.

b

Our driveway's gravel and Dr. Kirby bobbed and lurched, slipping and skidding on loose stone. He was faster than I thought he would be and he might've gotten to his car if Mr. Anderson wasn't a runner. In six lunging strides, Mr. Anderson closed the gap, snagged Dr. Kirby's collar, then whipped him around like a sack of laundry. Dr. Kirby gave a startled yelp and half-turned, his arms flailing, but Mr. Anderson was strong. Dr. Kirby's feet left the ground as Mr. Anderson slammed him against a minivan. The van rocked and then there was the keening wail of an alarm, and Dr. Kirby was screaming the same high note, swatting at Mr. Anderson, trying to land a punch. Mr. Anderson's fists bunched in Dr. Kirby's lapels and then he was cursing and smashing Dr. Kirby against the van once, twice—

"What the—" Someone swore, blew past me: my father. I didn't know he could move that fast. In another second, he and another man had Mr. Anderson's arms and were dragging him off: "Break it up, break it up, break it—!"

That pretty much killed the party.

c

Afterward—after Dr. Kirby realized he had a split lip and started howling about suing Mr. Anderson, after my father got Dr. Kirby ice for his lip, after the guests spawned for their cars—the adults went into my father's study and talked for twenty minutes. I waited in the kitchen and watched the catering crew clear dishes until my father called for me.

My father's study is paneled oak and red leather and framed diplomas and pictures and floor-to-ceiling bookshelves crammed with leather volumes he's never read. The room smells like oranges from the oil the housekeeper uses on the wood. My father was sitting behind his desk, a massive mahogany antique like the kind the president uses. Mr. Anderson and Dr. Kirby were in the wing-backed chairs my father reserved for visitors. Meryl and my mother perched on a small love seat to one side. My mother was wringing her hands and her skin was so pale her eyes looked penned on with a Sharpie. Meryl just looked disgusted.

Mr. Anderson stood as I entered. The reddish-blush of a bruise stained his right cheek, but no one had bothered getting *him* any ice. "Take my seat," he said.

"She's fine," said my father.

Mr. Anderson gave him a searching look, then shrugged but stayed on his feet, moving just a little closer to me. After an awkward pause, my father—annoyed—said, "Jenna, do you or do you not have money Dr. Kirby gave you?"

The hundred dollars. I'd completely forgotten. The bill was still crumpled in my breast pocket. I nodded.

"There, you see?" Dr. Kirby's lower lip was the size of a sausage. "I told you, Elliot," he said. "I was giving her a tip—"

"That's not what it was," Mr. Anderson interrupted.

"—just like I've done before," Dr. Kirby continued. I couldn't think of any time before that he'd ever given me any kind of tip, but he pushed on: "Elliot, for chrissake, I've known

Jenna since she was a baby. Can't a godfather give his goddaughter a tip for all the hard work she's done this evening? We were just giving each other a little hug good-bye and that's all. Now I'm willing to let this go—"

"I'll just bet you are." Mr. Anderson's voice was low and I was standing next to him, so I was the only one who heard.

"—because there's clearly been a misunderstanding. I'd hate for this to come between us, Elliot." Dr. Kirby spread his hands. "I mean, we have to work together. We've got the office to think of."

"And *you* have your daughter," Mr. Anderson said to my father. "Think of *her*."

"Oh, believe me, I do." My father's tone was brittle as dried leaves. He heaved a long-suffering sigh. "Listen, I appreciate you showing an interest in Jenna, I really do. Heaven knows, she needs people to help her negotiate life. You're probably not aware but before Turing, she had . . . well, *problems* and—"

No, please, don't say it. I saw my father's lips moving but heard nothing over the sudden thump of my pulse. I wanted to melt into the carpet. The earth shifted, a dark chasm opened, and then I was falling and I thought, *Good, fine, swallow me up.*

"—so I think you can understand that she's got some special needs," my father was saying. "After her hospitalization, we'd hoped that Turing would be a way for her to start fresh."

"This has nothing to do with any of that," said Mr. Anderson. "We're talking about this guy molesting your daughter. Jesus, are you blind, or just stupid? Look at her blouse. Look at *her*."

"That does it. I've had enough." Dr. Kirby grunted his way to his feet. "Elliot, I'll admit to a bit too much to drink and a misunderstanding, but that's all. Now I'm going home. Tomorrow, I'm going to sleep late, read the paper, drink coffee, and forget about this. I'll see you in the office." He nodded at my mother. "Emily."

When he was gone, Mr. Anderson looked at my father. "She's your daughter."

"Yes, she is." My father stood and leaned across his desk to offer his hand. "I can't tell you how grateful I am that you've taken such an interest. Not enough teachers spare the time these days."

Mr. Anderson didn't move. "But she's your *daughter*."

"Yes. Well." My father's smile wobbled and he took back his hand. "I'll just say good night."

⫶

Mr. Anderson asked me to walk him to his car. My father opened his mouth to say no, but then he looked at Mr. Anderson just daring him to do it and so my father, for once, shut up.

Our feet stirred stone as we crunched down the gravel drive toward the road. The night was moonless, and Mr. Anderson only a shadow gliding alongside. It was also colder than I remembered, and an easterly breeze made the bare branches chatter. I shivered and hugged my arms.

"Cold?" Mr. Anderson asked.

"I'm okay."

"You say that too much." I heard a soft shoosh of fabric and then Mr. Anderson was draping his jacket around my shoulders.

The leather was warm from his body heat. "I can't. I'll be fine. It's not that far. It's your jacket."

"Yes, it is. If it'll make you feel better, you can give it back at the car and then shiver all the way back to the house, okay? Now be gracious and say thank you."

"Thank you."

"You're welcome." Then: "I'm sorry, Jenna."

All at once, I was *that* close to tears. I gnawed on my already-raw lower lip. At this rate, I wouldn't have any skin left. "You didn't do anything. I should be apologizing to you."

"No," he said, his voice rough. "Don't ever say that. You've got nothing to apologize for. I'm sorry I couldn't keep your father from embarrassing you more than . . ." He paused. "Look, nothing your father said makes a difference, all right? You're still the same person you were before."

"I should explain about what happened last year—"

"No." His hand reached out of the darkness and touched my shoulder. "Listen to me, Jenna. What happened doesn't matter. It's past. I don't need to know. All that matters is here and now, you understand? Sometimes it's best to let the past go, Jenna. Don't get so caught up in looking behind you forget to look ahead."

We started walking again. I could feel the words bunching up in my throat. What Mr. Anderson didn't understand was . . . all of a sudden, I *wanted* to tell him. I wanted him to know *me*: about Matt and the fire, about the psych ward. I thought of his knife now squirreled in my backpack because it was easier to get at that way and I could keep it close. I liked the feel of that secret in my hands, and I wanted to confess that, too.

But I said nothing. I let his jacket keep me warm, and I kept my mouth shut.

At his car, he said, "There's something I want you to promise. Anyone touches you, *anyone*, I want you to call me, you understand? Day or night, makes no difference. Even if it's because you only need to talk, I'll be there. I'll come get you wherever you are. I mean it, Jenna. I'm here for you. This—" His words thrummed with emotion. "This stuff . . . It's crazy; it's—"

"I think my mom is having an affair." The words flew past my teeth and there was no calling them back. "My dad's screwing one of his nurses. Matt's gone, and it's just me with them, and I'm scared they're going to get a divorce and then I think that would be a good thing."

"Oh, Jenna. Oh, honey, I'm sorry." He took a small step and I thought he might hug me, but it was dark and his face swarmed with shadows. So I'm not sure, even now. But I will be honest: I wanted a hug. I needed one, so badly. Nothing like that happened, though, and after a second or two, he said, "Listen, any time you want a break from your folks, you come over to our house, okay? Door's open twenty-four hours a day, seven days a week. You wouldn't be the first."

Our house. Right. He was married; I remembered my stupid phone call and wondered why his wife wasn't here. I was also very glad he couldn't see my face.

"Sure," I said.

€

Psycho-Dad was waiting just inside the front door. "What did you say to him?" he demanded.

"Nothing," I said.

24: a

Sunday, after the party.

At noon, I watched my parents' car rumble down the drive. Meryl was sitting in back and only she turned to wave good-bye, which pretty much summed up the general temperature of everyone concerned: chilly, just the near side of frost. I lifted my hand to Meryl and then my father hung a right at the bottom of the drive, tooled up the rise toward the highway, and passed out of sight.

I closed the door, listening to the silence settle in. Before Matt left, our family always made the trip up north to Meryl's farm on Madeline Island together. The drive was long, over eight hours, so we'd stay an extra day or two to kayak on Lake Superior, bicycle around the island, or just hang out on the farm, helping out with the sheep that Meryl raised for wool. Mom said that when I was little, I always cried when we left. That was probably true. I loved Meryl just about as much as I loved my mother, sometimes more.

Still, I was relieved to be left behind, afraid until the moment my father turned the ignition and dropped the car into drive that they might make me come along.

At that point, my parents weren't due back until Tuesday night. I had sixty hours of freedom, give or take. Other than homework and running, I didn't have a clue what I was going to do with all that time.

It was weird, when you stopped to consider that at this same time last year, I'd been on a mental ward. So, at best, my parents leaving me alone meant that they completely trusted me.

At the worst—well, I guess you could say they deeply didn't care.

Which, I thought, was closer to the truth.

b

For the first two hours, I finished up what little homework I had. I surfed the Internet for a while, looked at my former friends' Facebook pages. My own page hadn't been updated since before my hospitalization. I didn't even look the same. My hair was shorter then, and my breasts barely there. (I was a late bloomer. Mom always said I was an ugly duckling that someday would swan. She might have meant well, but every word drew blood.) Besides, what would I add to my page? *Free At Last? Forty-Seven Days Since Last Cut?*

Then I remembered Matt. I hadn't e-mailed him in days, and that wasn't right. But what could I tell him? That I'd flushed Dr. Kirby's hundred dollars down the toilet? That I'd thought of my old nail scissors but instead clutched the kissing knife as my skin begged? That as badly as I wanted to, I hadn't cut and that was because I knew now that Mr. Anderson was the only adult willing to protect me? Fight for me? That he would never, ever hurt me? No, I couldn't tell Matt any of this.

There were no DVDs I wanted to watch. We didn't own *Alien*, but I found the final sequence on YouTube, where Sigourney Weaver blasts the alien into space, and turned the music up. Mr. Anderson said it was from Howard Hansen's "Romantic Symphony," so I downloaded that and a couple other tracks: an album of Judy Garland, Duke Ellington. That piano piece by Cyrus Chestnut we'd listened to the other night. Wagner.

Then, I thought: *Go for a run.* I'd mapped out a ten-mile route from the McMansion, but I was restless and wanted something new. Pulling up Google Earth, I searched until I found the address.

Well, Mr. Anderson had said his door was always open.

Time to find out if that was true.

C

County Road J turned out to be mainly rolling farmland, the fields fallow now, the withered stalks plowed under to form dun-colored quilt blocks. Here and there, fields of pumpkins shone an iridescent, impossible orange under that clear, bright, October sun. I passed sad farmhouses and tumble-down barns and listing silos. Other farms were better off, the barns painted a deep russet or a flawless, eye-watering white.

Mr. Anderson's mailbox guarded the mouth of a dirt road that snaked north over a rise hemmed by hardwood forest and disappeared. From the map I'd pulled up on Google Earth, Mr. Anderson owned about a hundred acres and his house perched on the southwestern shore of a large kidney bean of a lake. The Google images had been taken during full summer because all the trees were leafed out and the open fields were a deep emerald green. The woods extended from the lake on all sides and then gave way to open land to the east but more woods running north and west. A small stream drained into the lake at its northernmost point and another coiled away to the south. There seemed to be at least one more building way to the west, almost drowning in the forest, so maybe it was a summer cottage or an old hunting cabin. The nearest house was a good three miles east, but there was parkland off Mr. Anderson's property, with another lake and plenty of running trails, and that's where I headed.

If you're thinking that I was daring something to happen, Bob, you'd be right. At the time, I told myself that I just needed some new scenery to keep my workouts fresh. But I know the truth. I was hoping I might run into Mr. Anderson on the trails. He said he ran on his property and in the park, and I was a runner and lived sort of out here. So we would just happen to run into each other and then . . .

Then *what*?

Come by, he'd said, anytime. Did he really mean that? I thought he did. I also half-sensed that we were dancing around something, doing a complicated series of steps to some ancient rhythm that he knew but I didn't yet understand. Or maybe I was dancing alone, the whole scenario unfolding in only *my* imagination. Like so many other things.

Even for a nice day in October, Faring Park was virtually deserted, with only one other car—not Mr. Anderson's. I changed into my running shoes, stretched, then took off at what I knew was an easy seven-mile-an-hour pace. I followed a meandering wooded trail that, in three miles, would empty onto another east-west trail and *that* would eventually take me to the edge of Mr. Anderson's property. Total distance, there and back, was a little shy of seven miles. Crossing onto Mr. Anderson's property—running to his house, say—would add another four miles there and back. So, eleven altogether. It was doable. I just didn't know if I would.

Like math and science, running has never been hard for me. I don't listen to music when I run. The more I sweat, the clearer my mind becomes, as if all thought, good and bad, oozes out in salty rivers. After a while, there is nothing but the surge of my heart. My muscles are warm, my strides effortless, and I am flying, skimming the earth. I don't think; my head empties, and that is best of all.

I met no one on the trail. I knew when I'd reached Mr. Anderson's land because there were placards stapled to the trees: *Private Property* and *No Trespassing*. I could've continued. The trail unfurled like a brown carpet. I could run onto his property, loop around the lake, just *happen* to be passing by as he stepped onto his deck, a steaming mug of coffee in hand, to admire the view. Then he'd do a double take and shade his eyes and his lips would curl in a happy, surprised grin:

Jenna, what are you doing out here? You ran how *far? How fast? Your split was . . . my God, that's* terrific *time! I didn't know you could run that fast. Hey, if you've got a sec, come on in; I've just put on a pot and I was thinking about how nice it'd be to have someone to share this. . . .*

e

I made great time back to the car.

f

That night, talking to my mother on the phone:

"Your father and I really need to get away," she said. They'd made it to Bayfield too late for the last ferry to the island, so they were staying in town and just about to head out to their favorite restaurant. "I think we might stay an extra few days. You don't mind, do you?"

"What about the store?" But what I thought was: *What about your boyfriend?*

"Evan'll handle everything. I haven't had a break in, well, I don't know how long. Thanksgiving's coming up and things will get even crazier. I need the time away."

"I understand. Don't worry about me. I'll be fine. There's plenty of food and whatever I need, I can always buy." I had a stash of birthday money I'd planned to spend on some new clothes, but my mother had been too busy and shopping on my own was too pathetic even for me.

"There's emergency cash." Mom told me where to find it and then added, "You'll be good driving to school?"

"We're out for the week."

"Oh." Pause. "Right. I forgot."

Big surprise there. "When do you and Dad think you'll be back?"

"Is Thursday all right?" After I told her that Thursday was fine, Mom asked again what I'd done all day but then interrupted to say that Dad wanted to go eat. "And have his first martini," she said. "Talk to you tomorrow."

"Sure," I said. "Tomorrow."

25: a

Monday.

There was no work I could pretend to have. I was way ahead in all my classes except English. High time I got serious about my project, though I didn't have a clue what I was going to write about. Alexis's book had arrived at the school library the day before break, and I had yet to crack the spine. So I turned the radio to an NPR station—Mozart, I think—and settled onto the window seat in my bedroom.

I expected something dry, a recap of what I already knew from my Google search with some anecdotes tossed in for interest. Instead, the very first chapter was about the rescue of a female beluga whale that had gotten tangled in a snarl of illegal lobster traplines off the coast of Canada near the St. Lawrence Estuary. By the time the rescue team arrived in Zodiacs, the poor thing had been struggling for hours to stay afloat. Belugas travel in pods and her podmates were frantic, crying in high-pitched whistles as they circled their companion. As Alexis watched, some tried slipping beneath the female to keep her from drowning but couldn't get close enough to help without getting entangled themselves.

The only way to free the whale was to cut the ropes and that meant getting into the water with all those whales. Belugas aren't huge, only fifteen feet when they're fully grown, but any given beluga may weigh as much as three thousand pounds. If the pod panicked when the divers got in the water, or the trapped female began to thrash, the divers wouldn't have a chance. But if they didn't help, the female beluga would drown. There really wasn't a choice. While the Zodiacs took up positions between the pod and the trapped whale, Alexis and three other divers slid into the icy water. As soon as they did, the trapped whale became virtually motionless, as if she knew she must. Silent now, the other belugas circled, waited, watched. For more than an hour and in brain-numbing cold, the divers hacked at the nylon rope, mindful that the beluga's podmates might swarm in to protect their companion; that a moment's lapse in concentration or careless placement of a knife might injure themselves or the whale.

When the beluga was finally free, she blasted out of the circle of divers. The pod chattered and whistled, and then all the whales converged on the divers so quickly there was no time to get aboard their Zodiacs. Alexis thought they were toast.

Instead, the whales circled as the one they'd freed gently pressed the bulbous hump on her head—*melon*, Alexis called it—against each diver. When it was Alexis's turn, she wrote: "At the whale's touch, I felt my questing soul calm. It was as if I had been asleep my entire life and then suddenly come awa—"

b

The phone jangled.

The sound catapulted me out of the book and back to the real world. I fumbled with the handset. "Hello?"

"Hello . . . Jenna?" A pause. "Are you all right?"

My answer was automatic, awkward: "Yes, I'm . . ." I was still so deep in the web of the story I had a hard time making sense of the words. Then my brain caught up, and I sucked in a breath of surprise. "Mr. Anderson?"

"Yes." He sounded concerned. "I was just calling to see how you were doing. I would've called yesterday, but . . . Are you all right?"

I swallowed, all thoughts of Alexis Depardieu pushed aside. "I'm fine. I was just reading. Something for English."

"Oh." A pause. "Well, okay. I didn't mean to disturb you."

"No, it's fine, really. I just . . ." I glanced at my clock: nearly noon. Two hours had evaporated. "Wow, I lost track of time."

"Must be a good book."

"It is, actually. I wasn't expecting it to be. Anyway . . ." I slicked my lips with my tongue. "I'm fine."

"Good. I was just checking in. You know, after what happened Saturday night, you've . . . you've been on my mind. I would've called yesterday, but I thought that was too soon and your parents—"

I jumped in. "My parents are away for a couple days. They left Sunday morning." I explained about Meryl then said, "So I've got the house to myself until Thursday."

"Oh." Pause. "Well, what are you planning to do with all your free time besides read?"

"Uhm . . . well, I've started running again." I screwed up my courage. "In fact, I went over to Faring Park yesterday."

If he was surprised, he didn't sound it. "Yeah? I run there. How'd you do?" I told him and he said, "So that's . . . hang on . . . about a seven-minute mile, give or take about four seconds. Not bad. You run today yet?"

I shook my head then remembered he couldn't see. "Not yet."

"Neither have I. Want some company?" He said it lightly enough and then added: "If you're not too busy. No pressure. I did a long run yesterday, so I'm going easy today, only five or so."

"No." My heart was racing. "I mean, sure, I'd love some company."

"Great. Well, you know where the park is, right? How about we meet there in, say, an hour?"

I said that would be cool, and he said to bring a change of clothes because he knew this little place for lunch, and then I said that sounded nice and hung up and was out the door in fifteen minutes.

Depending on how you look at it, Bob, you might say that was the worst decision of my life. Depending.

26: a

After the first mile, Mr. Anderson said, "So how are things with your parents? I mean, in general."

I'd already told him about the glacial freeze on Sunday morning, so I said, "How do you mean?" We were going at an easy ten-minute-mile pace, and I had plenty of breath for talking. Not that I'd done any, I was too tongue-tied and awkward. Before leaving, I'd obsessed on which outfit to wear. When I'd started running again, I'd ordered two new pair of compression shorts, pants and matching tops, along with new shoes. The shorts were broken in, but the tops not so much and I thought the grungier I looked the better. I mean, I was *running*—with an older *man*—not going on a date (which I'd never been on anyway). In the end, I paired navy blue compression shorts with a baby blue racerback tank that hid my grafts well enough in case I peeled a layer; a white running bra; a lightweight training jacket; and good wool socks for the trail. The day was a carbon copy of the one before, though a little cooler because Mr. Anderson had suggested a loop around Faring Lake. By the end of the first mile, my muscles were warm; I was sweating, my body moving in a comfortable rhythm, though I had to lengthen my stride a little to keep up with Mr. Anderson's longer legs.

"Well . . ." Mr. Anderson glanced at me, then away. That plum-colored bruise was nearly lost in the high color splashing his cheeks. Sweat was just beginning to bead on his muscled shoulders and his throat glistened. "Maybe none of my business, but you mentioned that you were worried about your mom."

My stomach knotted. I was glad we were running so Mr. Anderson couldn't really see my face. "I might be overreacting."

"Or maybe not. You'd be surprised how long people can trick themselves when the truth's right in front of them."

So I told him about the night we'd gone to the store and Mom hadn't been there, and what I'd started thinking about. What I'd seen at the party. "If they're not having an affair, then I think they're really close to one."

Mr. Anderson didn't answer for so long I worried I'd done something wrong. Maybe he hadn't bargained on this. It was one thing to ask how my parents were; it was another when the crazy girl spilled her guts. I wanted to say that I was sorry, but I worried that would make me sound stupid, like a little kid, so I just ran.

After another half mile, Mr. Anderson said, "So you think that's why your parents decided to take an extra couple days? Your mom wants a divorce and your dad might be trying to talk her out of it? It's just as likely that they're enjoying one another's company and need some time away."

From you. He didn't say that, but I heard it anyway. I knew he was right. My parents needed a time-out from their crazy lives which included their nutsoid daughter. How dumb was it, me believing that Mr. Anderson was doing anything other than just being nice to the whacko new kid. He had to be thinking about what my dad had said: that I'd been on a psych ward and had *problems.* Mr. Anderson was probably regretting he'd ever called and counting the minutes until we made it to the parking lot.

This is what happens. This is what happens when you forget that only Matt understands. You can talk to Matt. His e-mails never change, he never . . .

All of a sudden, I was sprinting, running as fast as I could, full out, legs thudding, arms pumping, my chest going like a bellows. I heard Mr. Anderson call my name, but I didn't look back, just kept going faster, faster, my brain yammering: *run, run, run faster, must get away, must run faster.* If I ran fast enough, maybe my skin would split, peel off, float away, and then I would be like that beluga whale, finally free to get as far from my life as I . . .

"Jenna!" Mr. Anderson had drawn even, but I didn't slow, didn't turn. "Jenna, what—?"

"Don't!" I gasped. Sweat stung my eyes—or were those tears? Was I crying? I was such a loser, I was so—

"Ugh!" A sudden sharp pain knifed my side and I grunted, wincing as a deeper cramp took hold, and then I was groaning, pulling up short, nearly doubled over with the pain. My heart thudded in my ears, and then my knees bit earth and I was hunched like a dog on all fours, panting. Bile, bitter and nauseating, pushed into my mouth, and I spat it out. The stitch grabbed me again, and I moaned.

"Hey." Kneeling, Mr. Anderson put an arm around my shoulders. "Hey, it's okay, take it easy, try not to pant."

"St-stupid," I managed, and tried spitting, but my mouth was dust, my tongue swollen. My arms were quivering, my calves were starting to cramp, too, and my whole body felt shaky and weak. I was dehydrated, I realized. What had I drunk today? Coffee this morning, then I started reading. I hadn't had anything else to drink and nothing to eat. Stupid, stupid, so *stupid*.

"Take it easy, I'm here," Mr. Anderson said. Somehow I was on my back, staring up at blue sky through gnarly bare branches. My vision spun and my legs throbbed. Mr. Anderson had my right leg in his lap and was pushing my foot back, working his fingers into the solid rock of my gastroc, trying to knead out the cramp. "Deep breath, in . . . and out . . . in and . . ."

"I'm sorry." Mortified, I draped an arm over my eyes. I was too dehydrated to cry and my skin was hot. "I shouldn't have gone so fast."

"Stop apologizing. It happens. My fault for not checking if you'd hydrated before we started. Here." He pressed something into my hand and my fingers closed around a gel. "I hope you like green apple."

I squinted at the gel packet. "I hate it."

"Tough. Come on, suck that down. I've only got the one, but we're not that far from the car. There are restrooms and I think the water's still on at the picnic shelter. We can at least get that into you."

I was so shaky I could barely get my fingers to work, and Mr. Anderson finally tore open the gel pack for me. Sour apple gel never tasted so great, but it left me thirsty and puckered my entire throat. Eventually my leg cramps eased enough that I was able to limp to the car, albeit slowly and with Mr. Anderson's arm around my waist.

After a long drink at the shelter fountain and three more gels Mr. Anderson had stashed in his car (all sour apple), I felt a little more human. The shakes weren't as bad, but I was still weak and woozy, and a headache was pushing against my eyeballs and beginning to leak from my ears.

"Absolutely not." Mr. Anderson shook his head when I tried to head for my car. "No way you're going home just yet. The last thing we need is for you to wrap yourself around a tree. Come on." He dug around in the backseat of his Prius and came up with a fleece. "Put this on. We're going to my place. And shut it," he said, as I opened my mouth. "I'm the coach. No arguments."

So. I shut it.

27: a

Mr. Anderson's house was a rambling two-story contemporary, all cedar and stone and glass. I had a general idea of its shape from Google Earth, but the satellite photograph had been taken in full summer. Now, with the leaves gone, the house seemed massive, almost a mansion on a small rise above the lake. Stone steps led down to a dock. There was a slip where a boat would've been, but that was empty now. A long wooden walkway off the back deck led to a three-season boathouse. There was a stretch of brown sand at the water's edge, and two beached kayaks.

Over my objections, Mr. Anderson grabbed my pack and led me upstairs and then down a back hall to what he called a guest room but which turned out to be a series of three rooms laid out in a semicircle, each opening into the next: sitting room with a television, a bedroom that was bigger than three of mine, and a bathroom with a Jacuzzi bath and shower stall with four heads that was large enough to fit an entire relay team.

"Take your time," he said as he headed back down the hall. "And use as much hot water as you need." He grinned. "I have three sisters. There was never any hot water by the time they were done. I decided that when I got older, I would install *three* water heaters and name them after my sibs."

The shower was heaven. I was chilled to the bone and decided that this was no time for restraint. Dare to be decadent. I cranked on all the heads, dialing the water as hot as I could stand. The water thundered onto my shoulders, streamed over the scars on my abdomen and sluiced down the butterfly patches of skin graft on my back, washing away my sweat and grime and fatigue.

My embarrassment.

God, I'd been stupid. What an idiot. I hadn't followed the rules every runner worth her salt knew. I was just lucky that Mr. Anderson was a coach and understood what to do, how to help. He was being cool about it.

So why couldn't I follow his example and cut myself a break? Not everything was my fault. Something my shrink once said bubbled up from memory: *believing that everything is your fault is like saying that the world revolves around you and that is pure narcissism and no less destructive.*

So, okay, okay, I thought. *Like the man said: shut it.*

b

Incredibly, I was cleaned up and dressed before Mr. Anderson was. As I took the stairs to the first floor, I heard the distant rush of water from a shower at the opposite end of the house. The house was laid out in a giant H: bedrooms on the right, the rest of the living area to the left. I headed left, down another carpeted hall to where I thought the kitchen must be.

Classical music floated out of hidden speakers. The air smelled a little like roses and some kind of spice that nipped at my nose. Light splashed through windows and skylights. In what I thought must be a family room, one wall was just this huge picture window framing the lake like a painting.

A clutch of photographs hung on the opposite wall above a leather sofa: a younger Mr. Anderson flanked by an older man and woman who, from the resemblance, had to be his parents; Mr. Anderson when he was closer to my age, in swim trunks, suspended at the peak of his dive; Mr. Anderson, sprinting, chest out, legs scissored wide as he crossed the finish line first. A shot of Mr. Anderson underwater, in dive gear, his hair fanning like seaweed.

At the far left, near a stone fireplace, were three more pictures. One was of Mr. Anderson on his deck: in profile, standing at the railing, looking out over the lake with—yup—a coffee cup in hand. Mist rose from the lake and the trees were bare, so a shot in late fall or early spring, I thought.

It was a nice picture and looked as if it hadn't been taken all that long ago.

But, of the three, it was not the most interesting.

C

There was only one other photo like it in this room. Maybe there were similar pictures throughout the house, but I doubted it. The halls were lined with paintings, not photographs. On the other hand, perhaps two were all that were required to tell this particular story.

In the earlier photograph, Mrs. Anderson was as beautiful as a princess: slim and rosy-cheeked, with a long river of dark curls. Her wedding dress was v-necked and low-cut, and instead of a veil, she wore a wide-brimmed hat perched at a jaunty angle. Mr. Anderson sported a long-tailed tuxedo and a bright blue cummerbund that brought out the color of his eyes. Both of them were smiling and had their arms around each other, looking as happy as you'd think newlyweds ought to be.

The second, later photograph was a soft black and white. From the furniture, I could tell that the picture had been taken in this room. Mrs. Anderson stood to the left of the picture window, one hand on the back of a chair and the other draped over her stomach. A fan of sunlight made her skin glow and turned her blouse translucent. So there was no mistaking the bulge.

Or the scars.

₫

To be fair, Bob, only someone with my history would know what she was looking at. Most people—even you—would've missed the one on her throat because of the way the photo had been doctored. But look at the close-ups in an old, pre-Photoshop picture or movie next time, Bob, and you'll see what I mean. Guys' faces are always sharper, more chiseled, angular. But in the old black and whites—*Mildred Pierce, Stella Dallas, Casablanca*—the women's faces are much softer, a little dreamy. That's because the close-ups were filmed through fine gauze draped over the lens to hide imperfections makeup couldn't: freckles, zits.

Scars.

The only reason I spotted the one on her throat was because Mrs. Anderson wore a filmy Indian-style blouse with a scoop neck and long, bell-shaped sleeves. The scar was more like a dimple and very small, about the size of a nickel and a shade paler than her skin. In normal light—in color—it would probably be as pink as a newborn mouse. I knew because I'd been on a ventilator for a long time, too. My trach scar had been just like hers until Dr. Kirby took a scalpel to it. What I've got now is, well, invisible. You'd never know I'd had a hole cut in my throat for that tube at all. The doctors are right, too: I scar so nicely.

But, for whatever reason, Mrs. Anderson still wore hers, just as she'd chosen to keep that thin worm along the underbelly of her left wrist. I didn't know if she'd cut her right wrist because that hand rested on her stomach. Ten to one, she probably had sliced and diced that wrist, too, although maybe not as well. Most people are right-handed. So, statistically speaking, she'd have done her left first. By the time she switched, the bleeding would've started, and she might have been pretty shaky, light-headed. Now I've never done anything like that, but I knew more than a couple kids, boys and girls, who had. So trust me on this one, Bob.

My gaze ticked back to their wedding picture.

No scars.

Well.

C

A door opened from far down the hall. When Mr. Anderson walked into the family room, I was studying a psychedelic landscape: a bird's-eye view of blinding white farmhouses with electric blue roofs caught in the orange slant of a setting sun. He said, "You like it? I love that painting."

"It's really interesting," I said. Mr. Anderson looked the way he had the first day we'd met: fresh from his shower, hair moist and a little curly at the temples. Of course, he was fully clothed this time around: jeans, moccasins, a forest-green turtleneck that brought out the auburn in his hair when he crossed beneath a shaft of strong sunlight. I cut my eyes back to the painting. "I like the way it changes depending on the light. Who's the artist?"

"Harold Gregor. Obama has one of his paintings in his office, too, so I guess I'm in good company. Hungry?" He led the way into the kitchen, still talking about the evolution of Gregor's technique. I followed, but my mind wasn't on art.

Because I now knew things no one else did or had ever mentioned at school.

Sometime during their marriage, Mrs. Anderson had tried to kill herself.

Then Mrs. Anderson had gotten pregnant.

So where was the baby?

And, really, where was *she*?

28: a

Mr. Anderson decided we'd had enough adventures for one day and made lunch. I remember it perfectly, Bobby-o: goat cheese omelets and a green salad with preserved pears in balsamic vinegar, strawberries and slivered almonds. While I tore lettuce for the salad, he disappeared into a pantry and reappeared a few seconds later with a baguette that he sliced, drizzled with olive oil, and then popped into the oven to toast. After spinning the lettuce dry, I rubbed the toasted slices with garlic, and then Mr. Anderson spooned on a mix of chopped artichokes, roasted red peppers, and diced mozzarella. A minute before he turned out the omelets, he told me to put the bruschetta under the broiler to melt the mozzarella.

Lunch was delicious and, despite everything, I was ravenous. I was so used to thrown-together meals and leftover pizza, I'd forgotten what really home-cooked food tasted like. You could tell that Mr. Anderson was comfortable around a kitchen, the way he handled the knives and pans, even flipping the omelet and doing a pretty good imitation of Julia Child: "*You must have the courage of your convictions!*" He got me to laugh, which felt good, and we had fun. I ate every last bit of my omelet and had seconds on the salad and four pieces of bruschetta. We ate in a nook that looked out on the lake and didn't talk much, we were both so hungry. Then Mr. Anderson pulled out a freezer bag of homemade chocolate chip cookies to go with hot mint tea.

When we were done, I started to clear the dishes, but Mr. Anderson waved me down. "What's the hurry? You got somewhere to go? That's the trouble with people." He fingered up another cookie and bit into it. "They don't take time to just enjoy the moment."

"Sorry," I said, sitting back down.

"And stop apologizing," he said with mock severity, and when I laughed, he grinned. "You look a thousand times better than you did on the trail. You had me worried there."

"Sor—" I stopped myself, tried again. "I've never had that happen before. I mean, I've had cramps, everyone does, but never bad enough I couldn't run."

"Maybe your body's trying to tell you something, like . . . stop running." His words hung there, charged and loaded with meaning. When I glanced over, he was blowing on his tea, his gaze fixed on the lake, but the invitation was clear. The silence stretched and thinned. He sipped from his mug, said, "We don't have to talk about anything you don't want to."

Danielle had said he liked the broken ones. Mrs. Anderson was proof of that—wasn't she? Well, maybe. Not everyone wears their scars on their skin. Perhaps Mr. Anderson hadn't known right away or been able to help her enough once he did understand. For all I knew, he was really sensitive now to how people hurt inside, where no one could see, because of what she'd done to herself. That would explain why he tried so hard with someone like me. Maybe Danielle, too.

But . . . really? Who cared? Mrs. Anderson wasn't here, and neither was Danielle. Mr. Anderson was the first person in what felt like forever to give a damn about me. Fine, he liked to help people who were hurting. So BFD, you know?

It was all so push-me-pull-you, Bob. Like I was in this game of tug-of-war with myself.

Because the other problem was how could I tell him that it wasn't a question of just *one* thing? If this was only about dirty old Dr. Kirby, that would be easy. But there was Matt and my parents and Grandpa MacAllister, the psych ward, the thoughts I *still* had. The urges to cut—and I couldn't tell him that the kissing knife was kind of keeping me from doing that either because then I'd have to admit I'd stolen it. And there was also school, trying to fit in, wondering if I should even bother.

Thinking about all that was exhausting. Despite the hours I'd spent getting shrink-wrapped, I still wasn't sold that talking did a whole heck of a lot except let everyone else know what was going on inside your head. It's not like talking ever made anything go away.

The other thing was . . . I didn't know what the rules were, not yet. Come on, Bob, you know: some friends you only talk to about clothes, while others keep your secrets and vice versa. Every relationship has rules. Ours was just beginning. No, that's not right. My relationship with Mr. Anderson was turning into something different than it had been.

Yet, whatever his motives, who *cared*? I *liked* the change. I liked *him* just for who he was. He made me laugh and feel more comfortable in my own stupid skin. No way I wanted to blow that.

"Thanks," I said, finally. "For the offer. It's nice knowing there's someone who . . ." I wanted to say *cares* but settled for something not so loaded. "Someone who wants to listen."

"Always," he said.

b

As he washed and I dried, he asked what my plans were for the rest of the vacation. I told him about my English project, which he'd heard about from other students, and Alexis. It turned out that he'd read her book a while back, when he was in college.

"And had great ambitions." He gave a rueful laugh. "I was going to save the world. I really got into all that Jane Goodall, Dian Fossey, Alexis Depardieu stuff. *Born Free* was one of my favorite movies." I'd never seen it, so he told me about Joy Adamson then said, "Look, before we go, remind me to look in my study. I think I have something about Depardieu you might not have stumbled across."

"Were you going to be a marine biologist?"

"Mammalogist?" He hunched a shoulder. "Maybe. It was a dream. When I was a sophomore at Stanford, I did a summer internship with this guy who studied dolphins. We ended up in Japan. We were trying to document this massive dolphin hunt, but we got caught. Believe me, there's nothing worse than spending a couple nights in a foreign jail."

"Wow. Were you scared?"

"Yes. I believed in what we were doing, but I was still just a kid in college. All I could think of was what my dad was going to do to me when I got out. The guy from the American embassy came on the third day and sprung us in two more. Then he packed us on a plane and that was that."

"What did your dad do?"

"He pulled me out of school and sent me to Madison. Don't get me wrong. It's not like Madison is a bad school, but California . . ." He shook his head. "People are so different there, much more open. The light's different, too, and the air in the mountains is cleaner and you feel . . . *bigger* somehow."

"What made you get interested in dolphins?"

"*Flipper.* And I thought the fourth *Star Trek* movie was a heartbreaking work of staggering genius," he said, so seriously that I cracked up. He grinned. "Honestly, cetaceans are *so* cool. Those stories about how they rescue divers and swimmers? I saw it happen my freshman year."

"Really?"

"Dead serious. There was this one guy, a sophomore, who had this fascination with great whites. He must've seen *Jaws* a hundred times. We took diving lessons together and we surfed. So, one day we're out with another friend and he's on his board, and this baby great white just wallops him. They do that, you know, this head-butt thing where they try to knock out their prey. Then, while you're unconscious, they eat you. So my friend, he's paddling along and then." He slapped his hands together. "Just *wham*. His board kicked into his face and then he was flying one way and his board was going another. I heard him scream and I jerked around just in time to duck as his board shot over my head. I saw him in the water, maybe thirty, forty feet away. At first, I thought he'd hit a rogue wave and gotten thrown, but there was blood on his face and in the water—and then I saw this gray torpedo closing in fast, and I just knew."

My eyes were probably as big around as saucers. "What did you do?"

"After my heart stopped? My other friend and I stayed on our boards and hauled ass, screaming our lungs out." At the expression on my face, his lips twisted in a grim smile. "I don't have a death wish, but the reality is that a shark won't go for multiple targets. They're completely fixated. They're really remarkable engines of death. Besides, I had a knife. I always wore one just in case my kook cord got fouled. By the time we got there, the shark had Ken by one leg up to mid-thigh."

Like that scene in the movie, where the shark has Quint. I shuddered.

"I think the only reason Ken didn't die was because that shark was still young. His mouth just wasn't quite big enough. Anyway, my other friend jabbed with Ken's board, and then I stabbed the shark right behind the dorsal fin and ripped. I guess if I'd been in the water, I would've gone for the eye, but . . ." He ran a hand, wet from dishwater, through his hair. "Anyway, the shark let go and then we tugged Ken out of the water and onto our boards. Blood was gushing from his leg. By that time the lifeguards were coming, but there was all that blood and you could see the color just draining out of Ken's face. So I grabbed my surf leash, slipped it onto his leg and cinched it down tight. That stopped the blood. The lifeguards finally got there, but there wasn't room in the Jet Skis for my friend and me. We watched them rooster-tailing it back to shore with Ken, and we're still in the water with all that blood."

I gasped. "Oh no."

"Oh *yes*. Maybe a minute later, I spotted these fins coming right for us, and I thought, oh boy, more sharks, we're gone. But that's when I realized they were bottlenoses."

"What did they do?"

"The whole pod circled us and our boards, and then they followed us until we were in the shallows. Pods are always led by the dominant male, and I swear I saw one dolphin checking us out to make sure we made it. Once it saw we were safe, they left. And that," he said, handing me the dripping omelet pan, "is why I got interested in dolphins."

"Wow," I said again. "So why aren't you studying them now? Even if you were at Madison, you could've found a way."

"Maybe. If I'd been smart—as in *brave*. But I wasn't. I was pretty spooked after Japan. My dad was a chemical engineer and he wanted me in the family business. God, he threatened to cut me off I don't know how many times. He always said he was waiting for me to come to my senses and stop chasing dreams that could never pan out or earn me a living. . . . That kind of real destructive crap. To be honest, I think he was just as happy that the experience kind of . . . *broke* me, you know? A person can only stand so much pressure. So I did what he wanted. I came back home, changed my major to chemistry and then," he said, dropping a rattling handful of wet cutlery onto the drain board, "I got married."

C

By the time we made it back to Faring Park, the sun was nearly gone and the woods were black. Mine was the only car in the lot. As Mr. Anderson pulled up alongside, I unbuckled my seatbelt. "Thanks for lunch and . . . for helping me." Then I blurted, "I had a really good time."

"Me, too." In the failing light, I couldn't make out his expression, but he sounded sincere. "So are we running tomorrow?"

My heart surged. "Sure."

"Great. Nothing huge, though. We'll save huge for a couple days from now. How many tempo runs you done in the last month?"

"None? I do mainly distance."

"That's not good. Endurance is great, but you ought to be doing tempo runs to improve your speed. How about we do that tomorrow? Say, forty-five minutes?"

Ah. The magic words: *endurance, speed, tempo.* I knew where he was going. Never too late to join the team, especially when your lead runner's having the crappiest season of her life. Well, why not? The season was two-thirds over; I needed the exercise; Danielle could suck it up. "Okay."

"Excellent. I want to clock you at peak for a 5K. You do well with that, we'll go to an interval run day after. Of course, when school starts back up . . ."

"I join the team for workouts."

"That's the idea. We'll move indoors when the really bad weather hits, but I run outside most days unless it's downright dangerous. If you want . . ." He hesitated then continued, "You could keep running with me."

Was it my imagination, or did I hear a note of worry, that I might refuse? "Okay."

"Good." He sounded the tiniest bit relieved. "So, how about tomorrow morning? Early, like eight? I'll pick you up and we can have breakfast after. Promise, I won't cook. We'll go to a café I know. The pancakes are to die for."

"That would be great." I popped the door. The dome light flicked on, washing the interior of the Prius with light. Scooting out, I turned back to lift my pack from the footwell, except Mr. Anderson had bent and was already handing it up. Our gazes met. I don't know why, but we both went still. Neither of us looked away, and there was something there. I know he felt it because I saw some emotion chase across his face. My mouth had gone so dry, I had to slick my lips. "Thanks again. Really."

"No." He let go of my pack. "Thank *you*."

He waited until I had my car started and then he followed, not turning off at his house the way I expected but staying with me all the way to the main road, like he wanted to be sure I got out okay, or that nothing happened. We met no other cars on the road and I went slowly, mindful of deer which would start moving around once the sun went down and the temperature fell. By the time I saw the sign for the interstate, it was full dark and the deer were out, their eyes bright as green coins in my headlights. Mr. Anderson honked once and then I watched in my rearview as his Prius swung around and headed back for his house. I slowed, watching the twin red eyes of his taillights until they were out of sight.

Then, I got mad at myself. Like, okay, obsess much? Even so, as dumb as I felt, I kept glancing into my rearview, half-hoping he might magically appear.

He didn't.

But I kept hoping anyway.

Okay, sidebar.

Yes, I knew what was happening to me. I had no idea what was in Mr. Anderson's head, but I'm not completely clueless, Bob. I'd been fighting against the feeling since that moment I saw Mr. Anderson bathed in sunlight, a demigod in khaki pants and Ralph Lauren. I might be weird, but I'm not stupid. I knew—and I let it happen.

And why?

Because.

Just . . . because.

Okay, fine. Because I felt *bad*. Okay, Bob? My mother was a self-involved drunk, my father was a psycho-asshole used to getting his way and Matt . . . Matt was gone.

I was alone. I was sweet sixteen, the age when a mermaid finds her prince. I believed in magic and love at first sight and fate. I was every girl who ever lived. So now I had an adventure all my own, a deliciously agonizing secret.

Want to know how girls think, Bobby-o? Well, here's the inside scoop. It's the torture of *not* knowing that fuels a romance and that kind of pain is sweet, so sweet. It's the *longing*, stupid. Unrequited love is the best of all. Look at Shakespeare. He tells you, right up front, that Romeo and Juliet are star-crossed lovers. (You really want to get down to it, Romeo's first lines are all about getting into Juliet's panties. The boy has his priorities.) You know it's not going to work out, but you root for those crazy kids anyway. They kiss, a *lot*, and she's *fourteen*. They *finally* get each other into bed and then, by nightfall of the following day? They're history. No morning breath for them or kids in diapers or Romeo dragging home after a hard day dueling. They get a taste of heaven and *when* they die, what you think is that, for them, one night of bliss was worth it.

Here's what Will and Jane and Charlotte and all those writers knew, what every person who's ever fallen in love gets, Bob: nothing's ever as good as the build up to that first kiss. Obsession is an engine all its own, a torment of the most pleasant kind. The rest is just . . . a real letdown.

Come to think of it, obsession—*anticipation*—is the glint of a razor, the wink of a knife poised above unblemished skin. The moment when you've reached that proverbial fork in the road: cut, or not. Bleed. Or not.

So, yeah, Bob, I was letting myself obsess. I'd even had flashes of thinking about Mr. Anderson *that way*. When he kneaded my calf and then slipped his arm around my waist to help me back to his car, his touch was electric, his fingers fiery. My heart thumped harder; this wonderful zing buzzed in my chest. I understood *why* his food tasted so wonderful, why sharing the preparation was so intimate. Why I watched his hands as he washed the dishes, thinking how those hands might feel on me.

You getting off, Bobby? Think it's going to get all *graphic*? Like I'm going to make it *fun* for you? Hah. Keep dreaming. But thoughts like that? Yeah, I had them and they felt good. Mr. Anderson was a nice person; he had a great house; everyone liked him . . . and he wanted to spend time with me. *Me.* Yes, I knew this was partly some campaign to make sure I joined the team. Danielle said Mr. Anderson picked up strays, and I qualified. For all I knew, he had kids over to his house all the time.

But what if I wasn't *just* a stray? The way he'd rescued me from Dr. Kirby; that moment when our eyes met ... What if the emotion I saw in his face wasn't simply a reflection of my own?

What if ... what if ... what if ... round and around and around. Push me, pull you.

I didn't care. I liked how I felt because longing made me normal.

Even if I felt kind of pathetic at the same time.

29: a

Hello, honey. Your father and I have decided to stay up here until the end of the week. We're having such a relaxing time and it's been forever since I went kayaking and hiking. . . .

There'd been seven calls, three from Mom but she'd left only one message. Her voice was so bubbly, I almost didn't believe it was her.

Anyway, you don't have school, so you don't really need us there, right? If you want to reach us, you can call my cell, or Dad's. . . .

Someone in the background now: my father, sounding as petulant and whiny as a little kid. Mom's voice suddenly muffled as she put her hand over the phone, but her laugh was flirty and buoyant as a girl's: *Aren't you tired out yet?*

Okay, too much information. After a sec, Mom came back: *Anyway, hope everything's okay and you're keeping busy. How's that report coming? Love you. Bye.*

Click.

The ID for the other four calls was blocked. No messages at all.

D

It was still early, only a little past eight. I picked up Alexis's book but couldn't concentrate, my thoughts winging back to Mr. Anderson's run-in with that shark. I could never be that brave. The only person I knew who came close was Matt the night he rescued me from the fire.

Oh, Matt. I hadn't written for the longest time and wondered what was wrong with me. Writing to Matt had always been a priority. It didn't matter that Matt's letters never changed. What mattered was the lifeline *my* e-mails provided. Maybe Matt could treat himself as if he was already dead, but I couldn't allow myself to think that. One of us had to believe he was still alive. I just couldn't face the alternative.

So I was sitting there, staring at the list of Matt's e-mails in their special folder. My e-mail account was open, my laptop softly humming to itself—and I couldn't think of a thing to say. There was no way I could really talk about Mr. Anderson and I'd already written the same boring stuff to Matt a million times before. I was suddenly so *tired* of playing this stupid game. . . .

The phone rang, making me jump. The caller ID said *no data sent.* Normally, I wouldn't have picked up, but this time I grabbed the handset, thinking: *Maybe he's . . .* "Hello?"

"Emily?" A man, not Mr. Anderson, and he sounded pissed. "Emily, damn it, why the hell haven't you picked up?"

"My mom's not here." (Idiot. What was the first thing they taught little kids? Never admit you're alone in the house?) "May I take a message?"

"Oh." Pause. "This isn't a cell? Is this Jenna?"

"Who's calling, please?"

"It's Nate Bartholomew. We met a few nights ago at your mom's . . . your parents' party."

"Yes, I remember," I said, thinking: *yes, I remember Mom touched your hand, and I remember how you whispered in her ear and the way she looked at you.* "My mom's away and won't be back for another couple of days."

"Oh." Another pause. "I thought this was her cell. Well, uh, look, do you have that number?"

"Sure." I gave him the number and then put in, "My dad's with her." (I know: mean.) "I can take a message and have her call if she's got a minute."

Bartholomew hemmed and hawed over that one, and then gave me some bogus story about how Mom was supposed to arrange a signing only his publicist didn't think the date would work . . . something stupid like that. He was lying; Evan always arranged signings. But I let him tell his story and said I'd have Mom call. "Or you can try her cell."

"No, no, that's okay. Just the message, thanks." He hung up fast, probably worried I'd make another suggestion.

Replacing the handset, I toyed with the idea of saying something to my mother and gauging her reaction. Then, I thought, you know, mind your own business. What did they say about sleeping dogs?

C

In the end, I called Evan. The store was closed, so I helpfully left a voice mail all about poor Nate Bartholomew.

And try explaining that, *Mom*.

Really, Bob, I never could take my own advice.

30: a

Tuesday dawned colder but still cloudless. We ran on Mr. Anderson's property, a counterclockwise loop from his house skirting the lake and then west into the woods and toward Faring Park. As Mr. Anderson promised, we did a tempo run: fifteen minutes of an easy pace, then twenty of pushing to peak, and then a fifteen minute cooldown. We didn't talk. Mr. Anderson said that distracted me from paying attention to how my body felt close to peak, something he said I needed to recognize: "You have to understand when you still have more to give. Winning is a combination of ability, determination, and strategy. You won't win unless you know when to pull the trigger."

Whatever. I was just happy being outside. The run was better than the day before; the stinging air smelled of juniper and fir. My body felt sleek and powerful. I was a panther gliding over the earth, racing through the forest.

Our return route had us going southeast and then north around the top hump of his lake. By then it was past nine and I could see the lake through the trees, the surface of the water mica-bright now that the morning mist had burned away. That's when I noticed a meandering side trail, hemmed with balsam and tamarack, leading down to the lake. Bolts of sunlight speared through gaps in the trees, and I thought I saw a sparkle of glass. I remembered the images I'd pulled up on Google Earth, that small cabin nestled in the woods.

Back at the house, there were fresh towels in the guest bathroom and orange juice in the kitchen. Afterward, we went to a farmhouse ten minutes past Faring Park that had been converted into a bistro, with a tinkly little bell above the door, a display case of homemade bread and buns, and a small kitchen. The lady behind the counter looked up as we came in. "Mitch," she said, and then her gray eyes slid to me. "One of your girls?"

The way she said *girls* made me squirm. Mr. Anderson only chuckled and put a proprietary hand on my shoulder, just like a coach. "What's the matter, Adelaide? Jealous?"

Adelaide snorted. "Twenty years too late for that. Isn't this a little late in the season?"

"Never too late to add a great runner to the team. Adelaide, Jenna. Jenna, this is Adelaide, best short-order cook in the county and a notorious gossip."

"Hello," I said. "Nice to meet you."

"I doubt that very much. On the other hand, Mitch is right. I *am* the best short-order cook in the county." Adelaide showed Mr. Anderson a thin smile. "And how's Kathy?"

"She's fine. Visiting her dad in Minneapolis again," said Mr. Anderson and then that got Adelaide talking about the time her father got the cancer and how long he'd taken to die. Then we ordered, filled thick white mugs with coffee and wandered into a small dining room. A cheery fire snapped and popped in a stone fireplace. Other than two older guys in coveralls at a far table near the window, we were the only customers. We took our coffee to a table right in front of the fireplace.

For a few awkward moments, we didn't say anything and I think it struck me then how strange this was, like I'd slipped into an alternative universe or something, a place where people called Mr. Anderson by his first name and knew what he liked to eat (pancakes with strawberries and link sausage) without having to ask. I bet there was a bartender somewhere who knew just exactly how Mr. Anderson liked his martinis, if he drank them. As I thought about that—about the sly way Adelaide had brought up Mrs. Anderson—a tiny nip of jealousy bit the back of my neck. One of Mr. Anderson's *girls*? That made me sound like a, well, a prostitute or something.

"I'm sorry about that."

I blinked away from my thoughts. Mr. Anderson was watching me. "I'm okay," I said and then took a sip of my coffee. It wasn't as good as Mr. Anderson's.

"Yes, but it bugs you."

"A little."

He sighed. "I should've known Adelaide couldn't keep it buttoned. Summers especially, I sometimes get the team together for a run and then bring them here for breakfast."

"You don't need to tell me this," I lied.

"Yes, I do. I don't like the way Adelaide treated you. I don't like what she implied and when I come back, *alone*, I think she and I will have a little talk."

"I don't want to get her into trouble."

"Adelaide makes her own—" He broke off as another woman brought our food. We thanked her, waited until she'd refilled our mugs and gone, and then Mr. Anderson began buttering his pancakes. "Kathy's been gone an awful lot. At this point, you might say she's moved back to Minneapolis for the duration. Her dad's pretty bad, and her mom's dead and she's the only kid, so . . ." He doused his pancakes with syrup, forked out a bite, and chewed. He smiled and said, "Adelaide may be a bit tough to take, but she *does* make one helluva pancake." He thumbed his plate toward me. "Want a bite?"

Yes. The pancakes smelled warm and strawberry-sweet. Saliva puddled under my tongue. "No, thanks."

"Don't know what you're missing. Besides, a runner needs her carbs."

"About that . . ." I salted my eggs, over easy, wishing they were pancakes. "I haven't decided to join the team."

"Look, I think you'd be an asset, but I'm not going to pressure you. There are five races left. If you don't run for me this fall, maybe you will in the spring. Spring comes and you don't want to join up, it's fine. That won't change anything. I'll be running for most of the winter and if you'd like to keep running together, that would be great. If not, that's okay, too."

"I'd like to keep running. It's nice to run with—" I chickened out at the last second. "Someone else," I said, and hated how lame I sounded.

Mr. Anderson's smile seemed genuine. "I like running with you, too. Now, eat before your food gets cold."

Adelaide was a jerk, but her food was terrific and I vacuumed up my eggs, sausage, and hash browns in record time. Mr. Anderson watched as I cut a slice of buttered whole-wheat toast into long strips. "Soldiers," I said, sopping up egg yolk with one. "Meryl says that's how they eat runny yolk in England."

"Yeah?" and then Mr. Anderson reached across, fingered up a soldier, swirled it in yellow goo, popped the drippy bread into his mouth, gave a meditative chew. "Not bad," he said around bread. He swallowed, then licked a dribble from his right pinky. "Trade you a couple soldiers for some pancake."

"That would be nice," I said.

♭

Over a third mug of coffee:

Mr. Anderson asked about my parents, Meryl, Meryl's farm, what it was like to paddle around Lake Superior. "I've always wanted to do that," he said, toying with a sugar packet. "When I moved out here, I meant to make the drive, but things always got in the way."

"Where did you live before?"

"Kenosha. I wasn't supposed to be a teacher. My dad's company was down there. They manufactured electroless nickel, the stuff they use to coat hard drives, automotive differentials. I was supposed to take over right out of grad school. I did, for about three years. As soon as my old man retired from the board of directors, I sold the damn thing and made more money than God." He chuckled. "I thought my father was going to have a stroke, but I got the last laugh: money and my freedom. Well, most of it. I would never be young again, but . . . I guess you could say I got back at him for yanking me out of Stanford."

No adult had ever talked to me so frankly before. "You couldn't have stayed? At Stanford, I mean?"

"Sure, but I didn't think I could at the time." He tossed the sugar packet back into its little wicker basket. "That's one thing you learn as you get older. Parents expect they'll have the same influence when you're thirty as when you're ten. Some parents, the good ones, are able to let go. Others don't like becoming obsolete and do their best to convince you that you can't get along without them. That's where I made my mistake. I was afraid, pure and simple. I bought into my dad's idea that I couldn't make it without his help. True, things have worked out okay. Anyone looking would think I have this perfect, fairy-tale life: money, land, a lovely house, a great wife. But all that's surface stuff. It's like watching someone on the water who you think is fine because there's no fuss, no screaming, when, really, the guy's about twenty seconds away from drowning."

"But if you're rich," I said, "you could do anything."

"It's not that simple."

"Why not?"

"For one thing, you can't turn back the clock. For another, we're not talking just me anymore. I've got a wife and responsibilities. There comes a point, Jenna, where you have to let some things die." He shrugged. "Anyway, that's where I figure I can help people younger than me avoid my mistakes."

I wanted to ask him how many he'd made, other than abandoning his dreams of becoming a marine mammalogist. I thought I had an idea. And now I knew something else, Bob: despite everything he had—in spite of his wonderful wife—Mr. Anderson was unhappy. He had regrets, things he wished he could do over. I wondered if that included getting married.

He straightened out of his slouch. "Enough about me. What are your plans for the rest of the day? Other than doing your English thing."

"Nothing," I said.

"Terrific." He grinned. "How do you feel about glass?"

C

Glass turned out to be rooms and rooms of paperweights, different shapes, different sizes, some antique and others contemporary, in a riot of colors. The museum was in Neenah, housed in a limestone Tudor mansion squatting on a tiny peninsula off the northwest shore of Lake Winnebago, not far from Appleton. I'd never been past Fond du Lac, which was down south, and I'd certainly never heard of a museum devoted to nothing but paperweights. An informational display at the entrance said the museum had over three thousand, more than six hundred from this one lady whose husband was filthy rich or something and so had all this money to throw at his wife who'd been obsessed with paperweights since she was a kid.

Most of the glass *was* beautiful and the art of how you made a paperweight was pretty interesting. Mr. Anderson found me staring at a rectangular weight perched on a lone pedestal.

Suspended in the glass, honeybees hovered over four clusters of multicolored flowers. The flowers floated in the glass, their roots trailing in graceful swirls. The bees were so lifelike their hind legs bulged with yellow pollen sacs. But there was something odd about the roots and when I looked more closely, I realized why.

"They're people," I said to Mr. Anderson. "The way he's positioned the legs and arms, they look like roots, but they're really . . . *bodies*." (I hadn't wanted to say *naked*, but they were: a confusion of swelling breasts, round buttocks, large bellies, and, well. . . . Come on, you don't need me to draw you a map, right, Bobby?) "Like that painter who does all those people tangled together."

"Hieronymus Bosch? Hunh. I never thought about that before but now that you mention it. . . ." Mr. Anderson smiled. "You have a good eye, Jenna."

Afterward, we browsed the gift shop but didn't linger long. They did have a paperweight by that artist who did the root people, but it was something astronomical, like over three thousand *dollars*. Besides, I felt a little weird shopping with Mr. Anderson. Like it was *too* close, if you know what I mean. But it was also exciting. People who liked each other shared things: what they enjoyed doing, their interests, stuff like that.

Mr. Anderson treated me to lunch a half hour south in Oshkosh at a restaurant with its own microbrewery and about two dozen slips where boaters could dock and come ashore. On nice days, you could eat outside at picnic tables alongside the water, but it was late in the season and very cold for October. The picnic tables were stacked, the umbrellas folded and only a few boats trolled back and forth on the slate-gray water. Mr. Anderson eyed the tables and then scrutinized my jacket (which was nowhere near warm enough, not if you also counted the breeze lifting off the water). "Here," he said, shucking out of his coat and holding it out to me. "Put this on."

"I . . . I . . . I can't . . ." I didn't know what to do.

"Take it. Come on. I've got a sweatshirt in the car. The turtleneck's Under Armour, so I'll be fine. We'll pretend we're skiing."

Uhm . . . okay. Considering that I'd *never* been skiing and didn't have a clue what he was talking about . . . But I let him push the coat into my hands. It was the same sheepskin he'd worn the night he saved me from Dr. Kirby, and while he was jogging out to his car, I put my nose to the collar and inhaled. It had a . . . a *man's* smell. Like if I closed my eyes and had just that scent to go on, I would know that the only man I would see when I opened my eyes again would be him. I can't explain it any better than that.

When I slid my hands into the pockets, I found folded slips of paper, three nickels, seven pennies, and a half-dollar piece in the left—and a small Swiss Army knife in the right.

At that, I felt a little prick of guilt. He must be missing the kissing knife, which I always carried in my knapsack now, like a good luck charm. Probably he wondered what the hell had happened to that knife.

Or maybe . . .

Maybe he *did* know; had put two and two together, how that knife had disappeared the first and only morning I'd been in the back room—but had decided *not* to do anything about

it. To let it go. To let *me* keep the knife. Kind of like a present,
I guess.

It was a nice thing to imagine, anyway.

d

We huddled at a table in a splotch of sunlight but out of the
wind, and had burgers. I'm sure the waitress thought we were
insane and maybe we were, but I felt free and decadent, like this
is what adults did. When we were done, we just sat and watched
the water. There was a drawbridge just off the slips. A bell began to clang, and then the bridge split as some kind of big white
boat approached.

Mr. Anderson had his feet up on his bench. His chin rested
on the points of his knees as he stared at the boat floating
by. "I used to boat all the time," he said, a little dreamily. "A
walkaround." A brief glance my way. "The kind Quint had in
Jaws. Kathy never liked it, just never got into it, but I'd be on
the water for hours, sometimes a few days. Fishing sometimes,
but I was just as happy not. When I was in California, I used to
dive. I even dove Lake Tahoe once, this place called Rubicon
Point. I'd never seen anything like that. The wall's very steep,
goes straight down eight hundred feet, so far you can't dive to
the bottom. The water's green at the surface and then it gets
colder and bluer as you descend and you're still feeling okay,
like what's the big deal, just a bunch of rocks. Only right around
seventy feet, the bottom just goes away." His hands pulled
apart, carving out an expanding cloud. "Just . . . *gone*. There's
no bottom and you're floating over this abyss. For a minute, you
think you're going to fall. There's an anvil of water above and

water below, and you're just *there*. Then you follow the great wall, this massive jumble of boulders and vertical rock, straight down. You go deeper and deeper and it gets colder and colder until you're at a hundred and ten feet, and it's below forty and the light's completely grayed out, and you can't believe you'll ever be warm again."

His back was to me. His voice was hushed. I barely breathed. I waited.

He finally let go of a long, sad sigh. "Lake Michigan is too cold, too dark, and has too many wrecks. I never got into that kind of diving, never saw the point of gawking at all that death. The only wreck I ever did was in Belize, about a hundred feet down, but only because I wanted to see the continental shelf. I remember looking off to my left and seeing how the white sand bottom went on for a ways and then it just stopped. Like you'd come to the edge of the world. The ocean beyond wasn't even blue. It was *black*. We were following a guide rope and pretty far back because the currents at the shelf will sweep you away if you're not careful. There, you really *will* fall into the abyss."

"It sounds scary," I said.

"It is. Most things worth effort like that are, but what's the point of never taking chances? I don't know if I could stand living my whole life afraid. I'll tell you what did scare me at first, though: night diving. The idea of voluntarily slipping into the dark was really spooky. But it's . . . magic. At night, when you swim, the water sparkles with these bright green flashes, like stars, from these bioluminescent organisms. Cold fire, divers call it." His tone turned wistful. "It's like visiting another galaxy."

He sounded, I thought, like Alexis. I wanted to tell him that if he missed that and had the money, he should just go. I should've said that he should do what made him happy. But what came out was: "You make it sound like something I'd like to do someday."

He turned to stare at me. "Maybe we will," he said.

e

I don't remember what else we talked about. But we sat together in the cold for almost two more hours: him in his sweatshirt, me wrapped in a warm coat that smelled of him. We were out there long enough that when I looked up, the waitress was eyeing us through the restaurant's tinted windows.

Like *we* were the ones in glass rather than the other way around.

31: a

Mr. Anderson dropped me back at the McMansion a little before 7 P.M. The kitchen's handset display said I'd missed two calls, both from numbers I recognized.

First message: *Jenna? It's Evan. I, uh, I got your message and . . . well, I could be wrong, but I'm not aware that we're doing anything more for Nate. So . . .* (Pause.) *I don't know what he's talking about. Unless he and your mom . . .* (Pause.) *I'll give his publicist a call and see what the story is. Just . . . this isn't worth bothering your mom about. Okay? Bye, honey.*

Second message: *Hi, sweetie, it's your mom. Listen, we've decided to come back Saturday night. I know you don't mind. What teenager wouldn't kill for a week off from their parents?* (Pause.) *Anyway, have a good week. Love you.*

Click. Dial tone.

Mom was right, too: I didn't mind. I didn't care.

At. All.

b

I tuned my radio to a station Mr. Anderson liked, the one we'd listened to in his car. They were playing a Bach fugue. I thought about how Mr. Anderson might be listening to the same thing at this very moment. So we were kind of enjoying the music together, even if we weren't in the same room, and that felt good.

As I listened, I unfolded the papers I'd palmed from his pocket. He'd written them in real ink—with a fountain pen, I thought. There was something about the shape of the letters that reminded me of calligraphy and was so different from his familiar scrawl which I'd seen a hundred times on the blackboard or graded papers. It was somehow intimate and thrilling to imagine him forming each letter with exquisite care. One was obviously a grocery list: eggs, strawberries, milk, flour, everything he'd need for pancakes. Which meant he'd been thinking of me when he wrote it. That felt . . . private and special, like this was a note only I would understand.

The other note was very brief: a single letter and then a word.

J.

And: *lover.*

I read it twice over but knew there was no mistake. You'd have to be brain-dead not to get it.

I was *J.* And *lover* was . . .

This was about me, Bob.

It was about me.

32: a

By Friday, it felt as if Mr. Anderson and I had been together for months instead of only a few days. We had a routine going: run in the mornings, then a shower and breakfast. (Mr. Anderson said we should stay away from Adelaide's—not because we were doing anything wrong, but who needed the headaches?) I didn't mind. Making food together felt homey, like I belonged. He showed me how to make omelets and I showed him bangers and mash. We talked a lot, mainly about him, his family. He didn't ask a lot of questions about where I'd been last year or what Psycho-Dad had meant, and that was good because it was like we had this unspoken agreement. If I wanted to talk, I could. If I didn't, fine.

On the other hand, there was stuff about him we didn't touch—his marriage, his wife. I really wanted to know and then again, I really didn't because, honestly? Talking about her would remind him that he probably didn't need a friend like me.

Afterward, we'd go to a museum and then lunch and then either another museum or maybe we'd go for a walk and then have coffee and pastries—like they did in Europe, Mr. Anderson said. When he was a kid, his family went all over, and what he remembered most was how people there took their time and enjoyed life. In between his junior and senior years in college, his father had let him spend an entire summer in Italy, probably to make up for yanking him out of Stanford. Mr. Anderson said the best part of the day was late afternoon when you could sit at a little café in a piazza just about anywhere and have a grappa or cup of coffee and pastry and people-watch, maybe make up stories about them. Like Mr. Anderson would spot a guy and think that maybe he was waiting for his girlfriend because he kept checking his watch. He said he could tell which couples were going to stay together because of how close they sat and if they ate off each other's plate, which he said you only did when you really trusted someone. He really paid attention to things like that.

After coffee, we might go back to his house and walk around the lake, which I really liked because it was so peaceful, like the lake and his house and land were a whole other world for just the two of us. I loved how the landscape changed at dusk, the woods and fields graying out, the air smelling suddenly sharp and wet and cold enough so it was only natural for us to walk closer together, our arms unexpectedly brushing in a way that made it hard to breathe. The world would fade; the chatter of the birds drop away; and the day—and what I was in the light—slide toward night.

Who we were fell away, too, until we were like shades, ghosts of the people we'd been. Sometimes we stood on the opposite shore and looked back at his house, its windows fired with yellow light so it glittered on the mirror of the water.

And once Mr. Anderson said, very softly, "It's like looking at another country from very far away."

I wasn't sure what he meant, but he sounded sad again, like the day he talked about how people can drown and you would never know by looking because things seem fine. I wanted to reach out and take his hand, let him know I was there to help. Of course, I didn't.

But I loved it all, everything, every moment. I loved that Mr. Anderson always had fresh towels for me and gave me one of his old robes. He always let me shower first. Then, while he cleaned up, I would wrap myself in that robe and lie on the bed in the guest room and listen to the distant rush and thrum of the water. Sometimes I let myself imagine what he might look like, his muscles and bronzed skin wet and glistening. I never quite let myself form a *whole* picture, if you know what I mean. But ... almost. Enough that the robe felt almost unbearable against my skin. Enough that I imagined walking into his bathroom and letting the robe slip from my shoulders and then, somehow, he would see me and only stand there and let me look at him as the water flowed around his body and there was a mirror and my skin was flawless and white, no scars, no grafts and then I would step under the water with him and then ...

And then, for a few seconds—in my mind—I was almost beautiful.

Of course, I would never do that. It could never happen anyway and besides, it would be wrong. He was married. He had a wife and, maybe, a baby. Mr. Anderson was my friend. I tried to tell myself that he cared about me the way a teacher would who was going out of his way to make the crazy kid feel good about herself. Such a friendship didn't come around very often. I had to be careful not to wreck this.

Still, every night, I unfolded that scrap of paper and re-read the words Mr. Anderson had written that gave the lie, and I wondered if he was awake in a tangle of sheets, staring up at shadows, thinking of me.

b

And then it was Saturday.

When my alarm went off and classical music swelled, the first thing I thought was: *This is our last day. By this time tomorrow, nothing will be the same.*

I almost didn't want to get out of bed. What was the point? Tonight, my parents would come back. Monday, I would start school again. I would go back to being me. I would avoid the cafeteria; Danielle would continue to hate me; David might drop by the library again, but . . . well, whatever. Of course, I'd see Mr. Anderson again. Friday, he'd asked, one more time, if I would *please* be his TA, although he'd been smiling. He knew he'd won that particular battle just as I knew I'd show for cross-country practice on Monday afternoon if for no other reason than to be near him.

But I knew nothing would be the same. There would be other kids, more and different demands on his attention. His wife would come home, eventually. When that happened, I doubted he'd be inviting me back for breakfast—if we still ran together at all. As soon as I left this afternoon, he'd strip the sheets from the guest bed even though I'd never slept there and toss the towels in the wash, maybe even that old robe. By this evening, my presence would be erased from his house.

But I'm here now. She isn't. School's not. Don't ruin this.

The weather had been turning steadily colder all week and I could feel it in the McMansion now. It was still dark when I slid from beneath my blankets, which made it feel ten times colder. Walking on my bedroom floor was like crossing an ice rink in my bare feet and I shivered as I pulled on my cold-weather running gear. Downstairs, I made oatmeal in the microwave, sliced up a banana and threw in a handful of almonds, and then washed it all down with a cup of tea I made as hot as I could stand, just to have something warm to hold in my hands. I felt stiff and creaky and *angry*, like Saturday had rolled around just to piss me off.

I tuned to an NPR station on the way over. Usually that early, they played something easy on the ears—Mozart, Bach, Vivaldi. What came out of the speakers was movie music, violins and clean high brass. I recognized it immediately as Hansen's symphony, the part they'd used right after Ripley blasts the alien into space. Which is a very weird scene, actually, because she's singing to the monster the whole time: *You are my lucky star, lucky, lucky, lucky.* Almost like the alien's her, well . . . her lover. (Watch it again, Bob. Listen to the way Ripley's breathing, too. It's kind of kinky.)

The piece ended by the time I was turning off onto Mr. Anderson's road. I didn't know if the music was a good or bad omen. I was afraid to think what it was.

We were doing a long run that morning, fifteen miles, and already planned to drive to the Lake Michigan shore to follow a route Mr. Anderson had mapped.

"But I don't like the look of those clouds," he said. "Change of plans. Let's run from here, but we'll go on this trail I know that winds north of the park. That way, if it storms, we'll have more protection. We'll still get wet, but just not *as* wet."

The trail was dirt, gnarly with roots, and hemmed by barren trees on either side. Even in the cold, a thick mist from the lake wound over the ground and between the trees. With no leaves to slow it down, blades of an icy north wind sliced my face, cutting tears. Neither of us said much. Our route took us steadily uphill. Then, maybe five miles into the run, a rumble of thunder rolled through the trees and the wind picked up, flinging needles of sleet at my cheeks. I glanced up at the patchwork of sky just as a flash of lightning stitched through gray clouds. The sky to the north looked like a fresh, black bruise.

Mr. Anderson pulled up, panting. "This is no good. We need to turn back." He blotted sweat from his forehead with the back of his hand. "If we run *really* fast, we might make it."

We almost did. We raced back, legs pounding the earth, arms pumping, and were just coming up to the last rise, a small bald cap of meadow. Below, there was the lake and Mr. Anderson's house on the far shore. Then the clouds just broke, cracked wide open, and the rain came straight down in icy, hard sheets that soaked us in seconds.

"Follow me!" The rain was so hard and loud, he had to put his mouth by my ear and shout. Water was streaming from his hair and sleet bounced off his cheeks. His clothes were soggy and dragged on his body as if he'd been fished up from the bottom of the lake. "I know a place we can go to wait it out!"

I followed him as he plunged into the woods. The trail was mushy, the mud squelching beneath our shoes, and treacherous with slick leaves. The sleet and rain were so heavy it was like trying to see through a sheet of steel. Ahead, I could just make out the lake through breaks in the trees, but I knew from experience we were still a good three miles out. Then Mr. Anderson veered right, away from the house, and I realized he was heading down the thin ribbon of that path I'd noticed earlier in the week.

"It's not far!" Mr. Anderson called over his shoulder. "Another half mile!"

A few moments later, the trees parted and the cottage— a two-story Cape with cedar shingles—appeared in a small clearing. The screen door gave with a loud squall and then we were ducking under the porch and out of the rain.

"That's better," Mr. Anderson huffed. "Just let me . . ." He knelt, dug around in a gray and blue wide-mouth jug and came up with an old-fashioned iron key. "I don't know why I bother. No one ever comes here but me," he said as he fitted the key into the lock. The latch gave with a loud, solid thunk and then Mr. Anderson was pushing inside and feeling along the wall for the light switch. "Come on. There are towels inside and a shower. Just give me a second and . . ."

"What is this—" I began and then stopped as the lights popped on. The cabin was like something out of a fairy tale: light hardwood, a scatter of fur rugs, a leather sofa facing a stone fireplace and windows looking down at the lake. To the left was the kitchen, complete with wood stove, rustic wooden table, and two straight-back chairs. A wrought-iron staircase wound to an open loft. To the right and leading off the living room was a door, open just a crack. I caught a glimpse of bookshelves and the corner of a table. "Wow. This is *great*."

"Yeah, I like it." Mr. Anderson was shucking out of his running jacket. Rainwater streamed from his hair to soak his shirt. "I guess you'd call this my home away from home, with all the comforts and none of the hassles. The original place was a hunting cabin, just this room and the kitchen with a bathroom and bunks where the porch is now. When I took over the house, I redid the whole thing. This is where I come to read and think and listen to music, write. Sometimes I hunker down for a couple of days, just to get away. I spent a lot of time here, actually, even in the winter. It's quiet." He grinned. "Well, now, anyway. The old cabin used to have a corrugated tin roof. Sounded like I was in pan of Jiffy Pop."

"It's beautiful," I said. I hadn't moved from the front mat where I was making an impressive puddle. "I'm going to get your floor wet."

"Hang on." Mr. Anderson pulled off his shoes, peeled out of his socks and padded, dripping and barefoot, to a bench. Lifting the seat, he reached in and pulled out an armload of towels. "Here," he said, shaking out a large beach towel. "Shower's upstairs in the loft, to your right. There are some dry clothes in the closet that ought to fit. I'll get a fire started and make us some tea."

I didn't need convincing. Now that I was out of the rain, the cold really had its claws in me, and I couldn't stop shaking. The loft was huge with another fireplace and a small sitting area with a fur rug, game table, and two upholstered chairs. Further back was a four-poster bed with a patchwork quilt and a rainbow of throw pillows. Below, I heard Mr. Anderson moving around, heard the dull thud of cabinet doors, the rattle of pots. The hardwood floor creaked when I walked across and I was suddenly self-conscious, knowing that Mr. Anderson could hear everything. I wondered if he gave that a second thought and then decided I was being stupid.

The bathroom was off the loft, down a short hall with a closet on either side, and it was all white: white tile, white pedestal sink, a glare-white shower stall. There was a mirror over the sink. I looked drowned, my hair lank and stringy, my lips blue. Even my scars looked shriveled. My skin was so cold it got these red blotches and started to itch and then ache under the hot water. Still, I got out before I wanted to. In the closet, I'd found a flannel shirt that was only a size too large and pulled on a pair of sweatpants that puddled around my ankles, but they were better than nothing. I didn't want to leave the bathroom; the air was toasty and moist and I was still shaking. Gathering my running clothes into my towel, I steeled myself and opened the door, wincing as a ball of cold air broke over my face. "Your turn," I called.

"Coming." I heard Mr. Anderson's footsteps and then saw his head as he mounted the stairs. His eyes ran down my body, taking in my clothes. "You still look pretty cold. Was that all you could find?"

"I-I'm ok-k-okay," I said, and then laughed. My lips were trembling with cold. "M-maybe n-not."

"Go downstairs. The fire's going and I made a pot of tea. There's a blanket you can use, too, and if you dig in that bench, there are some nice warm socks. I'll be down in a few minutes."

Downstairs, Sinatra was crooning softly about flying to the moon. A fire crackled and there were plates of cheese and crackers, nuts and dried fruit on a coffee table. A pot of tea and two mugs, sugar, some cream.

I also noticed that the door to Mr. Anderson's study was half-open, as if he'd slipped in for a moment and forgotten to pull the door shut. Or, maybe, wasn't worried about anything I might see. Look at it another way, this might even have been an invitation. Maybe.

I listened for a moment, heard the water still running and then eased into his study.

Just a quick peek.

C

A bay, plate-glass window, with a window seat and cushions, took up the far wall. Because the cabin was on a rise, I could see both the forest and the lake. His house was visible, too, though just barely because of the trees and that steel sheet of rain still coming down strong. Even so, I could make out the deck along the back, and he'd left a light on in the kitchen.

The other three walls were faced with floor-to-ceiling bookshelves and held an expensive-looking sound system and lots of books: hardbacks and expensive leather-bound editions with gold lettering, along with paperbacks. The shelves also held a collection of fossils and rocks—crystals, mostly—and glass paperweights like the ones we'd seen at the museum. There was one other chair, a comfortable burgundy leather with a matching ottoman, with a Tiffany-style floor lamp to the right. A glass perfume bottle squatted on a small dark table right alongside and I spotted a small stack of coasters for Mr. Anderson's mug or glass.

His desk faced the window. A laptop squatted dead center; a small printer sat alongside and to the left. The laptop's screen was dark, but the power light glowed green.

There was a fountain pen on his desk, fat and black, one of those fancy Montblanc jobs in a black glass holder. I teased the pen out. The nib was silvery metal edged with gold or brass. I touched one index finger to the tip and came away with a small dot of blue ink. I imagined him sitting here, admiring the view, carefully forming letters with this pen.

Yes, I could see how he might spend hours, days here curled up on the window seat or at this desk, cozy and safe, in his own little world. I would never want to leave.

His desk had only one drawer, locked, which was strange. I looked around for the place where he might hide a key but saw nothing obvious. I looked at his laptop for a long moment and then reached for the touchpad. . . .

Above, the sound of the shower gurgled and then cut out.

My hand hovered over the touchpad. I was itching to see what he'd been looking at. Just a touch and then I would know because I wanted to know everything about him.

But then I felt bad. Mr. Anderson trusted me. What would he think if he caught me snooping?

Best to let sleeping dogs lie.

And yet: at the door, I stole a last look back over my shoulder. Let my gaze brush over the shelves, those books, that desk. The view from that window.

There was something missing. Something that should be here but wasn't. I just didn't know what.

Not then, anyway.

33: a

"You look comfortable." Mr. Anderson stood on the stairs, scrubbing his hair dry with a towel.

"Mmmm." The tea had been hot and strong and sweet. I'd gotten as close to the fire as I could without singeing my eyebrows. Outside, the rain continued its ceaseless drumming. I was as drowsy as a lizard on a hot rock and happier than I'd been in years.

He laughed. "There's that bed upstairs, if you want to nap. We're not going anywhere for a while, not until this stops."

"Too cold upstairs. I'll be fine."

"Yeah, I've heard that from you before. Well, sleep here, if you want. I won't bother you." Mr. Anderson slid down next to me on the rug. He eyed the ravaged platters of cheese and dried fruit. "Someone was hungry."

"Hey, you said we had to refuel. Just doing what the coach said," and then I yawned.

"Jenna, honestly, go to sleep. It's okay."

"I don't want to sleep," I murmured, but I let my head fall back against the couch. "I don't ever want to sleep again."

"Why not?"

So I told him the truth. It just came out. I don't know why. Maybe it was because I didn't think there was anything to lose and . . . well, so much of my life was constructed of lies of one sort or another. But this was Mr. Anderson's private place, and I thought it might be big and safe enough to hold my secrets, too.

So I said to the ceiling, "Because this is our last day and I don't want to waste it. There will be plenty of time to sleep when I'm not with you. There'll be the rest of my life."

b

The fire cracked and sputtered. Rain slashed at the windows. Mr. Anderson said nothing. It was so quiet that when I swallowed, I heard thunder.

I couldn't look at him. What had I done? Why couldn't I keep my mouth shut? I'd ruined everything. Would he even want me on the team now? Who wanted a little girl making googly eyes every time he walked by? He was probably trying to figure out what to say so the little dorkette wouldn't go all suicidal on him. God, I should leave. Maybe I'd catch pneumonia and die and save him the trouble of getting rid of me.

But I couldn't move. Couldn't breathe. Didn't dare to.

Then Mr. Anderson let go of a small, slow breath that wasn't quite a sigh—more like something was coming undone in his chest. "Oh hell," he said.

The way he said that . . . it was like the world was a bell jar that had exploded, suddenly, in a shower of razor-sharp glass. I thought of my scissors, the kissing knife. I would cut and cut and cut right down to the bone and bleed, the way my heart was at that very moment.

I had to get out of there.

"I'm sorry." My voice came out raw and ragged and bloody. Hurriedly, I straightened, the blanket falling from my shoulders as I struggled to stand, but my feet tangled and I nearly crashed into the coffee table.

"Whoa, whoa." Mr. Anderson snatched my wrist and then he was standing, and I was looking everywhere—the floor, the fire, the door—everywhere but at his face. "Jenna—"

I pulled, but he wouldn't let go. "I'm sorry. I shouldn't have said that. I should go. Please."

"No." He didn't sound angry. His hand was still around my wrist. I guess I could've pulled harder, but I didn't. He said, "I'm the one who's sorry. I didn't mean what I said. It came out all wrong. We should . . . we should talk about this, how you . . . how you feel."

How *I* felt. Yeah, let's discuss how the crazy, pathetic little psychopath feels. It would be just *so* psychiatric. "What's to talk about?" I heard the note of desperation in my voice and, to my horror, the sob welling up from somewhere deep in my chest. My eyes brimmed. "I'm sorry; I should go."

"Jenna." I remember his voice was husky and low, and then his hands were gripping my shoulders. "Jenna, please. Please, look at me."

I did—and that's when I realized that eyes really are windows to the soul.

"Don't go," he whispered.

C

Okay, time-out.

I know what you're thinking, Bobby. You're thinking I made this one up, too. I mean, it's too perfect, right? The rain, the fire, the cabin that just happened to be where we needed it, the tea and cheese and blankets and blah, blah, blah. Only happens in fairy tales, that's what you're thinking.

But this happened, Bob. This is exactly the way it went down.

I know something else, too. I'm doing it again, buzzing around the moment, flitting away like a startled moth. Protecting myself from the memory, I guess.

Because if I could just stop the flow of time there or *anywhere* before that afternoon, the rest couldn't, wouldn't spin out.

And then I wouldn't be here, in this emergency room—and neither, Bob, would you.

d

"Don't go," he whispered again. "I don't want you to. Please."

When he touched me—held me like that—something unraveled inside, like my heart was the knot of a flower and all the petals had suddenly unfurled. My knees went watery and weak and wobbly, the way they did when I ran hard and fast and for a very long time. I felt like I had been running forever and ever and ever and then I was falling, so fast and . . .

And then we kissed.

Or I kissed him. Or he kissed me. I don't know. But I kissed him and he kissed me, hard, very hard, so hard it was like he was drinking me in and then it was as if some shuddering dam finally burst and we couldn't get close enough; we were pressing together and kissing and I had never been so thirsty and we were trembling and his hands were all over me and mine were on him, and his mouth tasted of smoky sweet tea and then, somehow, we were on the rug and he was moaning into my mouth and then his hands slid beneath the flannel shirt and touched me, me, only me, only my skin and then . . .

And then my scars *shrieked.*

I gasped. I went absolutely, completely rigid. I felt his surprise as his mind registered what he felt. He pulled back, his eyes wide with shock, and then it was like I'd been suspended above myself somewhere and come crashing back into my body.

"Don't." I turned my face away. I was so ashamed. "I'm so ugly. Don't look at me. Don't touch me. Don't."

"Jenna, Jenna, no, you're not, it's okay, shh, shh, honey," and then he'd gathered me up again, his hand smoothing my hair, cupping the back of my head. "Oh, Jenna, sweetheart . . . what the hell have you done to yourself?"

34: a

I told him. About the fire and Matt rescuing me and how Grandpa MacAllister almost died. About the hospital and the grafts and then the cutting that started up after Matt was gone and, finally, that awful day my English teacher stared in horror at the blood soaking my shirt. I hadn't tried to kill myself. The scissors had slipped, that was all. But no one—not the teacher, not the doctors, not my parents—cared about that.

I talked for a long time. I lay on my back on the rug, my face turned toward the fire because I didn't want to see how his face would change as the knowledge settled there—the way my parents' had when the shrink explained my *condition*, like I was this new and interesting bug no one had ever known existed. I talked until I was hoarse and the rain had stopped and Mr. Anderson . . .

Mr. Anderson listened. He didn't say anything, interrupt, or ask questions. He lay on his side, head propped in one hand. His other hand rested on my stomach. (No, *not* skin to skin.

Our clothes were on. The flannel shirt was buttoned. You are such a perv, Bob.)

"So I couldn't go back to my old school," I said to the fire, "not after all that. But I don't fit in at Turing either and I don't know what all this has been for. My family's falling apart; my mother's a drunk; my dad's screwing around; Matt's still gone. Things are better when I cut. That's the one thing I can control. God, I'm such a screwup."

"Do you want me to agree?" Mr. Anderson said. "Jenna, has it ever occurred to you that so long as you keep cutting, your parents stay together?"

My cheeks burned. "Rebecca, my therapist, said that. She said that my being ill was my way of making sure the family stayed together, but that all the cutting was symbolic. Not like a death by a thousand cuts or anything. She said it was like this fantasy. I could cut myself, but I would always heal. I cut when the family's falling apart, but then I heal and the family's back together."

"When was the last time you cut yourself?" When I didn't answer, he said, "Was it when that bastard at the party . . . ?"

"Almost." My mouth wouldn't make the words that should come after that: *But I didn't because I would've used your knife and I knew you would never hurt me, so I didn't and don't you see, you saved me.* "Labor Day. When Grandpa touched me."

He said nothing. The fire popped. I closed my eyes and studied the purple after-images of the fire scorched on the darkness. I heard his clothes rustle when he moved. Then he said, very gently, "Jenna, when was the last time he hurt you?"

No one, not even my shrink, had ever asked me that. That was because no one else knew, or was supposed to know because then bad things would happen—as they had already.

"Not for a long time." I still couldn't look at him. "Not . . ." I forced it out. "Not since the fire."

"So it was the fire that stopped him."

I nodded. "He . . . he had a couple strokes in the hospital and now he . . . he's just . . . he can't . . ."

"Who knows, Jenna? Who knows he hurt you, besides me? Who do you talk to about this?"

Now I did open my eyes. His were serious and held me the way arms never could.

"Matt," I said.

♭

What I wasn't prepared for was his reaction. Mr. Anderson's eyes narrowed, and then his eyebrows pulled together in a frown. He said, carefully now, "When was the last time you actually spoke to your brother?"

The question caught me off guard. A little finger of alarm crept down my spine. "About two years ago. Maybe two and a half."

"Before you started cutting." He said it as a statement of fact, not a question. "So . . . he doesn't come home on leave? He doesn't call?"

"No, I told you; my parents didn't want him to enlist."

"I'm not sure that answers my question. How do you keep in touch?"

"E-mail. I keep all his e-mails separate so there's no chance Mom will see. It would just . . . she would be upset."

"That a sister would keep in touch with her brother?"

I said nothing.

"When was the last time you e-mailed?"

"A long time. Since . . . pretty much since the night you drove me home from school. The night we . . . the night Mom was . . ."

He waited, but when I didn't go on, he said, "Do you understand why you haven't?"

"I . . ." Tears squeezed from the corners of my eyes and dribbled down, tickling my ears. "I've been—" *Thinking of you, been with you, with you, with you.* "I've been busy. I used to write to Matt every day, only . . ."

"Jenna." His hand moved from my stomach to cover one of my clenched fists. "When was the last time Matt *really* answered?"

Me:

Mr. Anderson: "Jenna?"

Me:

He waited. His eyes never left mine, but I saw what he knew and I hated . . . I *hated* . . .

Something exploded in my chest, hexane under pressure with no escape and now there'd been the slightest spark. I scrambled to a sit, *screaming*: "So now you're my *shrink*? Why are you asking so many questions? Why are we *talking* about Matt? Why are you *pushing* me? I thought you were my friend; I thought you *cared*!"

"Jenna, listen to me, I do, I *am*."

"Then why?" I dragged my arm across my streaming eyes. I would've, *should've* gotten up, blasted out the door, but I was backed up against the coffee table now and there was nowhere to run. I drew my knees to my chin and hugged myself. "Why are you *doing* this?"

"Because." He was facing me now, leaning forward, face intent, his eyes grabbing mine so I couldn't look away. We were like matching bookends, almost touching but with volumes between us and stories, so many stories. "Because I *am* your friend and I *do* care, much more than I should."

"Then you'd stop talking about this! You'd *stop*."

"No. Jenna, honey, I can't. I wouldn't be your friend if I did."

"Why *not*?"

"Because." He cradled my face in his hands. "Because Matt's dead, Jenna, and I am so sorry, sweetheart; I am sorrier than you can ever know. But he's dead, and has been for more than two years."

35: a

"Don't you think I know *that*?" I screamed. "Don't you think I *know*?"

They were questions with no answers, just as there had been none when my mother refused to open the door to the Marines in their dress blues. Because, Bob, you see . . . if they couldn't tell us, then—for her, for us all—Matt was a fly in amber, a flower in glass. If we never heard what the Marines had to tell us, then Matt was caught somewhere in some other *when*, in suspended animation: still alive just a little while longer.

Something huge and horrible ripped in my chest, and then I just couldn't stand it anymore: not the hurt or the grief or the lies or the wounds that wouldn't heal no matter how deeply I cut, or how often. Maybe they were all the same thing; I still don't know, Bob.

I hid my face in my knees and wept the way little kids do when their world is coming apart at the seams and nothing is safe anymore.

But Mr. Anderson put his arms around me and pulled me to his chest so I could hear his heart. He held me together and wouldn't let me go, and he saved me from breaking to pieces.

b

Eventually, the rain stopped because it always does, and so did I. We didn't move. We faced the fire: me leaning back into Mr. Anderson; him with one arm across my chest and a hand in my hair.

I was exhausted, sweaty, hollow. Maybe I should've felt better—people say that letting go is supposed to be good—but I felt horrible. My mouth was dry and tasted bad, like I'd vomited out something awful. Which, I guess, I had.

I had ruined everything. Mr. Anderson had known my secret all along. Maybe he'd hoped I'd gotten over Matt and this was a test to see if I was worth the energy and his time. In the last couple of days, he must've gotten hopeful that I was better, but now I'd gone all Drama Queen—and, well, crazy is as crazy does.

"I'm sorry." My voice came out croaky. My tongue was swollen and my lips wouldn't work right. "I shouldn't have dumped all this on you."

"How do you figure? I *did* ask."

"But you already knew the answer. Was it in my . . . ?"

"Your file? Yes, in the hospital summary."

"Why didn't you say anything the first time? Why did you let me—" *Make a fool of myself.* "Let me go on?"

I felt his shoulders move in a shrug. "I didn't know you well enough. Oh, I wanted to, a couple times, but I kept thinking who was I to take that from you? We all have our fictions, Jenna, little lies we tell to keep ourselves going from one day to the next. So I let it go until . . . until I thought the time was right."

His arm was hard and muscular under my hands and felt sturdy and strong and safe. My words came in a near whisper. "So what changed?"

His grip tightened. When he spoke, his voice was low and harsh almost as if he knew he should stop the words before they pushed their way out but couldn't, or didn't want to. "You. *Me* . . . how I feel . . ."

"Please don't hate me."

"Oh God, I don't hate you, Jenna. This isn't your fault. *I'm* supposed to be the adult here, not the other way around. You shouldn't be worrying about me."

"I'm sixteen."

"I didn't say you were twelve. I said this wasn't your fault. I . . ." His voice faltered. His arm slid around my waist. "Listen, I started out just wanting to be a nice guy, you know? You were new and I wanted you to get comfortable in school and know there was someone on your side, an adult you could talk to without worrying about your grades or it getting back to your parents, things like that. Most kids, they warm up fast, but it took work to reach you. I don't know why I kept trying so hard, but I did. There's something about you . . ." He trailed off.

I hung onto his arm. My heart hammered my ribs so hard, he had to feel it.

He said, "When I was a kid—maybe ten, eleven—I found this sparrow. Our cat had gotten hold of it. One wing was all messed up. I was this real Boy Scout; I'd read all about how you could tape a bird's wing to its body and then it would heal. So I took the bird and I put masking tape around it, really anchored that sucker. Well, maybe five minutes later, the bird just keeled over. Completely freaked me out. When I touched it, it woke right up, but then it did that two more times in maybe three minutes. The last time, it wouldn't wake up no matter what I did. That's when I realized it was dead. I didn't figure out until later that *I'd* killed it. I'd taped the wings too tight. The poor bird suffocated and I'd done that. I hadn't meant to hurt it; I wanted to *help*. But I, literally, killed it with kindness. That's always stayed with me. I swore that whenever I tried to help, I would be so careful, never hurt anyone or anything again. I would always try to do the right thing."

"I'm not a bird with a broken wing," I said.

"Yes, you are. You just don't know it. I could've said something about Matt a long time ago, but you wouldn't have heard. You'd have run away. You did, if you recall, a couple times over. I guess I kept hoping if I gave you time. . . . But then I saw how your father treated you and that made me so damned angry, I knew I had to force it."

"But why?" I twisted around so our faces were inches apart. "You said you didn't want to hurt me, but you did anyway. You took Matt away."

"No, an IED killed Matt. I got rid of his ghost so you'd finally see."

"See what?"

"Me, Jenna," he said. "So you would see *me*. And then you would know that you're not the only one who's lonely."

36: a

It was dark when we left the cabin and followed the beam of his flashlight around the lake and back to the house. (Oh, Bobby-o, I know what you're thinking. Sorry to disappoint but we only talked and when we weren't, we watched the fire and held one another, and that's all. Bob, you really do need to get a life.) He held my hand the whole way. We didn't say much. My parents weren't due home for hours yet, so I stuffed my wet running stuff into a plastic bag. I could change at my house. This time, Mr. Anderson didn't follow me to the road but bent down at the driver's side window.

"Maybe it's good that we can't see each other tomorrow. We both need to take some time and think about how we . . ." He looked away and then back and tried on a smile. "Besides, you've got that English thing, right?"

Oh God. He was regretting this already. "Yeah."

"So . . . you okay?"

"Sure." I started the car. "I'm good."

"No. Wait." He didn't back away. His fingers tightened on the door and he looked down at the ground. "*Damn* it . . ." When he looked up again, his lips were tight, his voice urgent. "Listen, I want you to promise me something. Don't you cut because of this. Don't you hurt yourself because of *me*, don't you dare."

His ferocity took my breath away. "I won't. I promise."

His face smoothed. "Good. I just couldn't bear to think that you would . . . that *I* . . ." He wet his lips. "If you ever feel like cutting, *ever*, no matter if it's day or night, I want you to call me. I mean it, Jenna. Promise me you won't hurt yourself. Promise me you'll call. Matt's gone, but I'm here, Jenna. I'm right in front of you."

His words tripped a hidden spring, and I felt my guts uncoil. "Okay."

"Promise me."

"I promise."

"Okay." He blew out. "Good. Another thing: the cabin? Anytime you need to get away, you go there. I never move that key. It's always there. You don't need my permission first. If you're in trouble and you can't reach me or I can't get to you right away, you just go. It'll be our place, okay? You'll be safe there."

I smeared sweat from my upper lip. My fingers shook. I was afraid I was going to start crying again, but with relief this time. "All right. Thank you."

"Okay. See you Monday." Not: *See you Monday bright and early.* Not: *Don't forget we've got that lab to set up and you said you'd be my TA and I'm counting on you.*

He took a step back and gave me a wave as I dropped the car into reverse. When I reached the rise and looked in the rearview, I could see his house and the lights in the windows, but that was all.

b

Mom and Dad blew in around nine. They were giddy as kids, and my mom was all over my dad, touching his shoulders, messing with his hair. Made my stomach twist. Dad poured them both nightcaps, and they couldn't stop talking about how much fun they'd had, what with all that kayaking around the Apostles and screwing each other blind. (Okay, they didn't say the last part, but—really—if I'd done anything remotely like that with a guy in front of *them*, Psycho-Dad would've locked me in a barrel and fed me through a tube for the rest of my life.) They'd even browsed real estate listings and Dad made noises about how a hobby farm might be nice when he retired and Mom gave up the bookstore. Then Mom laughed and told him she was never giving up the store and gave his chest a flirty little push, and it was all I could do not to throw up.

I interrupted Mom in mid-sentence. "I'm going to bed."

My mom stopped talking, drink in hand, her mouth this perfect little O. "Sure. Of course."

"You feeling all right, kiddo?" Dad asked. "What'd you do all week, anyway?"

"Nothing," I said and headed for the stairs. "Night."

c

I didn't sleep.

My parents came upstairs around midnight. I wondered

if they would stop outside my door, but they didn't. I heard their shower go on and then off. The house fell silent and dark. There was no moon and only the glow of my clock. I lay on my back, watching the inky shadows bunch and gather on the ceiling, and thought about Matt, how he was gone, really gone this time and for good. Worse than a ghost, Matt was first a fantasy and now a memory that would fade the same way I couldn't remember much about the fire or what came before or what my favorite flavor of ice cream had been when I was three.

Mr. Anderson said he would be there for me, but how could that possibly work? He was my *teacher.* I was just a kid. No matter what he said, that's what I was and he would see that and regret ever opening his mouth

Plus, he was married.

And his wife, where was his wife, really? Their baby?

I sighed. My eyes itched from crying so much. I wondered what he was doing, if he was asleep or maybe thinking about me. . . .

The sounds might have been going on for a while, but I guess I'd been so preoccupied they were like white noise, background that didn't become clear until someone laughed. I sat up in bed, ears straining. The sounds were disjointed, broken— and then my mother laughed again and my father groaned.

Oh God. My parents were going at it, and not quietly. Or maybe they thought they were being quiet, or just didn't care. Because Jenna was asleep, right? Jenna was a good girl. Besides, she'd been gone so many months in that psychiatric hospital, who could remember to keep it down?

I stuck my head under my pillow and screamed into my mattress.

d

My parents slept late Sunday. I got up, skipped breakfast, and went for a run far away from Mr. Anderson's house. The temperature had dropped during the night and all the puddles from the day before had frozen over. Crossing a bridge, I skidded on some black ice and nearly fell into the river, but I didn't care one way or the other. I ran far enough that I started to feel sick and had to swallow a couple gels. They were sour apple and made me want to puke.

When I got back, my parents were up. The kitchen smelled like eggs and coffee, and the windows were fogged. "Hey, you've gotten to be a real athlete there," said my father. His cheeks were ruddy and his hair was still wet.

My mom was puttering over a skillet, spatula in hand. "You hungry, sweetie?" She smiled at me. "I'm making omelets. Goat cheese."

If I didn't get out of that kitchen, I was going to throw up in my father's lap. "I've got to take a shower. I have work."

"Well, *I've* worked up an appetite," said my father, and winked at me. Then he grabbed my mother around her waist and she squealed and did the whole mock-fight thing again. They were like a couple of googly eyed teenagers.

No one noticed when I left.

e

I hunkered in my room the rest of the day and finished Alexis's book. Here's what I decided: the lady was certifiable with all her crap about ecstasy under the sea and hot blood and cool water, and I ought to know. Now to figure a way to say that in five pages.

But I never opened Word. Instead, I went to my ghost e-mail account (oh, how appropriate) and scanned Matt's messages, all the ones he'd ever written and then my replies. I saw how I'd changed all the date stamps as I went along, resending myself his e-mails over and over again, so what was old was new again: *You've got mail!* Running my eyes down the list was like reading a timetable of my . . . well, my breakdown, I guess you'd call it.

I reread one of the first messages he'd sent when he'd been alive-alive:

The only way I live through each day is to pretend I'm already gone. If you're dead, then the life you had before is dead, too, and all that remains is the horror of what's right in front of you. So I'm dead, Jenna. You have to think about me that way, okay? Because that's how I think about you and Mom and Dad. As long as I'm here, we're all dead and it has to be that way for me to do my job and come back.

Was that crazy? I didn't think so. Matt had protected himself as best he could. I would never be able to imagine what living there—dying there every day—had been like. The real irony is that Matt chose to kill himself every single day so he could come back to life, and then he died for good.

I deleted all his messages. I deleted my replies. Every. Single. One.

Then I deleted my ghost account and dumped the shortcut into my recycle bin and then I emptied that, too. I would've ripped out the hard drive and run over it with my car, but then I'd have to explain to my father why I killed my computer. I might be nuts, but I wasn't crazy.

f

Mom was on a roll. For dinner, she whipped up lasagna and salad and garlic bread. She and Dad popped the cork on a bottle of Chianti and chattered about their college days and how they met and blah, blah, blah. I pushed food around my plate and then asked to be excused and, when no one gave permission, left anyway.

When I went to bed, I screwed in earbuds and listened to "Learning to Fly" and then Death Cab for Cutie and then Black Sabbath. Screw Ellington and screw Mingus and screw Judy, and screw you, too, Wagner.

If my parents went at it again, I sure didn't hear.

g

Sunday night, I'd told Mom that some of the people on the team practiced early and it made more sense for me to drive myself. She said that was fine; she'd have tons of work anyway now that Thanksgiving was almost here and Black Friday and Christmas and blah, blah, blah.

I didn't care about any of that. I wasn't sure I would even go to school.

All I wanted was to be left alone.

h

And then it was Monday.

I left a half hour earlier than usual, at 4:30. My parents weren't up; the house was quiet; the streets were dark and there was virtually no traffic. If I actually made it to school, I told myself I could work in the hall outside the library if I had to; Harley was used to my getting there early and wouldn't give me grief. Hell, I might even beat Harley.

But I knew I was lying to myself. I had to know if Mr. Anderson was there. I had to know if he'd come in early because if we were on the same wavelength here, I thought he might. There was no other time to really talk except before school. So I'd cruise past the lot. If there wasn't a single car—or if I saw only Harley's truck—well, then, I'd know not to make a fool of myself. I could still TA and be on the team, but the rest of it—yeah, like the rest of *what*—would be as if it never happened.

But, if he was there, that would . . . it would mean something.

When I stopped for coffee, I thought about picking up one for him, too. But he always made his own, so that would be kind of lame. I did get two scones, though; then worried I was jinxing myself; then told myself to get a grip, they were just *pastries*.

The sky was cobalt when I pulled into the school parking lot. The stars glittered, diamond-bright in the cold. At first I thought there were no other cars in the lot, not even Harley's— and then my stomach clenched.

Mr. Anderson's truck was there.

He'd come early. Earlier than I had. God, how long had he been here? My eyes flicked to the second story above the library—and zeroed in on a dim, barely visible glow. Had he turned on a light? I didn't think so. But he was here. He was waiting for me.

I had all the power now. Go to him . . . or not.

One of the front doors was unlocked. I pushed inside. The halls were very dim, and my footsteps echoed. On the second floor, I saw no spray of light from his classroom, and there was no music. Okay, that was bad. Yet the hall smelled of coffee. So that might be good.

The classroom was completely dark except for a slim bar of uncertain light beneath the office door. When I stepped into his room, I don't know why... but I pulled the door shut behind me. Quietly. But I did it. Then I crossed to his office door and put my hand on the knob.

He was sitting at his desk, but looked up as the door opened. The only light came from that small desk lamp, enough to see by but no more. He stared at me for a very long moment and then stood. Was he relieved? I couldn't tell.

"I wasn't sure you..." He paused, cleared his throat. "I just put on a fresh pot. Do you want a warm-up?"

"No, I'm good." I held up the paper bag of scones. "I hope you like blueberry."

"I love blueberry." But he didn't smile. We looked at one another and then he picked up a book from his desk. "Here. It's that book about Alexis Depardieu I told you about. I meant to give this to you the other day, but we got kind of... sidetracked."

"Thanks." The book was slim, with no jacket. I opened to the title page and then had to angle it toward that feeble light: *Swimming with the Sharks.* "Who's Peter Lasker?"

"Alexis's lover."

I couldn't look at him. My pulse throbbed in my neck. "Before she was married?"

"Yes, if you believe him. Before, during... and after."

Now I did look up. "But she was married," I said, faintly.

"I guess that didn't make any difference to them," he said, carefully. "I think they were in love and didn't care. I think they felt that loving each other was more important than following the rules."

"Are we going to follow the rules?" I whispered. I honestly didn't know what answer I wanted.

"We probably should."

I closed my eyes, willing my tears not to fall. "I killed Matt. All his e-mails, my account, everything." I opened my eyes. "There's only you. All I can see is you."

Something in his face changed and then he took a step forward and then another. He was close enough to reach out for me, but he didn't. Instead, he stretched past, pulled his office door shut—and locked it. He took the book and then the bag of scones from my weak fingers and carefully squared both next to the coffeepot. Reaching around, he eased my knapsack from my shoulders and let it slide to the floor, and then he peeled off my coat, his fingers lightly brushing my neck, trailing over my wrists. He draped my coat over his desk chair and then, without taking his eyes from mine, felt for the lamp.

Click.

The room went black. I heard him breathing. My heart was pounding. He was so close we could've touched in that trembling darkness, but I couldn't move. A moment later, I felt his fingers thread through mine and my pulse jumped.

His voice drifted out of the dark. "Come with me. I know the way."

I did. My head was buzzing. He moved easily through the storage room, past the hulking shelves of chemicals so carefully arranged and cataloged, and then down the short hall to the old forgotten darkroom he'd shown me in what seemed like another century. The door was open, but he didn't step inside. Instead, he paused, my hand still in his—and waited.

In the ruddy blush of the emergency exit sign, I spied that cot where he must sometimes take a nap or rest after a run. The air smelled different, though: still Dove and him but, also, the round warm scent of vanilla.

Now was the moment to decide which rules mattered. There were choices. I had the power. I could turn around. I could leave. There was no mystery here. Once I stepped into that room, I would be crossing a line.

"I haven't been able to stop thinking about you." When I turned, he cupped my face in his hands. "I thought I was helping only you, but now I think I've been struggling to help myself, too. But you have to understand how serious this is, Jenna. No one can know. You can't tell anyone. I could end up in jail."

"We've been out together. We've been places together." I realized, belatedly, that after Adelaide, Mr. Anderson had been careful to go where no one would know either of us. "We run together."

"And we can keep doing those things, within reason. I'm your teacher. Your parents know me. I've been to your house. I'm no different from any other adult. Or . . . we don't have to do anything. We can be friends and that would be fine. I . . . I care about you, Jenna. The last thing I want is to hurt you. I won't force you. I *want* you to want me."

They felt like words *I'd* wanted—waited for—my whole life. "I do want you." My body was liquid, my skin so hot I

234

thought that one more degree and I would burst into flame. "And I know how to keep a secret, Mr. Anderson, I promise."

He nearly, *nearly* smiled. "I think that when it's just the two of us . . . you can call me Mitch."

ﬁ

We didn't talk after that. Not with words, anyway.

37: a

"*Where* is Danielle?" Mr. Anderson planted his fists on his hips. His words rode on breath clouds the wind tore away. "We start in five. Don't tell me she's still suiting up."

The rest of us knotted together, jamming our hands in the pockets of our warm-up jackets, doing the cold-girl two-step. We were in Wausau on a Tuesday and a week before Thanksgiving for the last cross-country meet of the season. Regionals would be the week after Thanksgiving, with state the week after that. The weather was crap, the temperature a degree above freezing—kind of typical for north-central Wisconsin this time of year. A thin salting of snow filmed the frozen ground. The weatherman was talking six, eight inches on the way, and everyone was saying that winter was going to be early, long, and hard.

The wind was steady. The air smelled like crushed aluminum. Every gust whistled through my warm-up jacket and sweatpants, slicing straight to the bone. I'd tried to keep as warm as I could, but I could feel my muscles stiffening up. I needed to be running already.

"I'll get her." When Mr. Anderson gave a curt nod, I jogged past the clutches of parents huddling together in the cold (not mine; Dad would never come and Mom was working maniac hours). David and a couple other stalwart boyfriend-types were there, too; when I trotted by on my way to the visitors' locker room, David looked the question, but I only shrugged and—

♭

Oh, what's the matter? Is widdle Bobby *mad*? Like, wait a minute, she skipped a *month*? Well, what were you expecting, Bobby-o, a blow-by-blow? Every *minute*? God, you *are* a perv.

Oh, all right, short and sweet: yes, this meet was about a month later. I'd run in three meets since . . . since *before*. (I'm not being coy here; I just don't see that it's any of your business.) I'd done okay: third in my first meet and second in the two after that. My joining the team seemed to have lit a fire under Danielle. Maybe that's what Mr. Anderson had counted on. If so, it had worked. She'd poured it on the last three races.

But I would catch her soon, and I knew it. Her splits were way off, and when we did flat courses on the treadmill, I could punch up a six-minute mile for five and she couldn't. She'd gotten surlier and more withdrawn, too. In the locker room—yes, I still changed in the handicapped shower—I overheard how she and David might be splitting up; how her older brother, who was in the local university extension and had suddenly taken to showing up to take her home from practice, had gotten in David's face the other week. I could believe it. The way her brother acted—wedging himself between her and any other guy, even Mr. Anderson when he was just coaching—you'd have thought *he* was her boyfriend. Stuff like that.

But with me coming on board, we'd done well enough. My teammates were pumped because we might make regionals after all, even state. Mr. Anderson—Mitch—was psyched. Me, too. I knew it was only a matter of time until I *really* came in first—not just first on our team, but for the race.

For him.

Which didn't exactly endear me to Danielle, who had even more reason to hate my guts and . . .

C

Oh, wait. *I* know. You don't care about Danielle, do you, Bob? Why is she wasting time with Danielle, you're saying; why isn't she getting down to the nitty-gritty, what's *really* important. Where's the *good* stuff?

Well, know what I say to that, Bobby-o? Screw you. This is my story, so get over it.

Oh, okay, I'll cut you a break. I mean, since you asked.

Yes, Mitch and I saw one another almost every day and I don't mean *just* in that way, although . . . yes, in *that* way, too. And you know what, Bobby-o?

It was wonderful. It was magic. It was a fairy tale come true and the best thing that ever happened to me, and you can't take that away. I know that's killing you. You want this to be a different kind of story, but it's not and . . .

d

Okay, deep breath.

Mitch and I were together nearly every day, most mornings and after school but very, very late, after everyone else had gone home. I studied in the library, or we set up labs for the next day. Yes, we really *did* work, shocker there. There was also practice, conditioning work, stuff like that. We were extremely careful and always made sure that doors were open and there was music and, usually, other kids. Like we had nothing to hide.

Although sometimes his hand would brush my arm and a little shock would zing through my chest. Our eyes might meet, and then heat would crawl up my neck and warm my thighs, and I would have to look away. More often than not, we both drove away when our work at school was done or practice was over, so everyone would see us go in separate cars. We'd meet up again: for dinner, coffee—

And other things.

In his car. In mine. Huddled under blankets in darkened fields, where we explored ways of keeping one another warm: when he showed me what he liked, and how.

We ran on the weekends, too. And, yeah, a couple times, we couldn't wait until we made it to the cabin. That's not to say that we didn't spend a lot of time in our hideaway. That was ours: a private, magical space where we could talk and fill volumes.

e

I remember one afternoon—a Saturday after we'd . . . well, you know. We were wrapped in a comforter on that window seat in his study: my back snugged against his chest, his arms hugging me close. No rain this time, but the day was gray and the woods so filled with mist, we might as well have been on our own little island. There was music, something as gauzy and soft as that fog.

"I love it when it's so still," he said. I remember that his fingers brushed and stroked my breasts, back and forth. Nothing grabby. Just a gentle touch you'd almost swear wasn't there but which sent tiny electric shocks dancing over my skin and stabbing through my thighs. "It always reminds me of diving, the way you hover between the water below and the world above."

"I wish we didn't have to leave." My hands were hooked on his arms the way they'd been that first afternoon when I told him everything. "It feels like we're floating. Everything's so calm."

"Mmm-hmm." He pressed his lips to the top of my head. "I'd forgotten what this was like, feeling really *at* peace and not just putting on a show for family, my father, my . . ." He paused. "You remember when I said you can look at a guy in the water and not know he's in trouble? That he's drowning? I saw it happen once."

"You saw someone die?"

"Mmm-hmm. There was this one guy, pretty experienced, and his dive buddy was this newbie-kid who'd sucked down his air pretty fast. So the kid surfaced and this guy kept on by himself, which might not have been a problem if he'd stayed close or partnered up again, but he didn't. So we're all back aboard and thirty minutes become forty and then forty-five and the dive master is starting to freak. Then, all of a sudden, the captain spotted the guy maybe a half mile away. Without binoculars, you could barely see him, but he was upright and floating. We all started waving, but he didn't wave back, and then the dive master was screaming that we had to get there fast. I thought he'd gone crazy. I mean, the guy seemed fine: not shouting or splashing or anything. Only by the time they got the boat turned around and over there? He was gone. That's why the dive master was so frantic. He understood the guy had about twenty seconds left."

"But he was on the surface," I said. "How could he not breathe? Why didn't he scream if he was in trouble?"

"Because you're thinking of the movies, and that's not what happens in real life," he said. "They call it the drowning instinct. It's when drowning doesn't look like drowning. In real life, if the water's very cold, a person can't help but gasp. It's reflex. The thing is as soon as water hits your lungs, your throat closes off, even if the water's warm. Your body's trying to protect itself, and the reality is that a lot more people suffocate than truly drown. Regardless, to people on land, especially when you're really close to the end, you don't *look* like you're in trouble. You don't scream, but that's because you can't, and you don't wave your arms either or expend a lot of energy flailing. You're just *there*. So people don't notice that you're dying." He was silent for a moment. "That's me. I think I've been drowning all this time and doing it so quietly, even I didn't know it."

That sadness was there again. For some reason, I thought back to those pictures of Mrs. Anderson: happy and beautiful as a princess on her wedding day; then pregnant but scarred. I wondered what had happened in the middle; if maybe she'd been drowning and Mitch hadn't known that either. Maybe they both had.

Despite how Mitch made me feel, I never quite forgot what Danielle said about him and broken people. You can't spend a million hours in therapy and not have it rub off a little. So was Mitch always trying to help because he hadn't been able to do the same first for himself and then for his wife? I could see where the shock of what happened to her—the pain and guilt— would . . . well, rip and then scar a person on the inside. Look at my parents. Look at Matt.

My therapist once said that everything I did was a repetition: a way of trying to make what was wrong with our whole family come out differently and right. So why should Mitch be any different? Maybe he couldn't help himself. He might not understand what he was repeating, or that he was even doing it. Adults don't know everything, Bob.

I only understand this *now*, of course: sitting here, still freezing cold, in this awful emergency room. Listening to the quiet.

Back then and at that moment, warm and safe in his arms, all I wanted was to help. But I didn't know what to say. I had this urge to tell Mitch that I would save him—that he could grab on to me—but that felt dumb. Mitch had so much already. What could I do or give that he couldn't find somewhere else?

"But I'm here and now you *do* know that you've been drowning." I sat up and when I turned to face him, the blanket slid from my shoulders and down my back. The scars were still there, on my stomach and thighs. They would never go away. I wouldn't be me if they did. "So you don't have to do that anymore, Mitch. You don't have to drown."

For once, I did the right thing. Something unclenched in him; I could see the strain and tension drain from his body. His eyes drifted over my face and then to my breasts, my belly, those scars, and then he was reaching for me—and then there was no need to say anything.

Except for the moment when he guided my hand to where he wanted: when I gasped and he sighed and said my name, and then we were drowning in each other.

ƒ

It was all so shockingly easy, as long as we were careful. I know you don't want to hear that, Bob. You want to hear that we felt guilty or lived in constant fear of discovery. You want to know about our near-misses and how awful we felt, how criminal.

But I've got news for you, Bobby-o. I felt fine, *fine*, better than I had in months and months and months. Who would suspect a good, quiet kid like me and a nice, open, friendly guy like Mr. Anderson? I had straight As; I wasn't a troublemaker. The Tank decided I'd adjusted just fine, especially after I joined the team. My parents were careful not to think too hard about anything. Hell, they were *glad* I was on the team. I was looking good, they said. I seemed so happy, they said. My dad told my mom to admit it, going to Turing was the right move, and what could my mom say? Personally, I think they were so getting into each other again and with Mom gearing up for the holidays—they were thrilled not to have to worry about one more thing.

I was happy and Mitch made me beautiful, Bob. He made me believe that we would keep each other afloat forever.

And no one asked questions, Bob. No one gave us a second thought. Everyone looked, and no one really saw. We looked fine, and none of you knew the difference.

9

So, the meet.

I trotted into the silent girls' locker room but didn't see anyone. "Hello? Danielle?"

A pause. Then a rustle, followed by a grunt. "What?"

Her voice had come from the bathrooms. I went past the showers, my spikes clicking on the tile floor, rounded the corner, and saw shoes under one stall. "Are you okay?"

"Like you care." Her tone hardened as she recognized my voice. I could practically see her chin jut out. "I'm *fine*. I'll be out in a second. I just . . . I've got cramps."

"Oh. Well, Coach wants you outside. We're starting in like five, ten minutes."

"Yeah, yeah, I'm coming, okay?" When I didn't move away, she growled, "You going to stand there until I come out?"

"Coach said I should wait for you." Technically, I could leave and let Mitch lay into her when she finally dragged her sorry ass out of the stall. She would deserve it, too. This was someone who'd been nothing but mean to me. I didn't owe her a thing. But, I reminded myself, I didn't need to be that way. This may sound stupid to you, Bob, but in a weird way, I felt like I'd already won. I was Mitch's go-to girl on the team. Danielle might *think* she'd had something special with Mitch, but he'd already told me that she had a lot of problems and didn't want to listen to what he had to say. (What problems? I didn't know.

Mitch was good that way. He never let on about anyone else. It was private.) Besides, Danielle had David. She had a brother. Her father was some high-power attorney. She had plenty.

The toilet flushed. The stall door opened and Danielle emerged on a cloud of vomit and sour peach. She elbowed her way to the sink. Under the fluorescents, her skin was yellow. The smudges beneath her eyes were black as runny mascara and her warm-up clothes hung like burlap. She'd shed a lot of weight since the beginning of the year—to keep her speed up, she'd said. The other girls on the team whispered that she was starting to look like one of those bobblehead dolls: all head on a spindly frame, like a runway model. A real sickly looking kind of skinny.

"You don't look so good," I said.

"Takes one to know one." She sucked water from the faucet, swished, then spit.

"Are you sure you should run?"

"Just shut up." She rinsed out, spat again, then dragged her arm across her chin to catch the drips. "Don't even pretend you care."

I shrugged, but didn't say anything more. If she wanted to keel over from a heart attack, what could I do? Besides, Mitch had to see the same thing we did. He was the coach. If he let her run, he must think she could take it.

At the exit, she turned. "Let me tell you something. The more broken you are, the better he likes you."

"You know, I've heard that somewhere before. I guess that explains you."

"Fuck you." Turning aside, she mumbled something under her breath.

"What?"

"I said your time's coming." Her eyes, laser-bright, probed mine and then her face set. "Just remember that when the next loser comes along."

"I'm not a loser," I said to her back, but she only flipped me off.

Mitch was giving last-minute instructions when we got back. His eyes flicked to me and then to Danielle, and I saw him wrestling with the decision.

"I can run," Danielle said, her tone flat. "I'm fine. If we don't make regionals, this is the last race anyway."

Mitch closed his mouth, looked at both of us in turn and then nodded. "All right. Danielle, you set the pace. Jenna, you follow her lead. The rest of you, cover their backs and then when you've got your wedge, you go for it, understand?"

We did the whole hand-pump-team-chant thing, but when Danielle put her hand on mine, she grabbed my eyes and then her nails bit, hard enough for the pain to needle and my flesh to tear. But I didn't flinch or pull away. She was an amateur. There was nothing Danielle could do to me that I hadn't done better—and worse—to myself.

h

The starter pistol cracked and we took off in a jostling pack, thirty-one girls spread across three teams. Danielle and I were the best runners on ours so we stayed in front while the rest of the team ran interference to our rear. The race was a tortuous five miles of rolling, uneven pasture with obstacles: two streams that were two and a half miles apart and a narrow rocky ridge up a ten-percent grade a quarter mile before the finish. No roads.

The first half was against a brutal wind, a steady gale so strong it was like running in place. The ground was hard and as unforgiving as concrete. Every step sent shock waves shivering up my legs. After five minutes, I felt the pounding in my teeth, and my head rang as my spikes shattered glassy ice rimming frozen puddles left from sleet and rain two days before.

Danielle's ponytail bounced back and forth in front of me. She was doing her pogo-stick routine again, and going too slow, already in trouble. Her right arm was tight against her side and her left was moving too much to compensate. But she wouldn't pick up the pace and—stupid me—I stuck to the plan.

Four runners passed us. Five. Seven. We hit the first stream in a herd. I eyed the five girls dead ahead. They were bunched way too close together, a disaster waiting to happen—and then it did when one girl stumbled on a submerged rock. Yelping, she pitched forward, dragging down another girl only a step behind. That slowed down the others, and everyone broke ranks, splashing around the girls still wallowing in the stream. The water was very cold, so icy it burned, but then I was through and running up the other side.

Nearly two miles gone, about three to go, another mile to the turn where the wind would be with me. Now was the time to start breaking away in a sudden burst of speed, when the others least expected it. But Danielle was still lumbering. If anything, she was slower than before.

I pulled up behind her left shoulder. "Go," I hissed, "go, go!"

"Shut up," she panted back. Muddy water beaded on her neck. Her jersey was soaked. "It's too early, I'll go when . . . when I'm ready . . ."

Two more girls passed us and then, finally, one of our teammates got tired of waiting and put on some speed and kicked out ahead of us. That seemed to be a signal because then the entire team went for broke.

So did I. Screw Danielle. I cranked it up, stretching my stride, my shoes pounding, thighs pumping, legs scissoring. The faces of the refs stationed along the way blurred to a smear. I imagined that I was running with Mitch and we were flying over the ground, skimming the earth, and his voice was in my head: *Go go go go fast go fast go faster go go.* I blew past Danielle in two seconds and then I was kicking it higher, blazing, a rocket streaking over the dead grass, shush shush shush shush. I bulleted past my teammates and through a mile, up a hill, legs pistoning, quads bunching and clenching. The wind whooshed past my ears and tore at my hair. I kept focusing on the girl ahead and then when I passed her, the next and then the next, and then I saw that it was just me and one other girl, her legs flashing, her spikes stabbing the trail. Stream ahead: I watched her hit the water, take a step then another and then both arms flew up and she was stumbling, arms windmilling wildly just as I crashed into the water. I tried veering left, away from whatever had grabbed the other girl, but slipped and staggered and almost fell. But then my spikes snagged the streambed, and I was through, plowing up the opposite bank.

My lungs screamed; my throat was on fire. *One more mile, one more, one more mile, go go go go go. Push off from the hip, punish the ground, punish it, punish it, punish it.* My heart was a fist, bruising my ribs; every step was a solid *bang* that shuddered up my spine. I remembered that first run with Mitch, how badly I'd done and I would not let that happen now, I wouldn't. He was waiting for me at the finish. He would see me crest the rise and then hurtle down the final stretch, pulling a phalanx of runners in my wake like the streaming tail of a comet all the way to the finish line. He would be there; I would make him proud; I would be *his* girl and we would—

"*Bitch.*" Somehow, Danielle was right there, at my left elbow. "No, you don't," she hissed, "no *way.*"

I didn't answer. I don't know if I could've. That she had the breath was a bad sign because that meant she still had more to give, and I was already digging deep.

We hit the ridge together, stride for stride, the trail only wide enough for three. The drop-off on either side wasn't precipitous or a killer. But that didn't mean you could recover from a misstep. The trail was rutted and uneven, a hard-bed scramble with rocky scrub flanking either side, as well as referees and screaming parents and friends spaced like beads on a string. Ahead, the ridge dropped then leveled out to a grassy fan, but a fall here and you could kiss the race good-bye.

Which was precisely what Danielle was trying to force on me. Running flat-out, she pushed in on my right, trying to bully her way into the lead. I shot a quick glance, saw how the muscles of her neck stood out like ropes. Her teeth were bared in a grimace. No more talk or taunts now. We were dead even and both running as fast as we could.

Faces flashed by. Below, I could see the crowd at the finish line; I picked out David and there was Mitch waving us in and I could hear his voice above the others: "*Come on, come on, pour it on bring it on go go go!*" I focused on that, on his voice, running to him, for him, only him. I blistered along that trail as the wind whipped my hair and sweat ran in rivers down my neck and over my back and belly. My muscles were fraying, unraveling, tearing themselves from my bones. But I was winning; I would win this for him, for him, for him. A fraction of an inch and then another, and then I was moving ahead of Danielle and still I went faster, faster, faster, the kettle drum of my heart pounding, pounding, faster run faster go faster go go—

Then I felt a quick blow just below my ribs, something swift and sure and sharp, and yet so fleeting I almost didn't register that anything had happened. In the next instant, Danielle's feet tangled with mine and then I felt a sudden laser-bright burn as her spikes sliced my right ankle.

I lost it: my balance, my speed, everything. We caromed off one another like bumper cars. Her elbow smacked my temple. My left ankle rolled, and then it was like I'd spiked a bare knuckle of bone into solid rock. A shout of red pain grabbed my calf and then I screamed along with it as the world swirled in a drunken spiral.

Danielle and I tumbled off the ridge in a sweaty snarl of arms and legs. The ground rushed for my face, and I twisted, but I'm no gymnast. My shoulder banged against rock, and then the back of my head smacked icy ground. My vision flickered like a faulty lightbulb and then I was somersaulting down the hill.

You know that old riddle, Bob, the one about what's black and white and black and white and black and white? (Answer: a nun falling down stairs. Or a zebra.) That was like this, only it was gray rock and brown earth and dead grass and slack open mouths and faces, lots of faces. There was shouting, there had to be, but I didn't hear. I'd lost track of where Danielle was. I don't know how many rolls it took for me to finally stop, but the next thing I knew I was sprawled flat on my back, my feet still above me on the incline, my aching head dragging below. My mouth filled with a taste of wet metal. There was a confused, muddled sense of people rushing forward, pushing in, dropping on their knees, shouting, the words all running together like broken egg yolks: *heyheyareyouallrightsomeonegettheemtsjennahowstheotherjennajenna* . . .

Leave me alone. My head was swoony. Everything hurt. *Too bright, too noisy, go away—*

Then someone shouted in my ear: "Jenna!"

That voice, so frantic and frightened and one I knew so well by then, called me back. I pried open my eyes. There were gray clouds. It was beginning to snow; I could feel the ice pecking my cheeks. Two EMTs with blue latex gloves swam into view. Their lips moved, but I didn't hear them. Didn't care. For me, all that mattered was Mitch's stricken face.

"I'm so sorry," I said, and passed out.

38: a

So they said I had a mild concussion. My left ankle was sprained. The ER doctor stitched a bad rip just above my right ankle, finishing off with a train track of staples. The doctor was nice and pretty professional. He asked about my skin grafts but not my other scars. Although he checked them pretty carefully, his gloved hands probing my stomach and hips and pulling at the skin, probably to see if any were fresh because then he'd have to call the shrinks.

Mitch came in once. His skin was drawn down tight on his skull. He asked if I remembered what had happened and I said I didn't know, which was mostly true. He said the way I staggered, it looked like I'd gotten shoved, only we were going so fast and were so close together, the refs couldn't be sure and said it was an accident. I told him that was probably right.

"You're sure?" If he blinked, his skin would rip. "You're absolutely positive. Nothing else happened."

"Nothing. We got tangled up. We were crowding each other." That was true. "We should've known better. It was an accident. I messed up."

"No," he said. His lips thinned. "*No*. I won't let her hurt you again. She can't keep doing this, she—" Then he was turning on his heel, wrenching the curtain out of his way so hard the metal rings chattered. Danielle and David were two bays down. I heard Mitch's angry rap and then her muffled reply, something else from David, but I couldn't make sense of the words. But I do remember her voice going watery as she began to cry, Mitch's low murmurs after that, and a whole lot of nothing from David. Then Mitch left them alone.

They'd called my parents and Danielle's and told them we weren't dead or anything. Since we'd come up in a bus, the doctors didn't see much harm in letting us go back that way. I don't know about Danielle's father, but Psycho-Dad went all doctorly on the phone with the ER people. I think he'd decided I needed exploratory brain surgery or something. As things shook out, I got an MRI, which the ER doc told me was completely bogus but did anyway, probably to avoid more headaches with my dad. So that delayed us leaving for another couple of hours. If we hadn't been in Wausau, I think a bunch of parents would've shown up to take their kids home. By the time our hobbit-sized bus pulled into the hospital breezeway and they wheeled me and Danielle out, it was dark, cold, snowy, and windy.

No one said much during the long ride back. Danielle sat up front on the left, with her right leg propped in David's lap and an ice pack draped over the knee which they'd Ace-wrapped. She even had crutches. (Me, they let gimp onto the bus, and I was the one who'd, you know, actually *bled*.) Mitch sat in the very back. I had a seat to myself and dozed off a couple times, but the girl across the aisle kept waking me up because she'd heard it was bad to sleep when you had a concussion.

Even though David had driven her to school, Danielle's father and brother were waiting when the bus finally chugged into the school lot at ten. Her dad was this hulking guy with stubby fingers. As soon as the bus rolled to a stop, he was hammering on the doors and then bullying his way on board, ignoring everybody: Danielle, when she said she could walk; David, who was trying to explain; Mitch, who'd started down the aisle.

"We're fine; we're fine," Mr. Connolly barked. He scooped up Danielle like she weighed nothing, which was just about true. David followed with her crutches, and then Mitch was blowing past my seat, right on their heels. I watched through fogged glass as Mr. Connolly handed Danielle off to her brother and then snatched the crutches from David like he was a servant. David was talking, but Mr. Connolly hacked at the air with the side of his hand to shut David up and was turning aside just as Mitch got there.

It might have ended right there, if Mitch had stayed out of it. But Mitch just couldn't let it go—not before, not then, or later—so we all saw the same thing.

Mitch put his hand on Mr. Connolly's shoulder and said something. What, I couldn't hear. You could tell from the sudden set of Mr. Connolly's back that it was some zinger that really stung. Because, all of a sudden, Mr. Connolly spun around, planted his hands on Mitch's chest and shoved.

Mitch. I gasped. My heart lurched into my throat. *Mitch, no.*

"Holy shit," someone on the bus said.

Mitch staggered. He would've fallen if he hadn't grabbed onto the car door and then Mr. Connolly was right there, in his face, screaming, jabbing his stubby fingers into Mitch's chest, bunching a fist just inches from Mitch's nose. Mitch was tall, but Mr. Connolly was a very big man and I didn't know if Mitch could take him.

No one tried to help. Danielle's brother stood to one side, wiping his mouth over and over again with the back of his hand, like there was a taste that wouldn't go away. I saw a bunch of other parents pop out of their cars like jack-in-the-boxes, but no one made a move, not even Mitch. He stood there and let Mr. Connolly scream. Call me crazy, Bob, but for just a second, I thought that, maybe, Mitch wanted him to take that swing. Like Mitch somehow thought better *him* than someone else, like Danielle or David.

The only time Mitch made any move at all was when David finally tried get in the middle. Mr. Connolly pivoted, elbow cocked, ready to let go with a backhanded swat, but Mitch got his hands up, fast, and snagged Mr. Connolly's wrist. Mr. Connolly's bull-face twisted; for a second, I thought he'd take that swing.

That was when Danielle leaned out of the car and screamed at her father. Whatever she said made all the fight drain from Mr. Connolly. He seemed to deflate, like a spent balloon, and then he jerked free of Mitch before whirling on his heel and shouting something at Danielle's brother, who followed Mr. Connolly to their car. And then they just drove away.

Mitch and David watched them go. Mitch's face was a stone. David looked like he wanted to cry. After a couple seconds, Mitch put an arm around David's shoulders the way a coach does to comfort a kid who's dropped the winning touch-down. Or as a dad might for the son whose suffering he can't bear.

b

Of course, my parents hadn't bothered to come for me. Actually, that's not fair; that's a lie. I'm sure they would have, considering I was banged up and all. But since I couldn't drive with the concussion, Mitch told them my car would be safe in the school lot and he'd drive me home, which was the best news I'd gotten all day. We could keep driving to Canada, as far as I was concerned. We could drive forever.

The snow was really coming down now, slanted ribbons slashing through Mitch's headlights. He took it slow, his eyes fixed on the road. I found a Louis Armstrong CD and slipped it into the player. After a couple minutes, Mitch said, roughly, "How you doing?"

"I'm okay. My head hurts a little."

"You should sleep."

"No. Mitch . . . I'm so sorry." Maybe it was the concussion, but I got all weepy. I bit my lip. "I really wanted to win for you."

"Hey, hey, it's okay. There'll be other races. No big deal. We've got the spring track season and then two whole years after that. We'll make it."

He meant to make me feel better, but I went cold inside. This was the first time he'd ever mentioned that our time together was limited. The only future I had imagined was amorphous and fuzzy, something *out there* and so far away it was forever. Two years is a long time and no time at all. Matt had been gone for longer. But, in two years, high school would end. I would go to college somewhere and become . . . something. Mitch already had a life. In two years, I would be sleeping in a strange bed and Mitch would be delivering the same lectures on saponification and free radicals. There would be new faces on the track team, but he would run the same route from his house to the park. When he wanted peace, he could tend his fire and drink tea and listen to Mozart and find shelter in his cabin. I would duck from my dorm to class, with my collar turned up and shoulders hunched around my ears as a chill rain needled my face.

Mitch sensed the change. "What?"

"I was just thinking how I wish nothing had to end. I wish we could live in a little cabin in the woods, and I'd make soup and you'd chop wood and we could be together. I would never have to leave for college and no one would—" I clamped down on the rest. I'd said too much. I didn't want to become a shrew, a nag, a person with morning breath. This was the way it went down in books and movies. The lovers were always Romeo and Juliet: happy to spin out idyllic futures for about two seconds before the real world shattered their glass bubble and killed them. Or one of them—usually the girl, stupid, stupid, stupid—got demanding or went all hysterical and whiny, and the guy did something equally dumb.

For a long time—God, it felt like forever—I listened to the rhythmic thump-thump-thump of the wipers. The snow came in billowing curtains and spun into whirling funnel clouds in the truck's headlights. The night beyond was complete and dense and black.

Finally, I said, "I shouldn't have said that."

"Why not?" He never took his eyes from the road. "I feel the same way. I think about you all the time. I sit down to do a lesson plan, and then an hour's gone by and I've been day-dreaming about you. I think about how I don't have to work. I have enough money to go anywhere, *do* anything I want—but the next day comes and I'm teaching about the chemical rearrangement of disordered solids. Jenna, being older doesn't mean I have all the answers. The world has rules. We aren't powerful enough to make our own."

"But we've broken some. Who's to stop us from breaking them all?"

"You're young," he said. "I know you don't want to hear that, but I've been around a lot longer. There's no way we can break every single rule, not yet. You have to be patient. You'll be eighteen in two years and then—"

"And then I'll be gone. I'll go to college and then may-be grad school. Even if I went to Madison, we wouldn't be together. You won't quit your job and follow me wherever I go." I didn't make it a question because I knew the answer. "So we'll be apart. You'll still be married." This was as close as I'd come to asking about his wife. She was out there, a blur, a potentiality that might, at any second, press her face against the glass of our little bubble. Or shatter it altogether.

"But maybe not," he said.

"No? Then why are you still married now?" I tried to keep the desperation, the despair out of my voice, and failed. "She's been gone for months. She doesn't visit, does she?" I was on a roll now, unable to keep the questions from tumbling out—and honestly, not wanting to. "Do you even talk to her? Do you still love her?"

"Jenna, it's not as simple as that."

"Then tell me what it is, and I'll try to understand. I'm not a child. I'm sixteen. I'm old enough to . . ."

"Drive," he said. "You are old enough to drive. You are old enough to see a doctor in private, but your parents still have to sign a consent for any procedure. You are old enough to hold a job. You are old enough to get an abortion in Illinois without parental consent or notification, but not in Wisconsin or Minnesota or Michigan. You are just old enough—"

"To sleep with you," I said.

39: a

Silence.

I wasn't angry. I was mainly afraid that I'd blown it. And, yeah, okay, maybe I was a little bitter. But I figured we'd come to my dark moment, the real turning point where either Mitch dumped me or we went on to live happily ever after.

Because wasn't that the way these stories went? Meryl said they teach this kind of thing to romance writer-wannabes: the setup, the meet, the dark moment, blah, blah, blah. Like, at school, Dewerman said *Jane Eyre* was a romance, but I always thought it was kind of tragic. The disaster isn't driven by external events but something living inside Rochester and Jane—the dark hand of some old disappointment or pain that makes things go from bad to worse. Think of it as always being darkest at the dawn before it goes pitch-black, Bob. That's why *Romeo and Juliet* isn't a romance, even though it's all about love and obsession and family rivalries, but a tragedy. Despite what Shakespeare says at the beginning—I mean, he tells you right off the bat the end's not going to be pretty—you keep waiting for those two crazy, desperate kids to realize that there are alternatives, that they'll grow up eventually.

I would grow up. I would have to leave, eventually, and that would kill us because Mitch and I would grow apart. For me, there was an end point, something real and tangible, far enough away to ignore but so close I could taste the end.

b

So what *could* I control? I couldn't stop time. The difference in our ages wouldn't go away, and neither would his marriage. Those were out of my control. I could keep after him, of course. Nag, complain, moan, bitch, whine. Turn into someone like Danielle, actually. Looking back, maybe I should've. We'd have ended in that truck, right there and then, and I wouldn't have met you again, Bob. I wouldn't be sitting here, half-frozen and filling the memory of a digital recorder with my sorry-ass story, and you could be at home with the missus and your faithful dog, Shep, and your kids.

Anyway. It was like that instant before I'd followed Mitch into that old darkroom, my personal Rubicon Point where I was poised over the abyss. There were choices only I could make, questions that were mine to pose.

So I said, not meekly, trying to be as grown-up about it as I could: "Can I ask you a question?"

"Always." Was there relief in his voice? Had he been afraid to say anything more?

I took a deep breath. My lips were dry and my tongue didn't want to unknot, but I *had* to know. "Did you sleep with Danielle?"

C

Okay, I got a news flash for you, Bob. I am not brain-dead and never have been. Did it occur to me that Danielle's, well, jealousy wasn't only because I'd gotten the TA position and she hadn't? Duh.

But there were things I kept coming back to, David Melman being the primary reason why I didn't think Mitch and Danielle had ever been together. Danielle and David had been a couple for over a year, since David was a sophomore and Danielle was a freshman.

Now, was it true that Mitch was friendly to everyone? Yes. Were people always coming to him with their problems? Ditto. Could Danielle have a huge problem she might've spilled, hoping Mitch could help? Well, maybe so. After a psych ward, not only can one crazy pick out another in a crowd, but the broken ones can, too. Honestly, Mitch and I were so careful, there was no way anyone knew. But Danielle had sensed something, and I thought that could only happen if she was a lot closer to Mitch than I knew.

Here's what kept flashing before my eyes: the image of Mr. Connolly jamming his finger into Mitch's chest; Mr. Connolly shoving Mitch—and the way Mitch stood there and took it.

Like, maybe, he deserved it.

d

Mitch said, "Is that what you think?"

"I don't want it to be true," I said. "But I want you to tell me the truth. I'm old enough for that, too."

"I know that." He darted a glance my way. His skin was gray-green in the lights from the dash and his eyes were glittery black, like polished obsidian. "No, I didn't, Jenna. I was never even tempted. You're . . . you're the only one, ever."

"But there's something."

"Yes. But . . . damn it. Jenna, honey, I can't tell you what that is."

"Why not?"

"Would you want me telling other kids about you, your mom, your father? What you've told me, you've said in confidence. Even if we weren't lovers, you trust me. It's the same for Danielle, sweetheart. She's dealing with a lot. I haven't been there for her the way I used to, and she's hurt and that's really my problem, not yours."

Lovers. I wasn't prepared for how that little word made me feel. Breathless, I guess, and a little afraid, too. Like the word was almost a promise. I was Mitch's lover; I was someone no one else had ever been. "Can you at least tell me what her father said?"

He hesitated for only a moment. "He told me to mind my own business," he said, then added ruefully, "and that she's too young to know what she wants."

C

The CD clicked off. The wipers thumped. The snow was falling fast, sheeting like a heavy rain through which the truck's headlights cored a cold, bright tunnel. Maybe the snow was a good thing, though, because it gave Mitch someplace else to look and, I think, made it easier for him to do what he did next.

Mitch said, so softly I almost didn't catch it, "I haven't told you everything, though. About Kathy and me."

My insides went still. I wanted to say that he hadn't really told me anything because I had been so careful not to ask. Kathy was a black hole whose event horizon would kill us. But, somehow, I found the words. "It's about the baby, isn't it?"

He said nothing for a moment, but I felt his surprise. "I'd forgotten about that picture," he said.

"Is her dad really sick?"

"With cancer? Yes. I wouldn't lie about that. It would be too awful. But he's not so sick that she needs to stay."

"So why is she? Is it because of the baby?"

"Yes and no." He went quiet for so long I thought he might not say anything else. Then he sighed. "The first time Kathy got pregnant, she also got very . . . depressed. I missed it. I chalked up her moodiness and all that to, you know, what happens when you're pregnant. I just didn't understand what I was looking at. I didn't even find out until a lot later that she had a history of depression. Been in a hospital, suicide attempts with pills, the whole nine yards. Anyway, she relapsed. Pills again, and she slit her wrists. Insurance, I guess. She's alive only because all the blood scared her and she called her mother."

"Where were you?"

"Away." He gave a bleak laugh. "Diving. I told you I gave that up when my dad yanked me out of Stanford, but that's not entirely true. Kathy and I argued about it a lot. We're . . . opposites, but sometimes you only really find out things like that when it's too late. I was mad at my family, and I got married too fast, too young, on the rebound, and for spite when you get right down to it. Anyway, I wanted to move, take our chances, go to grad school." He sighed again. "Try to salvage something. But Kathy wasn't having any of that. She lost that first baby—

miscarried right in the emergency room—and then getting pregnant again, having another baby, was all she could think about. She'd decided it was my fault, too, for not being there. Never mind that it was the pills that did it."

"Did you want another baby?"

"No. I hadn't wanted the first one, but I felt so guilty. Getting married was my idea; I rushed us into it. Letting go of what I'd wanted to be made me feel so . . . empty." He bunched a fist over his chest. "Like everything I'd ever been, every dream, was gone and now there was only this hole. I tried to fill it with all the things that are supposed to make you happy: a wife, a house, a job. Don't get me wrong. I'm not an asshole. I did love Kathy, but sometimes I wonder if I used her as a kind of distraction so I wouldn't dwell on what I'd lost. Anyway, after I realized my mistake, I wasn't brave enough to undo it and then all I could do was keep running in place, trying to fix us. And now, finding out that she was ill, I was so scared she'd try again that I couldn't say no even though I didn't see how she could handle herself much less a child. Know what her answer was to that?"

"What?"

"For me to quit teaching, be with her 24-7. But I couldn't do it. Teaching was the last thing that was truly mine. At school, I could be closer to what I always thought of as the real *me*, and now she wanted that, too. I felt like . . . Jenna, it was like drowning in slow-motion. Our lives were contracting, collapsing. And then she got pregnant again. I'm not blaming her for that." He paused then said, wryly, "Obviously, I helped."

He fell silent again. This time, I spoke first. "What happened, Mitch? To the baby?"

"It died," he said. "Stillborn. We knew it would be because I . . . I convinced Kathy to get a sonogram."

"I don't understand."

"Her mom had a couple miscarriages and her sister, too. She would never have told me either except it all came out after she tried to kill herself. So I know enough to know that a family history of miscarriages is sometimes a bad sign. She didn't want genetic testing; she didn't even want a sonogram. She fought me the whole way, but when I threatened to leave, she caved and I won that one." He gave a bitter laugh. "Oh boy, did I ever. The sono showed that the baby was anencephalic."

Anencephalic: no head. My stomach went cold. I didn't know medicine, but I know words, Bobby-o.

"The whole top half of the baby's skull just wasn't there. Not much of a brain either. The baby would either die right after birth or in utero. There's no way to fix something like that. Most people would have an abortion, but Kathy wouldn't do it. No matter what, she would deliver that baby and there wasn't a damn thing I could do about it. It was . . ." He swallowed. "It was horrible. The thing was a monster. You can't know what that's like, Jenna, to know you *made* something like that. I watched Kathy hold and cry over it as if it were the most beautiful child ever born . . . and I just . . . I couldn't . . ."

"Mitch." I put my hand on his thigh. "You couldn't know. You had no control over that."

"But I did, Jenna, don't you see?" He pulled in a shaky breath. "If I had said no . . . if I'd been half the man I always thought I was we'd never have made that baby in the first place. I told myself I was stuck, no way out, that this was kinder than a divorce, but that's not true. I made a choice. I won't say it was easier because that would be a lie. Everything I've done to fix this only breaks it just a little bit more. If I were really brave, I'd end it. No matter what my part has been, I can't be responsible for her happiness forever. So . . . that's where we are. I guess you'd say we're separated. I haven't seen her since February."

Almost ten months. "Do you want to get back together with her?" You don't know what it cost me to ask that, Bob. But I did it.

"Oh, God, Jenna, I don't know," he said. "Most days, I don't think so. She's nobody I recognize anymore. We tear at each other, bring out the worst, and I'm so tired. Not having her around is a relief, but that makes me feel guilty. Isn't that crazy? I mean, she's sick and so I should keep trying, right? That's what a good person does. But then there are other times when I sit in that cabin and stare at the lake and think about how my life was before . . . and part of me wishes I could go back and stop all this before it ever has a chance to start. But I'm stuck. I can't go back and be what I was, and we can't move forward because what I thought we were is a lie."

I heard what he felt. He might as well have been telling me the story of Rubicon Point all over again: whether it's true that you can fall in water or only hover over the abyss. He was there, all over again, and I was down there with him.

"Mitch," I said, "do you want to fix it?"

Silence. The thump of the wipers. The whirr of the heater. And silence.

Then:

"No," he said. "No, Jenna, I don't think I do anymore."

40: a

When we finally turned onto my road, it was nearly midnight. We'd driven behind a snow plow on the main interstate, but they hadn't gotten around to the smaller secondary roads and wouldn't for hours. Once off the highway, the road disappeared beneath a white carpet. Although I knew where other houses ought to be, it was like the trees had crept in with the darkness to swallow them whole. A hump of snow crouched over the mailbox at the end of my parents' driveway. I made out only the barest glimmer of light at the very top of the hill where the house was. Mitch slowed, but instead of turning into the driveway, he pulled to the side of the road.

"Mitch?"

No answer.

"Mitch?"

No answer. He only stared straight ahead. I have no idea what he saw, Bob. Then he killed the headlights and, after another moment, the engine.

Darkness swallowed the truck. A fist of wind grabbed and shook the chassis. Snow sizzled over the windshield.

I groped for his hand. The cab was warm from the heater, but his fingers were ice. At my touch, he said, brokenly, "Oh God."

"Mitch." As my eyes adjusted, I could just make out the dim outline of his head and shoulders. "Mitch. Talk to me. Are you okay?"

He gave a sudden, savage groan. "*Nooooooo.*" He jammed a balled fist into his thigh, hard: once, twice, three times. "No, no, *no, I'm not, I'm not, I'm*—"

"Mitch!" Now I was scared and so I did the only thing I could think of to try and make it better. I grabbed his fist in both hands before he could hurt himself again. "Stop, *stop*. Mitch, I'm here, I'm *here*."

At my touch, his shoulders heaved and I heard something claw its way from his throat. He began to sag; my arms opened to catch him before he could fall anymore and then I was holding him up, the way he'd once held me, as he let himself go.

I'd never heard a man cry before, Bob, but . . . it's awful. Maybe you cry all the time, I don't know. Given your job, I'll bet it's tough not to some days. But I think some men aren't used to it and don't know what to do with all that feeling. Their emotions are hexane ignited in a closed space: an explosion that detonates deep in their chests and rips them apart, and then they feel like they're going to die—just as something was dying, at that moment, in Mitch.

Everybody breaks sooner or later, Bob. Anyone can drown. Sometimes you see it. Most often, you don't because the body protects and the skin hides, so drowning doesn't look like drowning and some people scar so nicely.

Take it from an expert.

b

Anyway.

We were there for a while, long enough for the cold to leak into the truck. I listened to the hiss of snow against the windshield and the creak of the truck and Mitch's grief, and I cradled his head against my chest and hung on. Finally, he sighed and pulled back, but he didn't let go, not completely, and neither did I.

"Oh, Jenna." His voice was husky and tremulous. "When I saw you fall . . . when you went down, I was frantic. I was so scared. I wanted to *kill* Danielle, I was that angry. I was furious."

"It was an accident. I should have been paying attention."

"No. *No*, that's a lie. I have eyes; I know what I saw. I know what she did. But, in a way, she did me a favor, too, because it hit me that if anything happened to you, *really* happened . . . I don't know what I'd do."

"Mitch." I touched his face. His cheeks were wet; his skin jumped beneath my fingers. We were teetering on the brink of something. "I'm *okay* now. I'll be fine."

"But I won't. I'm *not*, don't you see? Because I'm in love with you, Jenna," he whispered. "I'm in love with you . . . and I'm so afraid to really let myself know what this means."

"Afraid." I didn't understand. I couldn't catch my breath. My head felt filled with helium, and I was dizzy again and my mouth was dry and yet every inch of my body was suddenly alive and electric. "Mitch, why—"

"Because you don't know how long it's been since I've wanted to say that to anyone. But I do and loving you changes everything—and I love you." He pressed my hand to his chest so I could feel the hard, fast thump of his heart. "This is what you do for me." He guided my hand, slowly, to his lap and I heard the hitch in his voice, the low animal sound he made in the back of his throat at the instant I found him. "This is what only you can do *to* me," he said, thickly, pulling me closer. "You're the only one, Jenna, the only one."

"All I see is you," I said, and then my hands pulled at his shirt and his slipped beneath my clothing to cup my breasts but so carefully, as if I might break. But I needed the taut muscles of his arms and back and his full weight; I wanted all of him because at that moment I knew I was strong enough to hold him in this new and different way: in this and what we were in the love and the world we made together in this space, at that moment.

"Please love me, Jenna, please hold me, please save me," and then he was groaning; his mouth was a fever trailing down my neck, his tongue teasing mine and then my breasts, his hands knotting in my hair, and then we began to move together, and there was nothing but this and this and this and this and him.

"Love me, Jenna, please," he gasped. "Love me, love me, love me, love me."

41: a

A little over a week later, it was Thanksgiving.

After Matt, Thanksgiving became all about Black Friday. Before Matt left, Black Friday was important but not all-consuming. Mom had more money on hand, her credit was good, and she had staff to handle most of the headaches. Then Matt left and things began to unravel. Black Friday became the reason why Meryl started coming down a day earlier, on Tuesday instead of Wednesday. If I've learned to cook at all, it's because of Meryl, not my mom.

Now I don't mean that negatively, Bob; don't go all Freudian on me. But I defy any person, man or woman, to manage a store that's more than an hour away from home and on a shoe-string, and still have the energy to slap on an apron and rustle up some gourmet grub in a half hour or less. I admit: when Matt was still alive—

b

Well.

I had to turn off the recorder there for a second, Bobby-o, because I just realized something. I'm actually kind of curious. This thing rewinds and I see the button to erase everything, but is there some kind of search function? You know, for phrases or certain words? The reason I'm asking . . . I'll bet if I went back and reviewed everything I've said so far, I'll bet good money this is the first time I've said *when Matt was alive*.

Like I've reached the point in my story when those words are okay to say out loud.

I guess, before Mitch, I'd been in stasis, another little bubble alongside real time but in which, somehow, Matt fought his endless war. Well, Mitch broke that wide, wide open. Matt was dead, and Mitch had pulled me out of a land inhabited by ghosts.

So whatever happens, Bob, you remember this.

If Mitch did nothing else for me, he did that.

c

So our routine at Thanksgiving now—with Matt dead and gone—went something like this. Mom worked her butt off Tuesday and Wednesday. Dad did the same. After Matt died, he frequently worked on Thanksgiving, too. Holiday traffic accidents are a shock trauma plastic surgeon's wet dream. We'd do a guilt visit to Grandpa MacAllister either on Saturday or Sunday, depending on when Dad straggled back.

And, for once, I didn't care. Because I had Mitch and all that couldn't hurt me anymore.

d

Thanksgiving morning dawned wintry and cold: two feet of new snow on the ground under a full sun so fabulously bright I had to squint against the glare. I lay under my quilt and thought about Mitch, what he'd said the week before. How our bodies fit together. How I still felt. Even more than the morning after we'd first slept together, I was transformed. I was a woman. I was loved and I loved someone in return. This kind of obsession was delicious and wonderful, and I never wanted it to end.

Eyes closed, I imagined that Mitch was there with me. What was it really like to wake up in the morning next to someone you loved? I wanted to find out. Mitch was down in Madison with one of his sisters for the holiday, and I wondered if maybe he was lying in bed, too, thinking of me. Then that stirred up more thoughts and other, better feelings.

I might have stayed there another drowsy hour, but the kitchen smells of coffee and baked apple pancakes (Meryl's specialty) were just too much torture to ignore. I rolled out of my warm bed. My ankle protested with a tiny little bark, then subsided. Definitely on the mend.

Whatever magic Mom and Dad had conjured together was still working because they slept late. So it was just Meryl and me in the kitchen. Meryl had the radio tuned to classic rock, and Robert Plant was singing about that stairway to heaven as I worked over the baked yams for a casserole.

Meryl said, "You're looking better."

"Thanks." I scooped out yam guts. "The ankle only hurts a little bit."

"I wasn't talking about your ankle." Meryl was patting the turkey dry. Before Meryl, I'd never seen anyone bone a bird and there was a certain art to cutting so the skin remained unbroken. She squared the turkey breast-side down on the cutting board and picked up a boning knife. "I meant you, in general. You're glowing."

"Oh." I picked up another warm yam and sliced it open. Steam curled as I dug out baked yam and added that to a mixing bowl. "It must be the running. School's going pretty well."

"Uh-huh." Meryl cut a deep slit along the turkey's backbone from neck to tail then whacked off the tail and tossed it to one side for the stockpot. Deftly scraping the knife along one side of the carcass, she used her fingers to tug the flesh away from bone. "So who is he?"

"Uhm." I debated whether to lie then thought that if I didn't mention names . . . "It's kind of not official. I don't want to jinx anything." It helped that this was mostly true. "Mom and Dad don't know." Also true.

"Oh, I don't doubt that." Meryl started on the other side of the carcass. "You aren't doing anything stupid, are you?"

"You expect me to answer that?"

"No. I just had to ask. Anyway, now I know: you *are*."

"Meryl." I changed the subject. "Mom and Dad are doing a lot better."

"For as long as it lasts." By now, the turkey was an unrecognizable mass of flesh and skin, dangling legs and wings. Meryl worked the boning knife along the softer breastbone, being careful not to rip through the thin skin there. I squashed yams and stirred in butter and cinnamon. On the stereo, Sting said he'd be watching me.

"Listen, I don't pretend to be an expert in romance. I've never been married, never had kids. But I know your parents pretty well." She paused to peer over her glasses. Her eyes were bird-bright. "You ever get tired of the craziness here, you come live with me."

"I'm okay," I said.

"For now." She cut through the joint of one drumstick and pulled out a thigh bone. "A boyfriend can make you feel like you're invulnerable, that nothing can hurt you. But everyone has to come down from that high, eventually. Sometimes, when you do, it's not very nice."

"Mmmm." I didn't know what to say. I wasn't sure what she was really saying. Right then, I was more rattled that she could read how I felt, even if she thought I was in love with someone my age. I had to watch that. I was thinking so hard about that I missed what she said next. "Sorry. What?"

She washed her hands and then reached for a large, blue porcelain bowl filled with oyster stuffing. Spreading out the turkey skin-side down, she spooned gray stuffing blobs onto the dark, pink flesh. "I said, that teacher of yours . . . Anderson? Your mother says he's taken an interest. He does seem to go above and beyond. First, the night of your mom's party and then driving you home after the meet last week. . . . Not many teachers I know would be willing to get that involved."

A little warning *ding* in my brain. Another thing therapy teaches you, Bob, is how to read between the lines and then feed people answers they'll accept. It's like makeup, Bob; there's an art to smoothing on enough truth so those ugly zits don't show. Or scars, for that matter.

So I shrugged. "Well, I like him a lot. Most everybody does. But I kind of worry that I'm imposing too much, you know? It's really embarrassing having to cover for Mom and

Dad all the time. I feel like I'm taking advantage of him, except Dad's been all over me to get close to my teachers for recommendations. What's worse is, I think some of the other kids think I'm a teacher's pet and I don't want that either and . . ." I sighed. "Meryl, I just don't know what to do."

And score one for counterintuitive responses. While I dumped brown sugar and butter into the yam mash, Meryl threaded a trussing needle and then gave me pointers on how to not look like a suck-up as she sewed that turkey back together again. By the time Mom and Dad stumbled down for coffee and warmed-up apple pancakes, we were onto my visiting her on the island during Easter break in time for spring lambing, and all talk of me and Mitch was over, covered, and done.

e

Everything that happened after that? I blame Green Bay.

The Packers played the early game and got their collective heads handed to them on a platter by Chicago. By halftime, when the score was 31 to 14 and Dad came storming into the kitchen to trade his beer for Scotch, we knew it was going to be a rocky afternoon. The turkey was out of the oven by the time Green Bay finished cratering. Twenty minutes later, Dad was grimly carving the turkey like it was brain surgery and spoiling for a fight. I think that's why he gave me white meat. He probably hoped I'd complain and then he could yell and blow off steam and maybe stab the giblets, and we could get on with the meal.

The dining room was silent except for the sounds of people chewing and the click-click-tick of silver on good china. My father gnawed morosely on a drumstick. He looked like Og.

Even not having run for the last week, I was still starving and white meat just doesn't do it for me. So I reached for the other drumstick and said, just for form's sake, "Does anyone mind if I—?"

"Not so fast," Psycho-Dad snarled. "You've still got food on your plate, young lady. You finish that first, then we can talk about seconds."

My jaw unhinged. Mom and Meryl stared. Mom said, reasonably, "Honey, you know she doesn't like white me—"

"Stay out of this, Emily." Psycho-Dad thrust out his jaw. "I am sick and tired of the way you coddle her. She's over all that . . . ." He gestured with his half-gnawed drumstick. Bits of flesh bobbed on strings of tendon and ligaments. "That psychiatric bullshit. She's not going to break. She gets everything she wants. Didn't we get her that damn phone? And a car?"

Mom stupidly, stupidly tried again. "Elliot, dear. Please. Lower your voice."

"Mom, it's fine," I said. "I'm not hungry."

Meryl put her hand on Mom's arm. "Emily, I think . . ."

Mom ignored us both. "She's sixteen, Elliot. You're treating her like a four-year-old. You need to stop bullying people."

"I am not a bully," Psycho-Dad seethed. He threw his drumstick onto his plate and swiped a heavy cut-glass tumbler, still a third full of Scotch. He drained the liquor in a swallow. "I'm her father," he said, sucking air through his teeth, his voice thin and strangled with the alcohol burn. "I pay the bills around here. I pay for the food on this table and the clothes on your back and that store. You're just lucky I've done that for as long as I have."

If only he had stopped there, we might still have been all right. I do remember that he paused, just for a moment, as if thinking about what he wanted to say next. Maybe he even considered that silence would be kinder, although I doubt it.

Instead, Psycho-Dad gave this small, very satisfied nod and pushed on. "But I'm sick of it. It's time things changed around here."

"What's that supposed to mean?" asked Mom.

I scraped back my chair. "I'll start clear—"

"Sit," said Psycho-Dad. He didn't say *stay*, but he might as well have. I sat.

Mom's eyes narrowed. "Elliot? What did you mean *change*?"

Dad's face was ruddy. He reached for a bottle, splashed wine into his glass and drank. Maybe he'd pass out before he did more damage.

"Elliot?"

Dad came up for air. His upper lip was wet. Red wine dribbled from the corner of his mouth like blood. "I mean that I'm pulling my collateral for your line of credit. That store is finished and I'm done, Emily. I'm done."

f

Mom went absolutely still. Meryl froze, and so did I. I knew that Mom had come to depend, more and more heavily, on credit to meet her bills every month. For the last half year, that was the only thing standing between her and no store at all. The only reason the bank let her keep it was because Dad put up some of his assets as collateral. Without my father, my mother would have no credit at all. Without that, she couldn't pay Evan or her rent or keep up a full inventory. She'd ordered massive amounts of books, hoping this Christmas season her business would turn around. Now, she was nearly at the end of the month, the day before what she hoped would be a huge shopping day but hadn't been for years—and now, if Psycho-Dad meant what he said, no way to pay down her debt.

"My God," my mother said, finally. "This is like when we pulled Jenna out of the hospital. You didn't just decide this. You already knew you were going to do this when we had the party, didn't you? A month ago! You knew *then*."

Psycho-Dad took another swallow. "What if I did?"

"Then this whole last month, our trip, everything you said, that we *did* . . . " Mom's lips compressed to a gash. "What did you think, Elliot? Did you think screwing me again would make it easier to fuck me over?" Coming out of her mouth, the words were so much uglier. "That I wouldn't *mind*?"

"Of course not." Psycho-Dad managed a look of indignation. "I'm thinking of us, of protecting our position. That store is a money pit, you've said it yourself. You should be relieved. I'm only thinking of you." But the way his eyes slid from my mother's, I knew he was lying.

"Thinking of *me*? This is about you and your precious money. You son of a . . ." She choked back the rest and then stood, slowly, as regally as a queen. "You do what you need to do, Elliot, but don't sneak around. Be a man for once."

My father blustered. "You can't talk to me like th—"

"Fuck. You. Elliot." She waited a moment, but my father had clamped his jaws so tight I'd heard the click. She said, "Do what you want. I don't give a damn." She swept out.

He didn't go after her. Neither did Meryl. Maybe I should have, Bob. Matt wasn't her only kid. If I'd reminded her that I was here, too. . . .

I wish I'd been braver, but I was paralyzed. And afraid.

Because what if I wasn't enough either? What if I had never been?

I didn't want to know, Bob. I didn't. Everyone breaks. Some wounds will never heal, and I just couldn't, I couldn't.

So, instead, I only sat and listened to her cursing and rummaging in the hall closet. When she slammed out of the house, the windows chattered. A moment later, the garage door grumbled; her car roared; and then she was gone.

42: a

After Mom left, Dad and his Scotch stormed off to his study. Meryl and I cleared the table. I scrubbed pots and pans and cleaned counters. I might have gotten down on my hands and knees to scour the tile if Meryl hadn't stopped me.

"I'm going after your mom." She'd already shrugged into her coat and was knotting a scarf around her throat. "Thank God, the roads are clear or she'd have gone off a bridge. She's probably at the store. You want to come with?"

I didn't. After Meryl left, I snagged a cinnamon roll and went to my room. I picked up Lasker's book on Alexis, then put it back down without cracking the spine. The book reminded me of how much I missed Mitch, and I ached to hear his voice. Normally, I'd have been able to talk to him, either in school or on the phone or a text. In person, if we were running—or after: showering, toweling off. Making love.

But Mitch was in Madison until Sunday night and while I probably *could* call or text, he wouldn't be able to talk. He might not even answer. After all, there were limits to what you could explain away.

I needed to get out of that house. Go someplace I could breathe. Incredibly, my car was still down at school. I'd missed school the day after the meet; and then it was break. We kept meaning to retrieve my car, but Mom got busy with the store and we just hadn't gotten around to it.

But there *was* Dad's Lexus.

After tucking the Lasker book, my wallet, and cell into my knapsack, I tiptoed into my parents' bedroom. Dad's keys were on the bureau, along with his wallet and pager. I worked the key off the ring and then crept down the stairs to stand outside his study. I heard the television and what sounded like another game, but Dad was talking to someone, too, probably his nursie-mistress or some moral equivalent because I caught a couple words: *inconsiderate bitch . . . want to . . . miss you, too . . .*

I honestly didn't care. What with Nate Bartholomew and Mistress Nursie, I think I'd decided my parents deserved each other.

b

Lucky for me, the Lexus was all-the-time four-wheel drive and had good tires. I took it slow as I drove to Mitch's house. I worried about how to explain away my dad's car in his driveway—but the hike from the park was a good eight miles. My ankle wasn't that bad, but I didn't want to push it. Anyway, Mitch's house wasn't visible from the road and his nearest neighbor was miles away. I should be okay.

It had snowed twice more since the week before, but the Lexus took the packed snow and hills easily and Mitch's drive had been plowed. I pulled up to the house, climbed out, and listened to a

283

silence broken only by the susurration of the wind that spun snow into icy dervishes. Mitch's house was all sparkling glass, wood, and stone under the full sun, and felt empty even from the outside.

I already had my boots, but now I buckled on a pair of snowshoes and trudged around to the back of the house and looked across the white expanse of frozen lake. Mitch said the lake froze completely in winter, but it was still early in the season, the cold temperatures of the last two weeks notwithstanding. I could halve my travel time to the cabin if I cut across the lake, and there were prints where animals had crossed. But Mitch said the lake was very deep and visions of breaking through the ice kept me on the path instead.

The only sounds were the squeal of snow beneath my snowshoes and the steady huff of my breaths. My ankle complained a bit, then subsided. Sweat trickled down my neck and between my shoulder blades, and as I began to warm, I unzipped my parka and then my fleece. I hiked along for a good hour and when I turned onto the cabin trail, I don't recall that I was thinking about much of anything other than stripping down and enjoying a hot shower before making tea and curling up on our window seat with Lasker's book. As I rounded the last bend, I looked toward the cabin—

And stopped dead in my tracks.

No, I thought. *No, that's not right.*

C

A thin rivulet of gray smoke trickled from the chimney. Two windows fired with a yellow light that was not a reflection of the sun.

Someone was in our cabin. Mitch? But he was down in Madison, wasn't he? I hadn't looked in his garage. I had no reason. Was Mitch—?

I wasn't watching the trail and my shoe caught in a branch and then the snow was rushing at my face. I managed to get my arms out in time to avoid a spectacular face-plant, but not by much. Spitting and snorting snow, I dragged a gloved hand across my watering eyes and got to my feet.

That's when I saw something white and ghostly dart across a window to the right of the door, and then the blurry oval of a face.

A face that was not Mitch's at all.

d

I went absolutely still.

I'd only registered a face: a general impression of dark eyes and the gash of a mouth. Then whoever was in the cabin backed away and out of sight.

I stood there as snow melted on my neck and my heart thumped. My brain churned. Someone must've found the key. A homeless person? Maybe a runaway. Either was possible. Mitch said that people broke into cabins all the time. Maybe some of those people were dangerous. Whoever was inside must have come in from the park or the opposite side of the lake because mine were the only tracks on this path. Either way, they'd either bypassed the house intentionally or accidentally stumbled on the cabin.

What should I do? If I called the police, what would I say? What *could* I say that wouldn't get Mitch and me both in big trouble?

It came to me then that I was completely alone. No one knew where I was. Mitch was gone, too far away to help. I had my cell, but I'd left it behind in the Lexus, figuring that if Psycho-Dad called, I could legitimately say I hadn't known or gotten the message until later.

I was on my own, and I'd been *seen*.

The thought stroked gooseflesh on my arms and raised the hairs on my neck. I shivered, partly from sweat chilling on my skin but mostly from fear. Whoever was in the cabin knew I was here.

Get out, I thought. *Get out now.*

You can't back up in snowshoes, but you can turn around and hustle pretty quick. Which is exactly what I did. Twice I looked over my shoulder to see if some crazy meth head was bursting out of the cabin, ax in hand. But there was no one, only the constant stream of smoke and sun-dazzle bouncing off the windows.

When I made it back to the car, there were eight calls from my father on the cell. All the messages were the same, more or less. Only the profanity changed.

43: a

It was full dark by the time I got home. Meryl was back and my father was snorting fire—just not at me.

"We'll talk about punishment for you later," he said, scrubbing away my explanations with the flat of his hand. "Right now, I want to know where your mother is."

"Uh . . ." I shot a glance at Meryl. Thought: *Shit, Mom really is with Bartholomew.* Decided to play dumb. "She's not at the store?"

"No, and she's not answering her cell," Meryl said. "Your father called all the hospitals, but of course, she isn't there and there hasn't been an accident. Elliot, calm down before you have a stroke."

He ignored her. "Do you know where she is?" he asked me.

"No," I said, which was mostly true. Sure, I knew *who* she was with, but not *where*. "Have you tried Evan?"

"Of course. He hasn't heard from her either."

"Then she's probably just driving around."

"That's what I told him," Meryl said. "Where were *you*?"

"I was driving around, too," I said.

My father seemed to see me for the first time. "You're wet."

"I fell in the snow."

"I thought you said you were driving around."

"I went for a walk." I was still freaked about the cabin and just so sick of their drama. "Look, I'm sure Mom's okay. She's just angry, Dad. What did you expect? She was going to be thrilled you decided to let her store crater?"

"Don't tell me you're taking her side in this. This is for her own good." My father's lower lip actually pouched. He looked like a three-year-old ready to take his ball and go home. "You and she will both see that, eventually."

"It's not important what I see. But you have to give her some space to be mad. Why is it okay for you to storm off to the hospital whenever you get pissed off but not okay for Mom?"

"She's got you there," Meryl put in.

"Stay out of this." Dad glared down at me, but for once, I wasn't frightened of him, maybe because I'd already gotten my allotment of having the shit scared of me. "While you were gone, we got a call from Pine Manor. Apparently, your mother went to see your grandfather after she left here."

That was a surprise. "Mom did that? Why were they calling us?"

"Because he was so agitated when she left they had to put him in restraints and they wanted to know if anything unusual had—"

"Restraints?" I interrupted. God, what had Mom said? "What did she *do*?"

"They don't know, and neither do we. I want you to call her."

"You said she's not answering her cell. Maybe she switched it off."

"No, it rings. She . . . she's clearly screening her calls. So it's me . . . my cell, she doesn't want . . . but maybe she'll . . . if it's you . . . if you'd just please . . ." My father's face mottled an angry, embarrassed vermillion. I'd never known him to be reduced to incomplete sentences. He was mortified to have to beg his daughter to do something. "Will you *please* call her?"

My eyes shifted to Meryl. "She won't pick up for me either," she said. "Much as I hate to side with your father, I think it would be good if we knew she's safe."

So I dialed, listened to the rings, then heard my mother tell me to leave a message. "Hi, Mom, it's Jenna. I'm going to hang up and call you again. Please answer." I punched out, counted to ten then redialed.

Mom picked up at the first ring. "I'm fine," she said. "I'm more than fine. I'm great."

"Uhm . . ." Dad looked ready to swoop, so I turned away. "Are you going to come home?"

"Maybe. Eventually. I don't know." Was that a slur I heard? The image of my mother squatting somewhere, with a Stoli bottle clutched in one hand, flashed before my eyes. "I have to decide what to do."

"Okay." I didn't have the slightest idea if she meant about her marriage, us, the store, or all three.

"Ask her where she is," Dad hissed.

"Shut up, Elliot," Meryl said.

"Is that your father?" asked Mom, and then she went on before I could answer: "Of course, it is. Lis . . . lishun, honey, lis . . . lishun."

"I'm listening," I said, but my heart sank. Her esses always went mushy when she drank. I could only hope she wasn't in her car. "Mom, are you driving?"

"No, no . . . I . . . lis-lishun. . . ."

"Where are you, Mom?"

"Jenna, Jenna . . . No matter what, I want you to know I only did what I thought was besh . . . right. I wash trying to protect you, but I didn't, I didn't *know*. . . ."

"Mom? Mom, what are you talking about?"

"Oh, Matt," she said, and then she was crying. "I don't know what I would've done without Matt. I couldn't have st-st-st . . . lived with my-my . . . myself if he . . ." Her words came out in a howl: "Oh, I mish my baby; I mish my boy . . ."

"Mom." My eyes were burning. "Mom, tell me where you are. I'll come to you."

"What's she saying?" Dad asked.

I smeared tears from my cheeks. "Mom, please; Meryl and I, we can come together. Mom? *Mom?*"

But there was only dead air. I called back twice, but Mom never did pick up.

b

There wasn't much to be done after that. We sprawled in the family room, me tucked in a comforter and my head on Meryl's lap, and Dad, rigid in his chair, staring at his cell and our land-line, willing either to ring. *The Wizard of Oz* was on, a film I normally love, but honestly, listening to Judy Garland made me think of Mitch. I was desperate to talk to him, if for nothing else than for him to tell me that everything would be all right, that he was thinking of me.

The next thing I knew, Meryl was shaking me awake and Dad was shouting into the phone: "What what what *where* . . . ?"

Fear slammed into my chest and I scrambled up, wide awake. "Meryl?"

"I'm sorry, honey." Meryl's face was whiter than salt. "But there's been an accident."

44: a

Black Friday.

Meryl drove as fast as she dared, but we still didn't make it down to Milwaukee until after two that morning. Dad was on the phone almost the whole way, talking with the doctors, and the only reassuring thing about that was it meant Mom wasn't dead. Yet. I sat in the backseat, clutching my knapsack. Dad didn't hang up until we'd blasted off the interstate onto the exit ramp for the hospital.

"What did they say?" Meryl demanded.

Dad stared straight ahead. "It sounds a lot more complicated than we know."

"What does that mean?" I asked, but Dad just shook his head again.

There were three other people in the ER waiting room: a drunk sleeping in a far chair with his head propped up on his elbow; another guy with a blood-stained towel bunched in one fist; and one man, in a rumpled gray suit, who looked like he really didn't belong because he wasn't drunk, bleeding, or in obvious pain. When we told the ER nurse who we were, the man's head came up and I felt his eyes on our backs. Then I forgot about him because the ER nurse made us wait a few minutes despite Dad's bluster. She was on the phone for what seemed a year before confirming that my mother was indeed a patient. She said we could go up, but wouldn't let Meryl through because she wasn't immediate family.

"It's okay, sweetie, I'll wait right here." Meryl wrapped me in a big bear hug that I never wanted to end. "Give your mom a hug and a kiss for me, okay?"

Even at night, the Burn Unit is never quiet but filled with monitor beeps and alarms going off and nurses and doctors in squeaky shoes shuffling in and out of various rooms. The nurse led us to Mom's room, which was right across from the nurses' station, and I knew what that meant, too, because I'd been there, done that, bought the T-shirt. They always put the sickest people where the nurses can get to them in a hurry.

We gowned up because the infection risk for burn victims is so high. The smell in Mom's room made my stomach churn because it was so familiar: disinfectant and cooked blood and the sweet stink of roast pork.

(My mother, shrieking, fighting with the EMTs: *Don't you save that son of a . . .*)

She looked so small, swathed in a nest of bandages. Her arms and legs were up on pillows, and what little skin was exposed—the places that weren't completely cooked but only second-degree burns—was shiny with antibiotic ointment. There were monitors and tubes coiling everywhere, IVs and catheters and a breathing tube down Mom's throat. Mom was out, sedated because she kept fighting the tube and the doctors wanted to control the pain.

Dad's skin above his mask was chalky. His eyebrows looked like smears of shoe polish on white marble. For once he only listened as the burn doctor talked in numbers and percentages: third-degree burns over sixty-five percent of her body, second-degree over twenty percent.

"Then there's the complicating fact of her drinking," the doctor said, his tone neutral. "Her respiratory status is also severely compromised. There's been extensive epithelial injury and she's developed significant pulmonary edema. We've got her on CPAP, of course, but—"

"Bottom line," my dad cut in. "What are her chances?"

"Given her age, fifty-fifty, maybe a little worse. If we can get her through the next twenty-four, forty-eight hours, then it will be a question of controlling infection and . . ." The doctor went on like that for a while. Then he said, "Our next biggest concern will be finding enough viable skin for grafting. There's just not a lot left to harvest."

"Take mine." I looked up at the doctor. "Take whatever you need."

"Jenna," my dad said.

"It doesn't work that way," the doctor said, kindly. "The only skin that will take is her own. We can cover her burn sites with cadaver skin or pigskin, but those are temporary measures. The skin over those sites will eventually die and need to be replaced. We can grow new skin for her in the lab, using her cells, but that will take time."

"But you can harvest mine, right? If you can use a dead person's skin, why not mine?" I asked.

"Because your skin will die, too." The doctor's eyes were sympathetic, but his voice was firm. "I'm sorry, but that's just not an option." Then he and Dad moved out of the room to talk medical strategy.

I stood by my mother. Her face was almost completely hidden by rust-splotched bandages and very swollen, just her eyes and part of her mouth showing. The machine breathing for her pushed air in and then sucked it out with a long sigh. I wanted to take her hand and tell her it would be okay, but I was afraid. I had images of her fingers breaking off in my hand. I felt so helpless and small. This must be what she'd felt like, too, after the fire at Grandpa MacAllister's that killed me twice over: once in the ambulance and then two days later, in a place very similar to this.

"How's she doing?"

I turned, blinking away tears. A man, in gown and gloves and mask, had come up behind me, so quietly I hadn't heard.

"Who are you?" Then I saw his eyes above the mask. "You were in the emergency room."

He nodded, stuck out his hand and said—

Can you guess, Bobby-o? Do you remember?

"We've met before, though you were a lot younger and probably don't remember. I'm Robert Pendleton. I'm a detective." Your eyes crinkled above your mask. "But, please, just call me Bob."

45: a

I don't remember if I shook your hand, Bobby-o. Chances are I did. Whatever else you may think of me, my mother brought me up right.

"Detective?" I asked. "Why?"

"How's she doing?"

"They think she might die." I started to cry. Saying it out loud felt like I was going to make it happen.

"Oh hey, hey, sweetheart, hey, I'm sorry. Look ... would you like a cup of coffee or something? Maybe a glass of water? Poor kid, you're all done in. I'll bet you haven't slept. Come on, let's go sit down in the waiting room. . . . It's just down the hall, okay? Come on."

I was alone. I couldn't call Mitch. Meryl was downstairs. My dad had disappeared. So I let you put your arm around me and guide me out of my mom's room. We shucked our gowns and gloves and little booties, and I let you take me to the waiting room. You brought me bottled water. You even unscrewed the cap.

You were so *nice*, Bob. Like Mitch, in a way, that first day at school. You were kind when I really needed that.

Of course, I was a complete fool. Cops aren't nice for nothing.

I took a sip of water just to be polite. "We've met before, Detective—?"

"Pendleton. . . . Just Bob. I was in a different department then. I investigated the fire at your grandfather's house, when you were eight. I came to see you in the hospital. Do you remember that?"

"I remember the hospital."

"So do I. Poor kid, you were burned pretty bad then, but you look great now. How are you doing?"

What a stupid question. "Why are you here?"

"It's like I said." You spread those big dinner-plate hands. "I'm investigating the fire at your mom's store. We always do, in cases where we suspect arson."

My ears perked up at that. "Someone set the fire? Who?"

"Well, Jenna." You gave a rueful smile. "God, I hate to say this, but we think . . . we think it was your mom."

b

I just stared. Your mouth was smiling, but your eyes were hard and bright, like light winking off scalpels. I know now that you were gauging my reaction: Did I know about my mother? Had I suspected? Oh, I knew you believed what you were saying, Bob. There was no tentativeness in *your* eyes at all.

The thing is, you put into words what I'd not allowed myself to think. As soon as they registered, I knew the truth.

Despite all her talk, I'd heard her desperation. My father was an asshole. My mother felt she had nothing to lose, I guess. Having been suicidal a couple times myself, you might say I've got natural empathy where that's concerned. I understand the impulse.

What I wasn't prepared for was the talon of pain that dug at my chest. My mother had decided there was nothing worth sticking around for. What had she said?

I miss my boy. I miss my baby.

Matt. Always Matt. There was Matt, and there was the bookstore. There was me, but I guess I wasn't enough. In her mind, she had no reason to keep on going. Not even for me.

Not even for me.

C

"I don't think I should talk to you anymore," I said. "I think I should find my father."

Your Officer Friendly smile remained, but your eyes stayed hard. "You do what you need to do, sweetheart. But let me tell you one more thing before you go. The pattern of the fire at your mother's store, certain characteristics? They're really similar to what we found at your grandfather's."

When the heart sinks, people fall. My knees suddenly wobbled and I knew I was going to collapse the same way my mother had crumpled when my father finally pried her away from the door and let in those Marines. I plopped down hard into my chair, a puppet without strings.

"I'm sorry, honey," you said. "This gives me no pleasure. Believe me. Your mom's on thin ice here."

I said nothing.

"Because the thing is, we found the remains of the same kind of bottle at both scenes. Stolichnaya, actually. At your grandfather's, the arson guys figured they'd been broken in the fire. The fire started with the curtains and there was broken glass in the sink; your grandpa was a pretty heavy drinker. It made sense. Who would burn down an old guy's house, anyway?"

I said nothing.

"But we thought . . . *think* your mom might be involved. We looked at her for your grandpa but, well, your brother was a witness. He swore up and down that your mom was with him all night, and the two of them went to pick you up from your grandpa's. You know what's really funny, though?" You cocked your head and looked puzzled. For a second, I thought you were going to pull out a little notebook and a stub of pencil, but you're not Columbo, Bobby-o, not by a long shot. "I never quite understood why *you* were there but not your brother. Why have your grandpa babysit only *one* of you? That never made sense, but your brother was older and pretty convincing. But here we are again. You can see why this bothers me."

I said nothing.

You leaned forward and pressed your hands together. "Let me tell you a story, honey. I've kind of pieced this together, talking to various people, reading between the lines. I even looked at your mom's poetry. Do you know how hard her book is to find? Finally tracked it down through the Library of Congress, of all things. You know, they have a copy of every book that's ever been published? So nothing ever really vanishes these days, not even if there's a fire. Anyway, you just listen, okay; see what you think."

I was quiet.

"See, *I* think there was this guy who was a drunk and one bitter, abusive asshole. After his wife died—after she hanged herself—he only had his youngest girl to keep him company. She was everything: cook, housekeeper, nurse, and . . . companion?" You said that very carefully, Bob, but that word was a bullet. That word was as loaded as a pistol.

I listened.

"Eventually, that girl got out of there. There were probably secrets because you never can outrun the past. I read somewhere that people are the accumulation of their experiences. Without your memories and secrets . . . you're nothing."

I said nothing.

"So she falls in love; she gets married, has her own kids. For the first time in a while, she's got hope. But there's the damn bookstore that keeps dragging her down and won't let go. Her asshole of a dad is still around and, maybe, up to his old tricks. Of course, she doesn't know for sure. She hopes it's not true. Until she finds out it is and then she decides to do something about that."

I said nothing.

"Otherwise," you said, "I really have to wonder why any mother would set fire to a house knowing her little girl was inside." You paused. "Unless she didn't."

Unless she'd carried her little girl, her princess, to the car herself before she went back inside. Unless she couldn't know that her little girl wanted her favorite Ariel doll and slipped back into the house, to the basement where she'd hidden from her grandpa to

begin with and that it was her brother who noticed she was gone. . . .
Her brother . . .

You may have said something, Bob, but I can't be sure.
Because, by then, I was screaming.

46: a

Nurses and doctors came running. Dad blasted in and then he was shouting at you to get out and not come back without a warrant or lawyer or . . . I don't know. Once you were gone, Bobby-o, my father tried to find out what you'd said, but I was curled up in my chair, hands over my ears, eyes squeezed shut. Fire licked my back; my nose filled with the stink of burned hair and the cruel flames cackled. . . .

(Mom, swearing, slugging the EMTs doing CPR on Grandpa: *Don't you save that son-of-a-bitch; don't you dare!*)

"What did he say to you?" Psycho-Dad was back, his hands clamped around my wrists, forcing my hands from my ears. "Damn it, Jenna, what did he *say?*"

"I think you need to give her a minute, Doctor," said a nurse. "Maybe if we gave her a little something?"

"Get out," my father said, only he actually didn't say it that politely. After the nurse scurried away, Psycho-Dad bore down.

"What did he say? Jenna, goddamn it, look at me. I need you to tell me what he said."

Even in non-Hulk mode, my father always has been virtually impossible to ignore. Whatever gumption I'd discovered back at the house had evaporated. So, between gulps, I told him. His eyes got narrower and narrower until they were nothing but burning, bloodshot slits.

"Is it true?" I whispered. "Dad, did Mom—?"

"Of course not," he said. "Don't be stupid. The fire at the store was an accident."

That wasn't what I'd meant, and Dad knew it. "That's not what I meant. I meant about—" My throat balled, but I forced myself to finish. "About Grandpa."

"No. Don't tell me you believe that idiot. He's like all police. They're just covering up for their own incompetence."

"But the detective—"

"Fuck him." His eyes blazed. He aimed a forefinger at my face. "*Fuck.* Him. You are not to talk to him again, you understand? The only talking you do to any detective, ever, is when I'm there and our lawyer, you got that?"

"Do you remember him? From before?"

"I don't recall. The fire at your grandfather's was an accident, open and shut, all right? I'm going to file a complaint with the police chief and the mayor. I'm going to get that guy's ass fired so fast. . . ." Dad cut the air in an angry, dismissive gesture. "Jesus, like I don't have more important things to worry about. Listen, I have to go back home."

"But, Mom—"

"I've got no choice. I'm it for our practice and there are no other doctors I can call to cover on such short notice. I have patients in the hospital. There's nothing more I can do here for your mother anyway."

"Then I'll stay. Someone should be here if she wakes up."

"Jenna, she's not going to wake up anytime soon." He didn't say *never*, but he might as well have. "But if that's what you want . . ."

"That's what I want," I said.

b

Dad must've bullied someone because they let Meryl come up. As soon as I saw her, I plowed into her arms and buried my burning face into her shoulder like a little kid. "It's okay," she murmured, as we tottered back and forth. She stroked my hair. "Whatever happens, I'm here, honey."

She'd brought my knapsack and promised to fetch clothes. "And your hairbrush," she said, ticking items off on her fingers. "Shampoo, conditioner, face soap . . . am I forgetting anything?"

"My laptop." I told her what books I needed. "Oh, and my car's still in the school parking lot. I think my keys are . . ." I stirred the contents of my knapsack and came up with the ring.

"Sure, sweetheart." She checked her watch. "It'll be daylight soon. We're down here, might as well. Your dad and I can dig it out—"

"He wants to go back."

"He can suck an egg. His patients will keep. I'll get them to run your keys back up to you. That way, you can come and go as you please, without having to depend on me or him. Monday comes, we'll see how things are. I can put off going back north for a while."

"I need to go to school on Monday."

"Why don't you just take it one day at a time? You might not feel up to school for a while. People would understand." She peered at me over her glasses. "You call him yet?"

For a weirdly confused moment, I thought she and I were on the same page. I nearly called Mitch by name but caught myself just in time. "He's probably not up yet."

"If that boyfriend cares about you, he won't mind. Besides, don't all you kids sleep with your cell phones glued to your ear? Call him, honey. That's what people who love each other do."

C

The nurse's name was Laurie. She got them to bring in a cot so I could sleep next to Mom. "People always complain how cold it is," Laurie said, carrying in an armload of blankets. "I swiped these from the autoclave in the delivery room. You should be nice and toasty. Anything else you need, you just say."

"Thanks." I knew I wouldn't sleep, but I let her cover me up. She'd been so nice, it seemed the least I could do.

"Oh, one more thing, honey. Hospital rules, you can't use that cell up here. You want to make a call, you have to go down to the cafeteria. Otherwise, you have to go outside, as in out of the building. Okay?" I nodded, and she dimmed the lights and left.

For a while, I lay on my side and watched the green and red lines that sketched my mother's heartbeat and blood pressure. The ventilator hissed and sighed and sucked air and let more out. The IV pumps ticked away, dribbling fluids into my mother's veins. My mother was still as death.

I checked my cell: almost 5 A.M. Meryl might be right; Mitch would want to know. I knew *I* would. But I decided to wait a little while longer. The idea of bundling up to stand in the frigid wind made me feel tired.

If you're wondering if I thought about what you'd said, Bobby-o, you'd be right. Deep in my heart, I knew my mother had killed her bookstore. I could imagine her turning a slow circle, her eyes cutting across the silent spines of the books that she loved so much. I wasn't sure she meant to kill herself. She was drunk. So that might have been an accident. Or not.

About what you'd said about the fire at Grandpa's . . . Bobby, Bobby, you didn't really expect me to go on the record, did you? Mitch guessed. You're not as smart as he is, but you can read between the lines. Come to think of it, I probably should've had *you* do my paper on Alexis; you seem to be pretty good at telling stories about crazy people. So, draw your own conclusions.

◌

I rummaged in my knapsack and dragged out the Lasker book, the one Mitch had given me. Now was as good a time as any, I guessed, so I propped myself up on pillows and started in.

The book was a very fast read. Lasker reiterated a lot of what I already knew about Alexis. If you believed him, they'd met at Stanford before Alexis hooked up with Wright, and it was lust at first sight. Lasker went into great detail about what Alexis was like in bed (a screamer who liked to use her nails and wasn't above a little blood); how often she wanted to get into his pants (every five seconds); how she made him feel: sore. . . . Okay, he really didn't say that. What Lasker wrote was *sated*,

*yet hungry for more of the drug that only Alexis infused in my veins,
oh sweet happy death.* Talk about hyperbole. Maybe it's me, but
I imagined a bloated Bacchus, with wine dribbling onto his
chest. Or a heroin addict.

The whole book was like that. I wasn't sure why Mitch
thought it would be helpful, then considered that all I had for
Alexis's frame of mind was what she said and what others, out to
protect her legacy, wrote. Lasker was all me-me-me, and maybe
there was something to that. If you believed him—and I kind
of did—Alexis cheated on her husband all through their marriage. The Alexis in these pages was vain, self-absorbed, blind
to everything but her own needs and passions, whether those
passions were for whales and dolphins, or a lover.

But then I came to something Lasker wrote that made all
this somehow noble and tragic, at the same time, and so good,
Bob, I copied it word for word:

*There are those individuals who die for a cause, and we say they
have made the ultimate sacrifice. We call them martyrs, and we never doubt their sincerity.*

*Yet many others search their entire lives for something—or
someone—worth dying for and this is very different. These are the
lonely and the desperate, fearful that their lives have no meaning.
They yearn for the bullet, if only someone else will pull the trigger.*

Knowing what I do now, Bob, I think that was what Mitch
wanted me to see, whether he knew it or not.

8

After two hours, my eyes were gritty and sore. I closed the book
and reached for my knapsack. Before I could grab it, the book

slipped off my lap and thumped to the floor. My eyes shot to my mother, but she hadn't moved. I bent to retrieve the book which lay facedown, covers splayed like a broken bird. As I retrieved it, I noticed a slip of paper that must've been tucked into the back of the book. The print was dim and the lettering tiny, so I had to hold it at an angle and squint.

Saul's Rare Books, it read. There was a snail mail address, as well as a phone number and web site. There was the title of Lasker's book followed by a column of numbers and a final tally: $127.57.

A sales receipt. My eyes snagged on the date: October 3.

I knew that date because my mom's party was on October 6. So that meant the day Dewerman gave me Alexis's name was the same day *Mitch* had bought . . .

Don't you have an English project?

No. *No.*

A week later, Mitch said he already *had* this book in his library. Hadn't he? I couldn't remember. I wasn't sure. But he knew all about Alexis.

All right, wait, wait. . . . My heart skipped a beat, then two. Wait, he hadn't lied, he *did* have the book, but . . .

I closed my eyes, replayed the moment I'd turned around and seen Mitch and Dewerman chatting in the doorway. Then I remembered the handwritten slip I'd stolen: *J.*

And *lover.*

A note to himself.

A reminder to buy the book?

"No," I said aloud. "No, it wasn't like that."

f

As I headed down to the cafeteria, I'd decided that I must've misunderstood. Either way, whether he had the book already or only *thought* he had it and then bought it because he cared about me, what did it matter? He'd been thinking of *me*. That was all that counted.

A few people were already filing through with trays. I smelled greasy bacon and eggs, and as I spied a cafeteria lady flipping sausage patties, my stomach complained. I hadn't eaten since yesterday afternoon, but my stomach would have to wait. I chose a table in the corner and, holding my breath, called Mitch's cell.

One ring. Two. Then: "Hello?"

"Mitch, it's—" The words died in my mouth as I registered that the voice wasn't his. "I'm sorry. I was looking for Mr. Anderson. Who is this?"

"This is Kathy," she said. "Mitch's wife."

47: a

The words were a punch in the gut. My knees went suddenly wobbly and weak. It was a good thing I was already sitting down.

"Who's this?" Mrs. Anderson said. "Is this the police again? Mitch has already told you everything he knows. Do you know what time it is? Who *is* this?"

What? *Police?* Why would they talk to Mitch about the fire? "I . . . I'm on Mi—Mr. Anderson's track team, and I'm his chem TA and—"

"Oh, I remember him talking about you. You're another one of Mitch's girls, aren't you? Or . . . wait." Her voice changed and she whispered, "Is this *Danielle?*"

I blinked. I actually pulled my cell away and looked at it. Then I pressed it to my ear again and said, "No. My name's Jenna Lord. I'm Mr. Anderson's TA? In chemistry? And I . . . I need to talk to him. About Monday."

"*Now?* It's Friday."

Think fast, think fast. "Uhm . . . it's an emergency. My mom's in the hospital and I probably won't make it to school on Monday. I'm sorry, I guess I'm just so worried and upset."

I think it helped that all this was true, because Mrs. Anderson said just a minute, that Mitch was in the other room and she'd go wake him up and give him his cell. I listened to muffled footsteps and then what sounded like doors opening, closing, and voices.

Then Mitch was on the line: "Jenna? What is it, what's wrong?"

"You're with your *wife*," I blurted, loudly enough that two women four tables away lifted their heads and stared. I scooted around until I was facing the cafeteria wall which was a nauseating puke-brown.

"In separate rooms," he said. "I didn't know she was coming down, sweetheart. She surprised me."

"She had your cell."

"She had some calls to make back to her family in Minneapolis and I lent her my phone. Jenna, what's going on?" He listened as I pushed out the words around tears and then said, "Oh honey, is there anything I can do?"

"Can you come?"

He might have shaken his head because there was a small gap and then he said, "Not right away."

"You want to stay with your wife."

"Did I say that? Jenna, *think*. It would look pretty strange if I, *your chemistry teacher*, took off at dawn to go hold the hand of his *student*, who clearly has a family of her own."

I knew he was right. "I'm sorry. Why . . . Mitch, what does . . ." I couldn't bring myself to ask the question.

"Hang on a second. . . . Okay, I'm back. I'm actually in the bathroom, with the door closed."

His voice was very soft. "Where are you?" I asked.

"Hotel, in adjacent rooms, as in she locks her door and I lock mine. It's a long story, sweetie."

"I'm not going anywhere." When he didn't say anything, I said, "Mitch? Are you and she—?"

"No," he said firmly. "*No*. We're not sleeping together. We are not getting *back* together, no matter what she wants."

I had to wet my lips. "But do you want to?"

A longer pause this time. "I would be lying if I said it hadn't occurred to me. You don't deserve lies."

Oh no, I only deserved sneaking around and being told I was too young to understand and a dead brother and a mother who'd tried to kill my grandfather and ended up nearly offing me. I deserved a lover who was my teacher and married and couldn't divorce his wife and might be lying now.

Then I had another, brighter thought. Maybe Mitch hadn't found a *reason* for a divorce, until now. Until me. Maybe that's why they were together now.

But that's not what I asked next. "Mitch, when your . . . when Mrs. Anderson answered the phone, she thought I was the police. She thought I was *Danielle*." He was silent so long I thought we'd been disconnected. "Mitch?"

"I heard you. Look, I can't talk about it this instant. I will, just not now. Honestly, sweetheart, you have enough going on, you don't need to worry about this. I'll explain it later, okay?"

"Are you in trouble?"

"No." Then Mitch said he had to stay another day and wouldn't start back for his house until Sunday. "But I'll call you later on today, okay? I'll see you soon, honey." He told me he loved me and then we hung up.

b

Ten minutes later, as I was stepping out of the elevator, I remembered that I hadn't told him which hospital Mom was in. So I rode the elevator back down. The ladies at the table were gone, but the cafeteria was getting busy, and I broke down at the sight of pancakes. It was fifteen more minutes before I navigated to a table with my plate and a cup of coffee.

Mrs. Anderson answered again, something for which I wasn't prepared. "Oh, hello . . . Jenna? I borrowed Mitch's cell again. I think he's in the shower. Do you need to leave a message?"

It would be strange if I didn't and there was nothing suspicious about the information. I told her where my mother was, and then she said her father had been a patient there, too, only not in the Burn Unit. "It's horrible about the fire. I'm watching the news right now. Such a shame about that old bookstore. Just one more bad thing this weekend. They say bad things come in threes, so I'm waiting for the last shoe to drop."

I had no idea what she was talking about, so I said, "Yeah, it's pretty upsetting."

"I wouldn't wonder. You poor kids . . . Does anyone have any idea what's happened?"

Oh, the detective thinks my mother did it. "No."

"Well, they will. I'm sure the police will find her. Anyway, I'm so sorry I never got a chance to thank your mother in person for the book."

What? It took me a couple seconds; it seemed fifty years since the party. "Oh. Sure. Well, she'll be happy to hear that you liked it." *If she doesn't die first.*

Then it hit me. "Mr. Anderson gave you the book."

She sounded bemused. "Of course. He doesn't read that kind of fiction much."

I knew that, of course. But *when* had Mitch seen her? She was supposed to have been in Minneapolis the whole time. Maybe she'd come down on a weekend, or something. The most logical explanation was that he'd given her the book just yesterday. Sure, that was it, only . . .

I never got a chance to thank your mother in person.

That didn't sound like something Mrs. Anderson would say if she'd only gotten the book yesterday.

Wait a second.

That night after Mitch took me home that first time, I'd called. A woman had answered and there had been someone else in the room right before the hang up. But Mitch told me on the way home that his wife was away: *I'm baching it.*

Was the woman I was talking to now the same person? I thought about it. Decided, no, I didn't think so. That other person had sounded . . . *young.*

Like someone my age.

"Anyway," she was saying, "I'll give Mitch the message, okay? How was the rest of your holiday? I mean . . . I'm sorry, what a stupid question."

"No, that's okay. It was fine," I lied. It was killing me that she kept calling him by his first name. To be polite—and change the subject—I asked, "How were things at Mr. Anderson's sister's house?"

"Mitch's sister?"

"Yeah. She has Thanksgiving every year? In Madison?"

"Oh, I think you've got Mitch mixed up with another teacher," she said.

"Oh. She doesn't live in Madison?"

"She doesn't live anywhere," Mrs. Anderson said. "We're in Appleton, and Mitch doesn't have any brothers or sisters."

I kept waiting for her to say the rest: *in Wisconsin*. But she didn't. So I said, stupidly, "So he doesn't have a sister . . . or a brother?"

"No," said Mrs. Anderson. "Mitch is an only child."

48: a

I'm visiting my sister in Madison.

My head was whirling. I left my pancakes.

My sister always does Thanksgiving.

I drifted out of the cafeteria in a kind of daze, floating to the elevator, punching the up arrow, staring at the numbers ticking in a kind of countdown: 7-6-5-4. . . .

Casey's in Afghanistan.

I stumbled into the elevator and stared dumbly at the panel. A hospital tech reached past me. "What floor?" he asked.

"Burn Unit," I mumbled. He stabbed the right button as I sagged against the back of the elevator and closed my eyes.

I have three sisters.

Girls always use more hot water than guys.

My brother's in Special Forces.

Small world.

God, what world had *I* been in? Planet Mitch? He'd lied. He was in Appleton with his wife. He had no brother, no three sisters who used all the hot water. He bought the Lasker book the day Dewerman gave me the assignment.

No, wait. Numb, I navigated my way down the hall from the elevator toward the Burn Unit. Mitch had done his undergraduate work at Stanford; he'd studied marine mammology, he said, and as a grad student, he'd already *known* about Alexis and he just *thought* he had Lasker's book. But why buy it? There was no reason he would need it—unless that reason was me.

No, he went to Stanford and then Madison, and there were sharks and diving and dolphins and—

And then I realized what else was missing from Mitch's library, what my dad had and Mitch didn't,

No pictures there, in that cabin. No diplomas either.

Stop, I had to stop. Not everyone advertised. There were plenty of people who didn't slap every credential on the wall for other people to admire, and the cabin was private space. Mitch wouldn't need a reminder. I had to slow down. There were things Mitch had told me that had to be true: he was rich; he was married; I'd talked to his wife; I knew she was with her sick dad in Minneapolis.

Police. She'd said *police*, and Mitch said that was a long story. And what else?

You poor kids.

Bad things come in threes.

I'd assumed she'd been talking about me, but—

"But she thought I was Danielle."

"What? I'm sorry, did you say something, honey?"

I looked up and saw a nurse, not Laurie, in my mother's doorway. All the nurses were different. Change of shift. The nurse said, "Are you Jenna?" When I nodded, she dug into her

317

pocket. I heard the tinkle of metal. "Laurie wanted me to give you these. You were down in the cafeteria."

"Thanks." I took my keys. Meryl had pinned a note to the ring: *Family Parking, Level 2, Row 3.*

"I heard about your mom's bookstore on the news this morning," the nurse said. "I'm real sorry."

Mrs. Anderson had seen the news, too. *Bad things come in threes.* "Is there a TV around?" I asked.

The nurse steered me to the family lounge, which was empty. I punched through stations with the remote until I found the local news, but it was nearly 8 A.M. and the only story featured was something about a dancing penguin who wrote opera. (Okay, it wasn't; I made that up, but it was something equally stupid.) I waited impatiently, jiggling my foot, and then the lady announcer said, "A deadly fire destroys a cherished downtown landmark."

"And authorities in Milwaukee investigate what they fear may be a suicide pact between a Turing High School athlete and her boyfriend," her male partner added. "All that, and the weather when we come back."

Danielle. And . . . *David?*

My heart iced.

Mrs. Anderson thought I was Danielle—because she'd been there when the police called Mitch.

49: a

I had to wait through the weather first, an obscenely cheerful
guy named Brian jabbering about Arctic cold fronts and more
snow by next week. The announcers got in on the act, pos-
ing inane questions to which they already knew the answers:
*"Brian, I bet there are a lot of snowmobilers just chomping on the bit.
What about those lakes and rivers?"* Setting up Brian so he could
warn us all about appearances being deceiving and the dangers
of thin ice, blah, blah, blah.

Mom's store was the lead story. There were aerial shots of
the fire—a great roiling inferno—and then ground level, but
either way you could see there was nothing left but a charred
skeleton. The only thing saving the block had been the cold
and snow melt that had wet neighboring buildings so they
didn't burn.

Danielle and David were next. I listened hard, trying to still
my mind. What I got was that David had picked up Danielle

at her house on Wednesday and then they both disappeared. Just . . . vanished. The newspeople were getting the suicide thing from one of Danielle's friends—I recognized her from school—who said that Danielle had talked about maybe not coming back after Thanksgiving.

"Police have interviewed teachers and students at Turing High for any information that might lead to the discovery of the missing teens. While it is too early to speculate on their whereabouts, unnamed sources tell Channel 4 that Miss Connolly placed a call to Child Protective Services as recently as two weeks ago. Miss Connolly reportedly declined to make a specific complaint."

Cut to Mr. Connolly, standing on his doorstep: "All we have to say to Danielle is, honey, we love you, come home, we can work it out." Shouts from assembled reporters; I caught *allegations of abuse*. Mr. Connolly, his face lawyerly and glacial: "No comment."

Cut to the announcer: "CPS could not be reached for comment. Police are investigating. And in other news . . . "

b

Another bright, freezing, cruelly beautiful morning.

There was virtually no traffic heading up the interstate, and I made good time. Within fifty minutes, I was only four exits away from Mitch's house. When I'd retrieved my knapsack from the Burn Unit, I saw that Mitch had called five times. On the way up, he'd called twice more, but I hadn't picked up. I wanted to time this just right. I wasn't avoiding him necessarily, but I didn't want him getting there ahead of me. Appleton was only forty minutes from his place. Twenty, if he floored it. I thought he'd do that.

My cell buzzed again: a text message this time. My eyes flicked down: *PICK UP.* Five seconds later, my cell chirped. I flipped it open. "What?"

"Where are you?" Mitch's voice was controlled, but I heard the urgency.

"I'm at the hospital."

"No, you're not. They said you left almost an hour ago."

I said nothing.

"Where are you?"

"In my car."

"Are you going home?"

I took a deep breath. "No." I waited a beat to let him answer, but all I got was silence. I said, "How many other lies have you told me? You don't have a brother. You don't have a sister, much less three. You're in Appleton."

"Because Kathy called and wanted to meet. She came down from Minneapolis and I came up."

"Were you ever in Madison?"

Silence.

"Mitch?"

"Jenna." Frustration. "Honey, you don't understand. I can explain."

"I'm listening."

"No. In person. I need to see you."

"Why?" I said. "So you can kill me the way you did Danielle?"

C

A long, *long* silence.

Then: "What?" His shock seemed genuine. "*What?* What are you talking about? Jenna, what are you *saying?*"

"You were angry enough to kill her. That's what you said."

"That was a figure of spee—"

"She was in your house! She answered the phone! She was at our cabin!" I shouted. "I *saw* her! But she won't be there now, will she? She'll be gone because she was waiting for you; she *knew* where it was, and the only way she could know that is if you'd taken her there!"

"Oh my God. You think that—" He sucked in a breath. "Jenna, honey, Jenna, no, it's not like that. You don't understand."

"Stop *saying* that! I understand fine and when I find the proof, when I *find* it . . . !" I think I heard him shout my name, but I thumbed <end>. My cell immediately started up again, but I ignored it.

By the time I pulled into Mitch's driveway, my cell hadn't rung for ten minutes. I was certain he was already in his car, heading home, but I had a head start. The last thing I did was punch up another cell, reading the numbers from a business card. The other line rang once, twice, and then: "Detective Pendleton."

"This is Jenna Lord." I gave the address and then said, "Come quick."

Then I tossed the live cell onto the front seat. I heard you squawking, Bobby-o, but I had no more time to give you. But I'd seen enough *CSI* and *NCIS* to know: you'd find me soon enough.

50: a

The snow was packed solid. There'd been plenty of traffic to and from the cabin since I'd last been there what seemed a century ago, but was only two days. A good thing, too, because I didn't have my snowshoes.

The first thing I noticed when I rounded the bend and saw the cabin: no smoke. The windows were dark, and the cabin felt as still and deserted as Mitch's house. What did that mean? Had Danielle and maybe David stayed there on Wednesday then left Thursday or Friday? Or had Danielle come to see Mitch and then Mitch had . . . Or maybe it *had* been a homeless person. . . . No, no, that I knew wasn't true because Mitch hadn't denied that Danielle had been at the cabin. Had he?

Had I given him time?

The key was in the jug. I fished it out, fitted it to the lock, and turned. The cabin smelled like tomato soup and peaches. There were dry dishes on the drain board: two bowls, two spoons, two mugs, a saucepan. Danielle and David? Danielle and Mitch? Mitch and . . . ?

The bed was made, but sloppily—not the way Mitch and I always left it. In the upstairs bathroom, two bath towels were draped over the shower stall and there was a discarded travel bottle of Herbal Essences Peach Shampoo and a wad of blonde hair in the trash, probably teased from a brush. Danielle was a blonde. I used toilet paper to pluck the hair out of the trash and then thought I should put it into something where the hair wouldn't be damaged. *Envelope*, I thought, and headed back downstairs.

I paused at the fireplace. Whoever had made the last fire had used newspaper. There was still a section next to the hearth and I bent down to check the date: Wednesday, the day before Thanksgiving.

The day Danielle and David disappeared, and the day before I'd seen the face in the window.

b

The desk drawer was locked. I debated a half second, then slid the kissing knife out of my jeans pocket where I'd put it right before I left the car. I wedged the tip into the lock and jiggled it around, not really expecting much, and nothing much happened. Maybe I could pry the desk open. The blade was very thin and slid easily into the narrow crack between the drawer and the desk. I remembered something from a book, about how burglars used credit cards to depress the tongue of a lock. Maybe that would work and—

Snick.

The drawer popped open. The desk did this little jump and Mitch's computer monitor winked to life. I hadn't noticed that the computer was on. Mitch's wallpaper was a seascape: bulbous corals and a rainbow of fish. One program was running: Firefox. I maximized it. The window exploded across the screen and—

"Oh my God," I whispered.

You're old enough to get an abortion in Illinois. That was what Mitch had said. *But not in Wisconsin or Minnesota or Michigan.*

And Mitch should know.

The list of the Illinois clinics was right in front of me.

C

Abortion clinics.

Oh my God.

He'd gotten Danielle pregnant and then . . . what? Had she threatened him? The way Mr. Connolly got in Mitch's face . . . God, her dad *knew*? No, no, wait, that couldn't be right. Mr. Connolly was a lawyer. Wouldn't he have gone to the police? But why else would Mitch—or Danielle, because I now knew she'd been here—be looking up abortion clinics?

He told me to mind my own business, Mitch had said. *She's not old enough to know what she wants.*

That didn't sound like Mitch was the father . . . but, God, I didn't know what to believe anymore.

I scanned the other folders on Mitch's desktop. There were lecture notes and labs for chemistry, biology. A folder labeled *Cross-Country Training Programs*; another for track; a third filled with tips on how to prepare for the Ironman.

Then I saw a folder tucked in the lower left-hand corner, labeled only with an initial: *J*.

No. I stared at that folder a long, long time. *No, don't do it, don't do it, walk away just walk—*

I double-clicked on the icon and the folder opened.

d

They were Word documents, mostly, but also several jpegs and one PDF. I remembered the digital camera in Mitch's desk at school, but I opened the PDF first because of the date.

Discharge Summary: Jenna Meredith Lord.

Rebecca kept it factual and extremely dry. There was my diagnosis—*Major Depression, severe, with psychotic features, in remission; PTSD*—and a bunch of other diagnoses, none of them flattering, I'm sure. She detailed my history leading up to my admission, then my course of treatment and my discharge recommendations.

I saw, immediately, what was missing.

Of course, I knew about Matt, Mitch had said. *It was in your discharge summary.*

No, Mitch.

It wasn't.

51: a

Well, Bob, that's not quite fair. Rebecca did say *unresolved grief over her brother's death*, but that was all. She hadn't said anything about Iraq, or Matt's being killed in action.

All that Mitch found out from the newspapers.

Using my date of birth so helpfully included on my discharge summary, Mitch worked backward. Matt's death had made the local papers for a week or so, and all that eventually led Mitch to the fire at Grandpa's because he had all that information, too. My whole life was on Mitch's desktop, like once he found out about me, he wanted to know *everything*. Interest becomes obsession becomes—

"I can explain."

I whirled. Mitch was in the doorway. His hair was mussed and he wasn't wearing gloves or boots. His sneakers were wet. He must've run all the way from his car. His eyes went to his desk. "I'd wondered where that knife had gone."

So many things I wanted to say, they all piled up behind my teeth. I finally managed: "Where's Danielle?"

"At a clinic in Evanston. I drove her there with David myself on Friday morning." He paused. "I told them they could stay here Wednesday and Thursday. Both of them had been to the house, so they knew the way."

That would tally. I'd come here Thursday afternoon. "If that's true, why haven't they called their parents? Why does everyone think they're runaways?"

"Because Danielle's afraid her father will stop her. He'd make her go through with having the baby. No girl should be forced to do that."

"Who's the father? David?"

"Don't you really want to know if it's me?" When I didn't reply, he said, "There are three possibilities, and I'm not one of them."

I remembered what the reporter had said about CPS. Three men orbited Danielle: David. Her father. Her brother. Of the three, only the last two made any sense when you factored in Danielle's call to CPS. "Aren't you supposed to go to the police even if you only suspect?"

"She would deny it. I can only do so much, Jenna. She needed help and I gave it. She and David will contact their families when it's done."

I thought there was a flaw in his logic, but I couldn't put my finger on it. "And what about their families in the meantime? That doesn't make sense, Mitch. You could tell them to call their families at least, or the police." The beginnings of a headache blistered my temples. "And what about all this . . . this . . . *stuff* about me? Don't try to tell me that you got interested afterward. These downloads are dated a full *month* before I showed up. Why did you do that? Why *lie*?"

His Adam's apple bobbed in a hard swallow and, suddenly, his eyes slid from mine. "I . . . I wanted to find a way to reach you . . . get closer . . . I knew you'd be lost, lonely. I thought I could help. I swear to God, when it started, I was just trying to find some common ground."

"You don't believe in God," I said. Danielle had pegged it: *he likes the broken ones.* I felt empty and ill, like someone had taken a melon baller and scooped out my guts.

"Was any of it real, Mitch?" I felt weak for asking; I hated how I sounded: pleading and small. Only a completely awful person would tell me it was all a lie, and I knew that Mitch wasn't awful. Oh, this was completely screwed up; it was horrible, I knew that. Mitch had stalked me in his own way. But Mitch had also made me feel good about myself. He'd given me confidence. Would a . . . a *predator* do that? No, *no.*

Interest becomes obsession becomes . . . *love*?

"Did you ever love me?" I said. "Or were you in love with the idea of being the good guy everybody liked and helping out the poor kid? Only then you got in over your head and couldn't figure a way to get yourself out?"

"God, how can you think that, Jenna? I've risked everything to be with you."

Was that true? Yes, it was. We'd gone places together; all I had to do was run to my parents and he would go to jail. "Then why were you with your wife?"

"I met Kathy because I needed to tell her that I've fallen in love with someone else, Jenna," he said. "To tell her, finally, that I want a divorce."

b

It was the truth.

I knew it was. All I needed was to look into his eyes.

Or it might have been a lie.

Because it was so perfect, just exactly what I wanted and needed to hear. And he had lied to me before.

And that was why, all of a sudden, I wasn't sure I could believe him. But, God, I wanted to.

I had to leave. I was drowning in there, with Mitch. I had to get someplace where I could think. I couldn't trust myself not to be swayed one more time.

Then I remembered why I'd broken into his desk to begin with: the hair, an envelope, Danielle—and then I thought: *Oh my God.*

Because I'd called you, Bobby-o, and you were on your way.

Something cracked inside my head. I had ruined everything. The police would come and they would wonder why a student knew so much about her teacher and . . .

"Oh Mitch, I'm so sorry," I said through tears. "But I called the police."

Then I darted around him and out of our cabin and into the snow.

52: a

Where was I going? Even now, I'm not entirely sure. I think I was running toward something as much as fleeing something else. Not Mitch so much, but I needed to think, and I couldn't do that close to him. I certainly wasn't flying toward salvation, exactly, or even rescue—although I knew you were on the way, Bobby-o. I would like to say that I rushed out to delay you, to pass the whole thing off as the hysterics of an overwrought teenager. I could pull that off.

Yes. I thought that if I could get to you first, maybe I could still save us, me and Mitch.

Yes. That's what I think it was.

b

So I ran. Mitch was faster than me, but I'd caught him by surprise. He grabbed for my arm, called my name, but I twisted away, and then I was gone, crashing out of the cabin and flying over the hardpack. In two seconds, he would come after me, and he would catch up, I had no doubt.

And what would he do? *Hold me, kill me, hold me, kill me.* My heart hammered. The icy air tore at my throat, but I kept running, punishing the snow, punishing it. *Save me, kill me, kill himself, kill us both. . . .*

I spotted Mitch's house, still so far away, through a stark grill of trees, and that was when I decided staying on the path would take too long. So I swerved, hurtling into the deeper, un-broken snow, making a beeline for the lake. My boots crunched through the hardpack but not as deeply as I thought they might, and I kept pumping, high-stepping, almost hopping, trying to stay as light on my feet as I could. Mitch was heavier; he would sink and have to work harder. That would buy me the time I needed to get across and into my car. I didn't know what I would do then. I hadn't thought that far ahead. Maybe head you off, Bobby? Yes, maybe I could.

I heard Mitch call and shot a glance over my shoulder. He was wallowing in the snow. I knew I would make it to the house first. I faced back, eyeing the house, thinking: *Get there, get there, just get there!*

"Jenna, stop!" he cried. "Don't go any further, *don't*—!"

I was gasping, pulling in lungfuls of air. Spiky branches cut and whipped at my naked face. Wood snapped and broke beneath my boots. Then, all of a sudden, the ground fell away and I stag-gered, my arms shooting out for balance as I stumbled the last few feet down the dip at the shoreline and spilled onto the lake.

"Jenna!" Mitch called again. "*No!*"

The snow wasn't as deep, maybe only six inches, maybe less because of the wind that snatched fistfuls away during the day.

The surface was crustier, too, because of sun melt that refroze every night. So I could go much faster and I did, picking up my speed, stamping down and then pushing off as I plowed across. My boots dragged furrows through the snow and then I was a third of the way across, almost at the middle and—

POP.

Oh, Bob.

C

I froze.

I, literally, honestly, froze in mid-stride, one boot above the snow, the other still planted on the ice, my arms squeezed tight against my sides the way a good runner should.

POP.

CRACK!

Then a long grinding groan, like Mitch, inside me, moaning in his ecstasy, a deep-throated sigh that went on and on and on: *OOOoooohhh. . . .*

Something came out of my mouth, a high, inarticulate exhalation—and even now I think, yes, that's what *I* sounded like when Mitch and I were together, and for the briefest of moments, I was no longer there but defined only by the limit of Mitch's arms holding me together, tight tight tight.

Crack. Crack crack.

I was afraid to move. My muscles were quivering. I couldn't breathe.

"Jenna." Mitch sounded close. Was he on the ice, too? I was too scared to put my foot down much less turn around. "Jenna, honey, listen to me, do exactly what I say."

"Mitch?" A film of cold sweat bathed my face. I closed my eyes and swallowed. I wondered if the icy water would burn. I wondered if I would die fast this time. My voice rose a notch: "*Miiitch?*"

"I'm right here, Jenna. I'm only fifty feet away. I won't leave—"

"Don't leave me, Mitch, don't leave me!"

"I won't leave you, sweetheart. I love you; I'll never leave you. But you have to listen. Are you listening?"

"Yes." I was crying—from fear, from love, from relief. "Yes, I'm listening."

"The ice is too thin. You have to come back the way you came, okay? Come back to me, Jenna, and then we'll get off the ice together, all right?"

"Yes." I swallowed, gasped again as the ice popped. "Okay."

"Put your foot down, honey . . . slow, *slow* . . . that's it, good girl. Now, Jenna, I want you to lie down."

My voice thinned to a wheeze. "Lie *down?*"

"Yes. Lie down on your stomach, spread as wide as you can, arms and legs as far as you can, and then you'll turn around."

"Mitch, I . . ." I gulped. "I don't think I can do that."

"You have to, honey. Please. It's the only way. You have to redistribute your weight so the ice can hold you. Then you'll turn around and shimmy back, okay? Come on, you can do it."

My trembling knees creaked. The ice popped and groaned. My teeth were chattering. My whole body was shaking as if I would never be warm again, exactly the way Mitch had felt in the abyss at Rubicon Point. But I did what Mitch said: first my knees and then my legs and then I was facedown, spread-eagled in the snow. Now I could see the fissures in the snow, radiating out from my body in all directions. The ice under my belly moaned.

"Good girl," Mitch said. "Now turn yourself around very, very . . . slow, honey, slow . . . I'm right here, I'm not going anywhere, you don't have to hur—"

CRACK.

A moan dribbled from my mouth, but now I was facing back the way I'd come. Maybe thirty feet away, Mitch was on his stomach, shucking his coat in slow-motion, rolling carefully from one hip to the other, but the ice beneath him was popping and snapping with every move. With dawning horror, I saw the same starburst of gashes in the snow and realized: the ice was breaking and ripping apart under him, too.

And Mitch was heavier than me.

"Mi-Mi-Mitch," I gasped. "The *i-ice*."

"I know, honey. It'll be okay," he said evenly. But I saw his face. I had seen Mitch happy, tender, rapturous, sad, and not five minutes ago, guilty and full of remorse. But I had never, ever seen him scared to death. "When I throw out my coat, stretch as far as you can and grab hold. Is there any way you can get your boots off?"

"My b-b-b-b . . . ?"

"Yes. Your boots are heavy and so is your parka. If you break through, I don't know if I'll be able to hang on to you." He didn't say that I might also drag him under. He didn't have to.

I did try to get those boots off, but every time I reached back, the ice complained and Mitch told me to stop. "But if the ice breaks," I began, "you won't—"

"I won't let go of you, Jenna. I will never let go, I promise," Mitch said. The sun had cleared the trees and was warm on my back, which meant it was also warming the snow and ice. Mitch skimmed his tongue over his upper lip. Sweat was dribbling down his cheeks. "Okay, honey, we've got to move now. Come on, start back toward me and I'll back up with you. We'll be—" *Snap. Pop.* "We'll be on the shore in no time."

I did what he said, with my fists knotted in the sleeve of his sheepskin coat, the coat that had kept me safe and warm and held his scent—and which he gave up now for me, without hesitation, just as he always had and always would.

I'm right here. See me, Jenna. I'm right in front of you.

All I see is you, Mitch. All I see is you.

We crabbed on our bellies, shuffling back by inches, but we were going so slowly, too slow! Heavy sunlight pressed our backs and battered the lake and now the ice was talking, a constant rattle and snap and crackle like brittle glass being crushed beneath a hammer. Mitch kept up a steady stream of patter—I was doing fine, fine, we were going to be okay, okay—but his breath was coming faster, and I heard the hum of his fear. We made a torturous ten feet, then twenty, but the shore seemed to recede, and meanwhile, the snow kept fracturing.

Then Mitch moved—and I saw the snow and ice buckle, actually *break*, and lift beneath his right hip.

"Mitch!" I choked. "Mitch, *stop!*"

"Oh shit." He closed his eyes, let his head drop to the snow. I saw his back move as his breath came in deep, hitching gasps, and when he lifted his face again, I saw him pushing back the panic, grappling for control. He tried easing back on his other hip, but there was an even sharper crack and then something that sounded like dry branches splintering under a heavy boot. Mitch's body jerked and then his hips dipped as the ice began to give.

And, suddenly, there was water: dark as blood, seeping across the snow, oozing from the wounds beneath Mitch's body, spreading fast.

"Oh God." He looked at me. "Listen to me, Jenna. When I go through—"

"No, you're *not*—"

"*When* I go through," he said, "unless there's a shelf, something for me to grab onto so I can hold myself up, you have to let go."

"No. No, Mitch, no, I can't, I *won't*!"

"You *have* to!" he shouted and now I realized that what I'd thought was sweat on his cheeks were tears. "Jenna, I won't be able to let go because I'll panic and I won't want to let go of the coat, but you *have* to, no matter what I say. Do you understand? I'm too heavy and you won't be able to hold me, honey, not this time. I'll just end up killing you, too."

"No, Mitch," and I was crying again. "Mitch, don't ask me to do that, I can't let you *die*—"

"Jenna, please, honey, you have to do this, you have to let me g—"

Suddenly, all around his body, the ice was crumbling to pieces, like a pane of brittle glass. There came a heavy sodden *sploosh* as the fissures widened and the ice tired.

And then the lake *screamed*: a high, grinding squall of rusty hinges, of rotted metal. Beneath him, the ice broke in a staccato clatter, like the rattle of machine guns: *CRACKCRACK-CRACKCRACKCRACK*!

Mitch's eyes found me and held on. "Jenna," he said, and he put everything into that one word. He put in a lifetime.

Then, in the space between one heartbeat and the next, the thin ice—that frail membrane that buoyed him up and kept him in my world—let go.

A few moments later . . . so did I.

53: a

So.

What else could you possibly want, Bobby-o? You know the rest. You're the one who found us. Me. What a picture that must've been.

Well, shall I tell you what it feels like to watch someone you love drown and not be able to do anything to stop it? Do you want to know how long it took, or if the water boiled? Do you want to know if he screamed?

Would it interest you, at all, to know that he *did* try to scramble back onto the ice? That his hands grabbed and his fingers clawed, but the ice—that treacherous, greedy, teasing ice—kept breaking and breaking and breaking, sketching a path straight for me? And that when he saw what would happen to *me*, he stopped trying to save himself?

Would you believe that someone could love anyone that much?

Or do you want to know what I said? How I felt? That it might be better to die with him?

Would it help you to hear, Bob, that all of a sudden, he went so still, so silent, that no one would ever have believed that this man was drowning?

Do you want to know what it was like to understand that this was the end? And that there was nothing I could do?

No.

No, I don't think I'll tell you about that, Bob. I don't think I will.

b

But here's the truth, Bobby-o.

I'm no angel. But if I could have sprouted wings from those grafts on my back and plucked him out of the water, and if I'd been strong enough to fly us somewhere far, far away, I would have.

But I couldn't, and so I didn't.

As for the rest?

Brush up on your Shakespeare, Bob. Then we'll talk.

c

I know science. I know that it is possible for someone to survive a cold-water drowning, and they've been working over Mitch for a long, long, *long* time. I think it was Rebecca who once told me that they work longer if they think you've got a good chance of pulling through. I guess that explains me.

But it's been awfully quiet these last few hours. Awfully quiet . . . and I am so afraid to really let myself know what that means.

Weird, how I didn't quite understand what Mitch was trying to tell me when he said that, but I do now. He felt the way my mother did when those Marines came to the door. Mitch's fear was fed by the same fire that kept me recycling Matt's e-mails over and over and over again.

Because if you can just hold off the moment when you must confront reality, time stands still and you can keep pretending that life will continue as you've known it: that nothing—not even something as wonderful and as terrible as love—has broken your world beyond repair.

So I think I'll stay here a little while longer. There's plenty of time to get off this gurney and open that door and rejoin the rest of you.

There's all the time I have left on Earth.

There's the rest of my life.

When I do leave this room, I don't know what will happen next. My mom's in a coma; she might die. Dad . . . I don't think he'll change, no matter what. Matt is dead. And Mitch—

d

I just thought of something.

If Mitch is . . . If he's really gone, they can use his skin for my mother. If he's an organ donor. Knowing Mitch, he would be. They'll parcel him out in little pieces, an eye here, a kidney there. So why not his skin? They could flay his body and cocoon her with him. That last living bit of all that he was would help heal my poor mother—and how ironic would that be?

For that matter, my heart is broken. So maybe they'll give me his. It's something to shoot for.

And maybe, in all that, Bob?

There is forgiveness.

e

I just remembered Danielle and David. It's still Friday. No . . . Saturday? I've lost track. But Monday will roll around soon enough, and Danielle will get her abortion. Or she won't. Either they'll get in touch with their folks, or Mitch was lying.

But I was on the ice with him, Bobby-o, and you weren't. So I don't think he was. I think everything Mitch said out there—every word—was the truth.

Every. Word.

f

You probably want me to regret Mitch. You want me to see that he lied, was some kind of predator; that I'm a *victim*, like you said. But Mitch was broken, too, in his way and just as much a hostage to his past and his mistakes. Maybe by trying to fix me, he was also healing himself in the only way he knew how.

Oh, I can just hear you now. You and every therapist who ever lived will say that I'm *rationalizing*, that I've *identified* with a monster, just like those kids do who are kidnapped and live in a cage for twenty years. You'll want to see me as *damaged* somehow, and then you'll try to cure me. Well, I got news for you, Bobby-o.

Cured is just a synonym for coming around to your way of thinking.

Cured is the word you use when I finally agree.

But here's the problem with that, Bobby-o. You and the therapists can yammer until you're blue in the face, but I just can't agree with you and probably never will.

Because Mitch gave me love. He handed me back my life and that doesn't make me a victim.

When I close my eyes, Bob, he's there, right in front of me, and all I see in the dark is him.

All I see is him.

∫

Oooo, you just knocked, Bobby-o. I know it's you. Oh, sure, nurses and doctors knock, but they never wait for an invitation. They just barge on in. I think they hate closed doors. Come to think of it, they're a lot like parents that way.

Anyway.

I know you're chomping at the bit to get at what's in this little machine. Well, Bobby-o, here's what I say to that.

These are my memories. They are my feelings, and you can't have them. Because you'll use them against Mitch, dead or alive, and I can't let you do that. Not everything Mitch and I had was a lie, and he saved me, Bob: first when he said I had to let him go, and again when he saw that I would die if he didn't stop trying to save himself.

So now it's my turn to save him.

You want to crucify Mitch? Find someone else. Because these words are mine, Bobby-o; they are mine.

That's not to say that I won't give you back your recorder, though.

Just give me a sec while I find that little red button, the one labeled <*era*

Acknowledgments

Every book is tough. Every relationship, whether it's between two people or a writer and her book, is about taking risks. This story was extremely difficult because my intent was to present a situation in which there are no stereotypical predators *or* victims. Only a very special editor tolerates and champions that kind of ambiguity. Lucky for me, Andrew Karre is of that rare breed and for this, I offer my sincerest thanks.

Jennifer Laughran has proven yet again to be a fabulous advocate and a writer's dream-agent. Thank you, Jenn, for getting what this was about and taking the plunge.

For my stalwart husband, David: I could tell you how wonderful and patient you are, and there still wouldn't be enough hours in the day.

One last word about this book: Are these damaged people? Absolutely. Are there monsters in these pages? Yes; one, for sure. Yet many relationships are bound as much by hatred as love; growth may come from damage; and reality is complex.

In my experience, the truly evil are few and good people, with the very best of intentions, often make very bad decisions and get in way over their heads before they know it. People drown, quietly, before our eyes, all the time.

About the Author

Ilsa J. Bick is a child psychiatrist, as well as a film scholar, surgeon wannabe, former Air Force major, and award-winning author of dozens of short stories and novels, including the critically-acclaimed *Draw the Dark* and *Ashes*. Ilsa lives with her family and other furry creatures near a Hebrew cemetery in rural Wisconsin. One thing she loves about the neighbors: They are very quiet and only come around for sugar once in a blue moon. Visit her online at www.ilsajbick.com.